# THE CYGNET AND THE FIREBIRD

*Ace Books by Patricia A. McKillip*

THE FORGOTTEN BEASTS OF ELD
THE SORCERESS AND THE CYGNET
THE CYGNET AND THE FIREBIRD

# THE CYGNET AND THE FIREBIRD

## PATRICIA A. McKILLIP

ACE BOOKS, NEW YORK

THE CYGNET AND THE FIREBIRD

An Ace Book
Published by The Berkley Publishing Group
200 Madison Avenue, New York, NY 10016

Book design by Todd Adams based on a design by Arnold Vila

First Edition: September 1993

Library of Congress Cataloging-in-Publication Data

McKillip, Patricia A.
    The cygnet and the firebird / Patricia A. McKillip.—1st ed.
        p. cm.
    ISBN 0-441-12628-6
    I. Title.
  PS3563.C38C9 1993
  813'.54—dc20                                        92-21149
                                                          CIP

PRINTED IN THE UNITED STATES OF AMERICA

10  9  8  7  6  5  4  3  2  1

For Howard Morhaim,
the Dark Knight of the Soul,
with love (and no cholesterol)

# CHAPTER
## 1

Meguet Vervaine stood at the threshold of Chrysom's black tower, swans flying at her back and shoulder and wrists, swans soaring out of her hands. She had stood so for hours. Dressed in black silk with the Cygnet of Ro Holding spanning silver moons on mantle and tunic, she held the ancient broadsword of Moro Ro, unsheathed, tip to the floor, guarding against stray goose and cottage child's ball and wandering butterfly, for within the broad, circular hall the councils from the four Holds had gathered to discuss their differences under the sign of the Cygnet and the formidable eye of Lauro Ro. In Moro Ro's day, the threshold guards would have faced both chamber and yard, prepared for violence from any direction, not least from the volatile councils. Meguet, armed by tradition rather than necessity, faced the hall to keep the sun out of her eyes. She had gathered her long corn-silk hair into a severe braid; her eyes, green a shade lighter than the rose leaves that climbed the walls of the thousand-year-old tower, kept a calm and careful watch over the sometimes testy gathering. Members of the oldest families in Ro Holding had made long, uncomfortable journeys to meet for the Holding Council in a place where, not many weeks before, Meguet had found herself raising the sword in her hands to battle for her life. She did not expect trouble; it had come and gone, but some part of her still

1

tensed at shadows, at unexpected voices.

But only the councilors themselves had provided any excitement, and that was contingent upon such complexities as border taxes. There had been sharp debate earlier in the day between Hunter Hold and the Delta over mines in the border mountains, which had kept everyone awake on the ninth day of the long council. Now, the heavy late-afternoon light, the pigeons murmuring in the high windows, and Haf Berg's young, pompous, querulous voice maundering endlessly about sheep, threw a stupor over the hall. Meguet heard a snore from one of the back tables. She stifled a yawn. A sudden wind tugged at her light mantle. The air was a heady mix of brine and sun-steeped roses on the tower vines; it seemed to blow from everywhere at once: from past and future, from unexplored countries where wooden flowers opened on tree boughs to reveal strange, rich spices, and sheep the colors of autumn leaves wandered through the hills. . . .

She felt herself drifting on the alien wind; a sound brought her back. The hall was silent; she wondered if she herself had made some noise. But it was only Haf Berg, sitting down at last, working his chair fussily across the flagstones. Lauro Ro watched him impassively. She sat at the crescent dais table, the Cygnet flying like a shadow through tarnished midnight stars on the vast, timeworn banner behind her. Her elegant face was unreadable, her wild dark hair so unnaturally tidy that Meguet suspected Nyx had bewitched it into submission. The Holder's heir sat at her right, wearing her enigmatic reputation with composure. Lauro Ro asked, "Will anyone challenge Haf Berg's painstaking examination of the problems of sheep pasturage on the south border of Berg Hold?" There was a daunting note in her voice. Only a pigeon challenged. Iris, on the Holder's left, consulted a paper and whispered to her mother.

Rush Yarr sat beside Iris, and Calyx beside Nyx. The two younger sisters, one fair and reclusive, the other dark and distinguished most of the time by extraordinary rumors, bore the intense scrutiny of the council members calmly. When Calyx

spoke, pearls and doves did not fall from her lips. When Nyx
spoke, toads did not fall, nor did lightning flash. But it had taken
days for the anticipation to fade.

The Holder spoke again. Linden Dacey of Withy Hold wished
to bring up the matter of . . . Meguet tightened her shoulders,
loosened them. A knot burned at the nape of her neck. She
shifted slightly, easing some of her weight onto the blade she
held. Across the room, the sorceress lifted her eyes at the flash
of light.

They looked at one another a moment: cousins bound by blood
and by secret, ancient ways. Memories gathered between them
in the sunlit air. The swans on the hilt and etched blade in
Meguet's hands had taken wing, Nyx had transformed herself
from bog-witch into Cygnet's heir so recently that the sorcery
in that hidden time and place beneath their feet must still be
rebounding against the labyrinth stones. The sorceress's eyes,
mist-pale in the light, seemed mildly speculative, as if, Meguet
thought, she contemplated turning her cousin into a bat to liven
up the tedium. Meguet, returning her attention to the proceedings,
half-wished she would.

Linden Dacey had brought up the matter of a border feud
between Withy Hold and the Delta. A river had shifted, or been
shifted; the south border, defined for centuries, was suddenly
uncertain . . . The great Hold banners swayed and glittered above
her head as she spoke; eyes caught at Meguet. The Blood Fox of
the Delta prowled on starry pads; one eye glinted as if thought
had flashed through its bright threads. The Gold King of Hunter
Hold, the crowned and furious sun, glared out of his prison of
night. Meguet, gazing back, felt a sudden chill, as if the face of
spun gold thread were alive again and watching.

Someone from the Delta interrupted Linden Dacey. There was
an interesting squabble on the council floor. Old Maharis Kell
jerked mid-snore out of his nap. The Holder let it rage a moment,
probably to wake everyone up. Then she cut through it in a voice
that must have brought a few cottagers in the outer yard to a
dead stop. Rush Yarr slid a hand over his mouth. Calyx, catching

a tremor in the air, glanced at him. Rush, Meguet noted, had recovered his sense of humor—or discovered it, she wasn't sure which, for he had loved a sorceress who was never home for so long that likely even he didn't remember if he had one. Calyx had entered the doorless walls of the tower he had built around himself, and he found her inside his heart.

Linden Dacey, finished finally, yielded debate to the chastened Delta councilor. Gold streaked suddenly through a west window. Meguet eyed her shadow, guessed at the time. Another hour, if that . . . The Delta councilor bit a word in half and was still. Meguet raised her eyes. On the dais, no one breathed. Behind her the yard was soundless. Not a child's shout, a groaning wagon wheel, an iron blow from the smithy, disturbed the sudden, bewitched silence. Meguet stared at Nyx, wondering if, bored or day-dreaming, she had thrown some spell over the council. But Nyx was entranced by the table, it seemed; she gazed at it, wide-eyed, motionless.

Someone had slowed time.

In the weird stillness, Meguet heard a footfall in the grass behind her. She whirled, her heart hammering, and brought the broadsword up in both hands. A man stood within the tower ring, staring up at the solitary black tower. The flaring arc of silver from the door as the broadsword cut through light startled him; Meguet felt his attention riveted suddenly on her. In the brilliant, late light, the stranger cast no shadow.

She drew a slow, noiseless breath, tightening her hold on the blade, trapped in a world out of time by his sorcery and by her peculiar heritage: the sleepless compulsion to guard what lay hidden within the tower's heart. The man's face, blurred by the dazzling light or perhaps by shifting time, was difficult to see. He seemed a profusion of colors: scarlet, gold, white, dust, blue, silver, that sorted itself out as he moved, crossing the yard with a strong, energetic stride.

Tall as she was, Meguet was forced to look up at him. His hair and skin were the same color as the dust on the hem of his red robe and his scuffed yellow boots, as if the parched gold-brown earth of some vast desert blown constantly through sun-drenched air had seeped into him. A strange winged animal embroidered in white wound itself in and out of the folds of cloth at his chest. The robe was belted with a curious, intricate weave of silver; silver glinted also at his wrists beneath his sleeves. A pouch of dark blue leather was slung over his shoulder; another, of dusty yellow silk, hung beside that. He stopped in front of Meguet's blade. She saw his face clearly then, as surprised by her as she was by him.

His eyes flicked over her shoulder at the motionless hall, then back to her. His broad, spare face was young yet under its weathering; his eyes, a light, glinting blue, were flecked with gold.

He said, amazed, "Who are you?"

Meguet, abandoned, with only a broadsword to protect the house against sorcery, found her voice finally. "You are in the house of the Holders of Ro Holding. If you have business with the Holder, present yourself to the Gatekeeper."

He glanced behind him at the little turret above the gate, where the Gatekeeper leaned idly against the stones, a motionless figure in household black watching something in the yard. "Him." He turned back. "He looks busy." He touched the blade at his chest with one finger, but did not turn it. He grunted softly, his eyes going back to Meguet. "This is real."

"Yes."

"Well, what do you expect to do with it? You can't keep me out of this tower with a sword. How can you have the power to see me through shifted time and still wave that under my nose? What are you? Are you a mage?"

"You have no business in this tower, you have no business in this house, and you have no business questioning me."

"I'm curious," he said. "You eluded my sorcery, and I had only thought to come and go so secretly no one would ever know."

"Why?" she asked sharply. "Why have you come here?"

"I want something from this tower."

She felt herself grow so still that no light trembled on the blade. "You may not enter."

"There are a thousand ways to enter a tower. Every block of solid stone is an open doorway. You can't guard every threshold."

All fear had left her voice; it was thin and absolute. "If I must, I can."

He was silent, puzzled again, at the certainty in her words. "It can't be the sword," he said at last. "The magic is in you, not that. True?" He caught the blade in one hand, so quickly that not the flick of an eyelash forewarned her. She wrenched at it; it might as well have been sunk in stone. "Not," he mused, "the sword, then." He loosed it as abruptly. She steadied herself, breathing audibly, while he studied her, his eyes quizzical, secret. "Perhaps," he said finally, "it's what you guard in this tower that gives you such power. Is that it?"

She raised the blade again, swallowing drily. "No one may enter the tower at this time without permission from the Holder. Those are my instructions. You may not enter."

"But the Holder will never know," he said softly. "What I want has been hidden for centuries. No one knows it is here, and no one will miss it when it is gone. I will never return to Ro Holding. Let me pass. If all you're brandishing against me is a point of honor, you won't be dishonored. No one will ever know."

"I will," Meguet said succinctly. "And so will you. Honor is a word you would not bother to toss at me, if it meant nothing to you. You may not enter."

He was silent again, so still he might have put himself under his own mysterious spell. His eyes had narrowed; light or memory flashed through them. "What made you time or honor's guardian?" he breathed. "You have seen a few of its back roads, its crooked lanes and alleyways. Haven't you. But you are not a mage. Or are you?" She did not answer. He stepped closer; she did not move. He stepped so close that the blade snagged the golden eye of the winged beast across his chest. He said, "If you do not let me enter, I will turn every rose on this tower into flame."

"Then you will burn what you have come for."

He moved closer. The blade turned a little in her hands as if the animal had shifted under it, and she felt the sweat break out on her face.

"I will seal every door and window in this tower, and turn it into a tomb for those you guard."

"It is already a tomb." Her voice shook. He stepped so close the blade slid ghostlike into him. Her shoulders burned at the sudden weight, but she held the blade steady under his expressionless gaze.

"If you do not let me enter, I will kill you."

"Then," she said, as sweat and light burned into her eyes, and the clawed, airy animal whipped beneath the blade like a desperate thing, "one of us will die."

He stepped back then, as easily as if the great sword were made of smoke. The animal turned a smoldering eye at her and subsided into the cloth. The blade trembled in her hands; still she did not lower it. The mage's face changed; the expression on it startled her.

"You deserve better than a doorway," he said abruptly. "What kind of upside-down house is this where no power but honor is pitted against the likes of me? You can't stop me. You can barely hold that sword. It is shaking in your hands. It is so heavy it weighs like stone, it drags you down. It is heavier than old age, heavier than grief. It falls like the setting sun, slowly, slowly. Watch it fall. Watch the tiny flame of light on its tip shift, move down the blade toward your hands. Watch it. The light trembles among the silver swan wings. What is your name?"

"Meguet Vervaine."

"Is it night or day?"

"I do not know."

"Are you awake or dreaming?"

"I do not know."

"Are you a mage?"

"No."

"Have you a mage's powers?"

"No."

"How do you have the power to see and move through shifted time?"

"I have no power."

"Then who gives you power?"

"No one."

"You have power. You are standing here talking to me when no one else in this house can move."

"I have no power."

"What gives you power?"

"Nothing."

"You are guarding something from me as steadfastly as you guard this door. I will enter this tower. Do you have the power to stop me?"

"You may not enter."

"Do you have the power to stop me?"

Meguet was silent. Wind brushed her face, a cool breeze smelling of twilight. For a moment she stared senselessly at what she saw: the inner yard, the towers, the outer yard through the arches, where cottagers' children flung a ball back and forth, and the Gatekeeper on the ground, his back to her, opened the gate to a couple of riders. Then she looked down at her hands. They were locked so fiercely, so protectively around the hilt of Moro Ro's sword that her fingers ached, loosening. The smell of roses teased her memory. *I fell asleep,* she thought surprisedly. *I had a dream. . . .*

Then the Holder's voice snapped across the chamber. "Meguet!"

She turned, startled. The sword slipped out of her hold, rang against the stones like a challenge, and she saw beside it the rose that had flung itself off the outer wall into the room to lie burning in her shadow. She dragged her eyes away from it to the dais.

Nyx had vanished.

Dream shifted into time, became memory; she felt the blood leap out of her face. She reached down, snatched up the rose and began to run.

* * *

On the dais, the sorceress had felt the sudden shift of time.

Intrigued, she simply sat still, not a difficult thing to do for one who had spent nights in the black deserts of Hunter Hold watching the constellations turn and the orange bitterthorn blossom open its fullest to the full moon. She saw Meguet bring up the sword in her hands, turn. The fair-haired stranger stopped at the threshold. Nyx's attention focused, precise and fine-honed, on her cousin, who was waving a blade of sheep grass against the wind. Their voices carried easily across the eerie silence.

She watched, unblinking, while the stranger came so close to Meguet only the swans on the sword hilt protected her. Light sparking off a jewel in Nyx's hair would have alerted the mage; when he forced her to move, he would not see her. But he backed away from Meguet, passed around her, left her defending a breached threshold in a dream. He had paused, for some reason, to pick a rose off the tower vines. He dropped it in Meguet's shadow. He passed among the councilors with no more interest in them than if they had been hedgerows. At the stairs, beneath the Blood Fox prowling between green swamp and starry night on the Delta banner, he hesitated. The power within the tower was complex, layered as it was with Chrysom's ancient wizardry, household ghosts, the impress upon the centuries of every mage or Cygnet's guardian who had left a trace of power lingering in time. Beneath that lay the entombed mage and the vast and intricate power within the Cygnet's heart. He would not recognize that power, but he would be aware, like a man stepping to the edge of a chasm at midnight, that something undefined was catching at his attention. To separate what sorcery the stranger had come to find from the emanations of power and memory within the ancient stones would require at least a walk up the spiral stairs. When the stranger had felt his way through the lingering magic beyond the first curve, Nyx rose. She formed an image of Chrysom's library in her mind, book and stone and rose-patterned windows, and stepped into it.

She waited.

The sight of Nyx reading at one of the tables made the stranger pause a heartbeat, as if his glance into the council chamber had snared her in his memories. But she gazed down at the page— a list of cows who had calved four hundred and ninety years before—with rapt attention. In that magic-steeped chamber he would not notice her mind working. He had reached his goal; his attention flicked like a needle in a compass toward what he had come to steal.

The stone mantel above the fireplace was littered with thousand-year-old oddments of Chrysom's that had somehow survived accidents, misplacements, pilfering and spring cleaning. Nyx had no idea what they were, besides volatile and unpredictable. The stranger glanced briefly at them. He stood in the center of the room, sending out filaments of thought like a spider spinning a web, into tables, hearth, book shelves, ancient weapons, cracked, bubbled mirrors, tapestries on the wall. He ignored Nyx, who, surrounded by mysteries, was reading about cows. He moved finally, abruptly, across the room to kneel at the hearth. His hands closed around one of the massive cornerstones that was crusted with centuries of ash. He tried to shift it. Now that he had shown her where it was, Nyx asked before he found it,

"What in Moro's name are you looking for in there?"

He was so startled that he nearly leaped back into his own time. Parts of him faded and reappeared; a wing on his robe unfolded in the air and folded itself back into thread. He did not so much turn as rearrange himself through shifting moments of time to face her. She recognized the white animal then, from some of Chrysom's ancient drawings: She thought he had imagined it, from some tale so old there was scarcely a word for it in Ro Holding. The mage, his face a few shades paler than dust, studied her while he caught his breath.

He said abruptly, "You were in the hall, down there. I remember you now. Your eyes."

She lifted a brow. "You saw me watching you?"

"No. I remember their color, when I passed the dais. Like a winter sky. You are a mage. It's hard to tell, in this house."

"People who belong in this house recognize me easily." She rested her chin on her palm, contemplating him. "You are a thief. You are not from Ro Holding, or I would know you by now; your remarkable power would have caught my interest."

"You have some remarkable powers yourself," he said with feeling. "You nearly turned me inside-out, scaring me like that."

"I know a few things," she said.

"You don't know what's in this stone. You never knew anything at all was in there. I can name it. That makes it mine."

"Fine," she said drily. "I will let you keep the name. You may take that and yourself out of this tower. How dare you bewitch this entire house and wander through it, pilfering things? What kind of barbaric country taught you that?"

"Only one thing," he pointed out. "One pilfering. That's all I need. Something you have never needed. Let me take it and go. I'll never return to Ro Holding again."

"You have more than theft to answer for. You disturbed my cousin Meguet. You threatened her and tried to coerce her." He opened his mouth to answer, did not. Nyx continued grimly, running one of Calyx's pens absently in and out of her hair, "You used sorcery against her."

"I'm sorry," he said. "I was curious."

"You were cruel."

He drew breath, his eyes flicking away from her; she saw the blood gather under his tan. "I was never taught," he said finally, "to make such fine distinctions. In my country, ignorance is dangerous; curiosity can be ruthless. But I would never have harmed your cousin. I only wanted to know—"

"I know what you only wanted to know." She paused, her own eyes falling briefly. She took the pen out of her hair and laid it down. She folded her hands in front of her mouth and looked at the stranger again. "But it's none of your business. Now leave this house in peace."

He paused, his eyes narrowed faintly, light-filled, hidden. "You're curious, too," he said slowly. "You want this thing only because you don't know what it is." She nodded, unperturbed.

For a moment their eyes held, calculating, and then, abruptly, he yielded, tossing up a hand. "I never expected to find this tower so well-guarded. And now I have run out of time. . . ."

And he was gone, to her surprise, as easily and noiselessly as light fading on stones. Distant sounds wove into the air again: children shouting, cows lowing as they came in from the back pastures. The Holder, she remembered suddenly, would be discovering the empty chair beside her. But Meguet would reassure her. Nyx knelt at the hearth, touched the stone with her hands, and then with her mind. Neither moved it. She wrapped her thoughts around the stone, feeling its weight and texture, its size: a single block of charred marble in a hearth so old the stones were all sagging into one another. As she studied it, she felt something watching her. She lifted her head. A crow winging out of the mantel gazed at her out of its black marble eye.

She reached up, touched the eye. Nothing moved. Above it, in relief, the Cygnet flew the length of the mantel through a black marble sky, its eye aligned with the crow's eye. She had to stand on air to reach it. The Cygnet's eye moved nothing. She stood thinking, her own eyes flicking across the scattered convocation of crows, until in all their black stone eyes the pattern formed.

It was a constellation: All the eyes were stars, depicting the Cygnet flying across the night. A riddle, she thought, no one outside of Ro Holding would have guessed. She felt a rare impulse for caution, but dismissed it immediately, too close to the mystery, too curious. One after another she touched the dark stars. The stone, its mortar sifting drily into the firebed, swung free.

She barely had time to look into it, when something struck her—a wind, a thunderbolt—and flung her at the mantel and then into it among the crows. She cried out, startled; her mouth was stopped with stone. She concentrated, found the face of one of the crows and gathered herself like a thought in its stony mind and then into a point of light within its eye. Beneath her, she saw the mage looking into the hollow stone.

Meguet, slamming the library door wide, knocked a shield off the wall. The mage, barely glancing up, flung a hand out impatiently, murmuring. The animal leaped from his breast, a sinuous blur of white that poured to the floor, bounded upward again, catching air with its wings, claws out, aimed at its prey. Meguet threw up her arm, wielding a rose against it. Something—the streak of red in the air, a sound she made—caught the mage's attention. His head snapped around. For an instant the rose stunned him. Then he spoke sharply. The animal halted in mid-flight; white embroidery thread snarled in the air. Nyx dropped like a tear out of the crow's eye, reappeared in front of Meguet. The air seemed to snarl in her wake as she dragged remnants of the mage's spell from the air and threw them back at him. The mage began to fray in different directions at once, as if he were spun of fine threads of time, all unravelling. He cried something before he vanished. The cry skipped like a rock across water, snatched the gently falling thread. Cry and thread whirled away into nothing.

Meguet sagged against the open doorway, felt air and brought herself upright. "Moro's name," she whispered. "What did you do to him?"

Nyx, her eyes flooded with color, untangling herself from her sorcery, looked bewitched herself, something only half human. "I'm not sure," she said. "I've never done that before."

"Is he still alive?"

"I have no idea." She drew a deep breath then; her eyes relinquished color, became familiar. She glanced toward the noise that had followed Meguet up the stairs. She touched her cousin, who, having fought some ancient and very peculiar sorcery not many weeks before, seemed oddly shaken by a tidy piece of work. "Stay here. Keep them out. If he comes back, this time not even that rose will stop him."

She crossed the room quickly, knelt at the hearth. Meguet, watching the air for a warning of color, was jostled by the first of the guard who, weapons drawn, flung themselves precipitously toward the threat to the house. Several of the more agile councilors were among them. Meguet heard the Holder's voice farther down the stairwell.

She turned briefly, stilled the guard with a gesture. They quieted, peering over Meguet's shoulders at Nyx, who was gazing
meditatively into a cracked, charred stone adrift from the hearth.
The silence spread; subdued whisperings passed it back to the
crowd at the top of the stairs, until it reached even the Holder.
Meguet felt her coming in eddies of movement as the guard
pushed a path clear for her. She joined Meguet, who was guarding
yet another threshold, eyed her daughter, and went no farther.

"What is it?" she asked. She had evidently flung a trail of
pins down the stairs; most of her hair had fallen loose. She was
frowning deeply; her black eyes were expressionless, wintry, but
she kept her voice low. "Was she harmed?"

"No. There was a strange mage, a thief, trying to steal something—she may still be in danger."

"Moro's eyes, she knows enough sorcery to make Chrysom
sit up in his tomb—why didn't she just let him have what he
wanted?"

"Because she doesn't know what it is."

"I thought she knew everything by now."

"She's trying to be careful."

The Holder stared at her. "Really. And how did this thief get
past the Gatekeeper?"

"He slowed time."

The Holder's response caused even Nyx, feeling through the
stone for mage-traps, to raise her eyes. The Holder, still furious,
lowered her voice mid-sentence, "—in the middle of the Holding
Council, wandering among us at will, it's unthinkable, intolerable.
You couldn't stop him?"

Meguet sighed noiselessly. "I tried. All he wanted was something of Chrysom's, nothing more serious. I had no power against
sorcery. Nothing but a sword."

The Holder was silent, gazing at her quizzically. Her eyes
dropped to the rose in Meguet's hand. Meguet, staring at it, felt
the color blaze into her face. She lifted her other hand, pushed it
against her eyes, and saw the rose again, lying beside the sword
in her shadow.

She let it fall, as if a thorn had pricked her. "I was bewitched."

"Apparently," the Holder said curiously. "But, I wonder, by what?"

A murmuring rippled through the crowd at Meguet's back; she looked up to see what the mage wanted so badly out of the stone that he had stopped the world.

Nyx held it in her hand: a golden key.

# CHAPTER
# 2

Nyx was crouched under a table in the mage's library a day later, picking at a crack in the stone floor with her fingernail, when the firebird flew over the gate. Engrossed, she did not immediately hear the effect of its arrival. The Hold Councils and most of the household were at supper; strings and flutes from the third tower played a distant, ancient music in the peaceful twilight that wove among the reeds and drums from the cider house. Nyx, dressed for supper, had forgotten it. Cobwebs snagged in her dark hair; absently, she had rearranged the elaborate, jewelled structure until pins and strands of tiny pearls dangled around her face. Her black velvet dress was filigreed with dust; she had walked out of her shoes some time ago. Her eyes, usually the color of bog mist, were washed with lavender. Her face had taken on a feral cast; she seemed to be scenting even threads of smoke ingrained in the ancient stone.

The disorderly clamor of people and animals finally intruded into her concentration. She straightened abruptly against the table top. Someone pounded on the door, then opened it.

"Nyx!"

It was Calyx, who, looking high and low in the shadows, finally looked low enough. Nyx, rubbing her head crossly, said, "I thought I locked that door. What in Moro's name is that racket in the yard?"

"It's a bird," Calyx said dazedly. "What are you doing under the table? And what have you—" Her voice caught; color washed over her delicate face. She found her voice again, raised it with unusual force. "Nyx Ro, what have you done with all the ancient household records I was studying?"

"Over there," Nyx said, waving at a cairn of books as she crawled out. "A bird. What bird?"

"They're all jumbled up! I had them all in order, a thousand years of household history—And look what you've done to this room!"

A pile of chairs balanced on a tiny wine table; shields and furs and tapestries hung in midair above their heads; bookshelves climbed up the stairs to the roof. Spell books, histories, accounts, diaries, rose like monoliths from the floor. Nyx, her arms folded, stood as still among them, eyes narrowed at her sister.

"Calyx," she said softly. "What bird?"

"Look at this mess! And look at your face! There are black smudges all over it."

"That would be from the chimney. Calyx—"

"You put your face up the chimney?"

"Evidently."

"Why," Calyx asked more precisely, "did you put your face up the chimney?"

"Because I'm looking for something," Nyx said impatiently. "Why else would I crawl up a chimney?"

"I have no idea. I thought, after studying sorcery for nine years, you'd pull an imp out of the air to do it for you. Maybe I can help you. What is it we're looking for?"

"Most likely a book."

Calyx stared at her. "Did you," she asked ominously, "look on the bookshelves?"

"Oh, really, Calyx." She wiped at ash with her sleeve, her breath snagging on a sudden laugh. "You do keep dwelling on nonessentials. After studying sorcery for nine years, I have learned how to clean up a room." She picked her way through the chairs to the windows. From that high place, she could see the parapet wall linking the seven white towers, most of the cottages clustered beyond the wall, and the vast yard with its barns and forges and craft houses that dealt with the upkeep of the household and the lands that rambled endlessly within the outer wall. One thing caught her eye instantly at that busy hour.

"The Gatekeeper is not at the gate."

And then she saw the flash of fire that scratched the air with gold and turned a rearing cart horse into a tree with diamond leaves.

Meguet had been sitting with the Gatekeeper in his turret when the bird flew over the gate. Dressed in corn-leaf silk the color of her eyes, strands of tiny jewels braided into her rippling hair, she had abandoned guests and musicians in the supper hall, pulled on her oldest boots and wandered into the summer twilight to talk to the Gatekeeper. She had seen nothing of him the day before; at the Holder's request she had stood watch in Chrysom's library most of the evening, while Nyx puzzled over the key she had found. Some of the gossip had evidently found its way to the gate; as she entered the turret, the Gatekeeper handed her a rose.

She eyed him; his lean, sun-browned face, with its silvery-green swamp-leaf eyes, was expressionless. She said, "It was red, not white."

"I hoped you'd like this better." Then she saw the beginnings of his tight, slanted smile, and she sighed and slid onto the stone bench next to him.

"I was hoping no one had noticed. Does gossip blow on the wind across this yard? Or do you hear through stone?"

"People like tales." He put his arm around her shoulders. "For nine days you've stood at that tower door with a sword in your hands. When you suddenly toss it aside for a rose, it causes comment. What was he like, this mage who gave you the rose?"

"You should know," she said grimly. "You let him in."

He stirred; his eyes flickered away from her, across the wall, where the lazy tide sighed and broke. "He did get past me. Odd things have, in this house. Tell me what happened. No one saw him but you and Nyx, and the tales being spun around this mysterious mage make me afraid to open the gate."

She smiled at the thought. "You'd open the gate to winter itself. Or time, or the end of it." She brought the white rose to her face, breathed in its scent. He opened her other hand, dropped his lips on her palm where thorns had left an imprint.

"You fought a battle with the red rose."

"I nearly lost it," she said, and heard his breath.

"Tell me," he said, and listened with the hard, expressionless cast that his face took on when something disturbed him. He applied a taper to his ebony pipe before the end of it, blowing smoke seaward, his eyes hidden. She told much of the tale to the rose, turning it in her fingers, finding memories in its whorl of petals.

"Is he expected back?" he asked. "Or did she kill him?"

"She doesn't know. She told the Holder that if he is alive he might return, since he seemed that desperate."

"For a key? To what?"

"Nyx thinks a book. Some secret magic book of Chrysom's."

"I thought she had all his books."

"So did she."

He turned his head, tossed smoke downwind. "What kinds of things would a mage keep hidden?"

"That," she sighed, "is why Nyx refuses to let the stranger have what he wants, which is the advice that, at some length, the Holder gave her. If she knew, she might let him take it and stop threatening the house. But she is spellbound by this book that she can't even find."

"So is the stranger, it sounds, stopping time and threatening to burn the house down for it."

"What was that like? Did you feel time stop?"

He shook his head. "Your corn-silk hair caught my eye; I turned to look at you. I was hoping you would turn. Then I blinked, and there was your face. Then you vanished into the tower, and what caught my eye was the blade of silver light on the stones just inside the door. A moment later one of the tower guards ran for help. And I guessed what the light must be. I nearly left the gate. But I didn't want to risk trouble letting itself out while I was gone, though it had wandered in without my help. So I waited. And the tales started flying like birds out of the tower, each one more colorful than the last." He touched the rose in her hand. "They all said you were safe." He paused, his eyes going seaward again, where white birds flashed over the water and dived. "I caught the gist of it: a mage, a key—"

"Don't say it."

"And a blood-red rose."

She looked at him, said recklessly, "You were watching; you must have seen him pick it."

He blinked, wordless, then pulled her close suddenly; she heard his heartbeat. "What do you think? That I would have stood here sunning myself like a tortoise while you defended a sleeping Holding Council alone against a mage who could have left you lying on your shadow as easily as the rose? Is that what you think?"

"Yes," she said, for there were gates within gates into the house, and she suspected he watched them all. "No. Yes. What I think is that you know exactly what comes and goes through that gate."

He was silent. His hold eased; he dropped a kiss on her hair, and said finally, "So I do. And in case the mage considers knocking at the gate next time, tell me what I should look for."

"A man," she said, "taller than me, by a few inches. With hair a dusty golden-brown and light eyes like water. The animal is embroidered on his robe." She paused, thinking back. "He wears silver at his wrists—"

"Old?"

"No older than you. Taller than me—"

"You said that."

"And he moves like a man accustomed to space."

"You noticed a lot in an eye-blink," he commented drily. She looked at him, her eyes still and clear as the sky where the sun had set and the memory of light lingered. He swallowed a word. His face dropped toward hers. Their lips touched. And then he turned abruptly, snatching her breath along with his, and she saw the firebird over his shoulder.

It seemed to blow out of the sea like spume, so white it was, and so fast it flew; then, as it passed the turret, she saw the fiery wingtips and the long, graceful plumes that trailed behind it like flame. Its talons were silver. It gave a cry of such fierce fury and despair that it drove the blood from her face and brought the Gatekeeper to his feet. The busy yard stopped as if it were spellbound again. With the cry came fire: a forge-fire, and a hammer, and the hand holding the hammer froze into silver.

Meguet hit the ground running before she realized she had moved. There were cottagers' children transfixed by the swooping bird; there were animals everywhere, it seemed—horses, cows still coming in to be milked, chickens, hounds. The bird, crying again, turned a corner of a barn into bronze, and nicked a hound's ear. The hound bellowed, blundered into the cows; there was a small stampede toward the bewitched forge. Stable girls hurried to take in the horses, ducking their heads under their arms as at pelting hail. The bird wheeled above a group of barefoot children who had twisted themselves into a knot with a piece of harness. Meguet and several of the cottagers ran toward them as they struggled frantically. The bird's fire missed the children, hit a cat slinking away into the shadows and turned it into a jewelled sword. Meguet snatched it up. Wielding it above the children, she startled them into tears. She cut them free of each other; they scattered, wailing, then turned again, too fascinated to find shelter.

She saw Rush Yarr and a few of the younger councilors on the tower wall with bows; household guards were racing to position themselves along the crenelation. She saw Rush fix an arrow, draw back and aim. She slowed, feeling a sudden, unreasonable dismay form like a shout in her throat. The bird, a swirl of white and red, cried its enraged sorrow; fire swept the wall, and all the archers ducked. The stones themselves turned gold.

"Nyx," she breathed. The Gatekeeper, struggling with a panicked cart horse, shouted at her.

"Meguet!"

"I'm going to get Nyx! Tell them not to shoot!"

"It's not the bird in danger," he retorted, holding the horse as stablers unhitched the lurching cart. "It's you standing there waiting to be turned into a silver rose."

"It cries so," she said, puzzled, hearing it again, a sound that made her throat constrict. The horse reared, throwing the Gatekeeper; it elongated itself as the fire hit it. Its dark hide turned to wood; harness rustled through its still, shimmering leaves to the ground. Meguet, hand to her mouth, stifling a cry, stared at the Gatekeeper. He glittered no more than usual, and, rolling promptly under the cart, seemed unharmed.

He shouted at her, "Go!"

She went, still carrying the transformed cat, out of habit, and dragging her skirt high above her boots as she ran. Nyx, who seemed to have fallen like a rose off the vines, appeared abruptly in front of her outside the dark tower.

"I'm here," she said, putting a hand on Meguet's shoulder to keep from being run over. The bird cried above them; transfixed, they followed it with their eyes. Calyx, hanging precipitously out a window, ducked suddenly inside. A shower of bronze apples scattered on the grass.

"Roses," Nyx said tersely, eyeing them. "Not Calyx."

"Moro's name," Meguet said, dragging at air. "What is it?"

"A firebird."

"It cries like wood might cry in the fire. Why does it cry like that?"

"They do, according to sources. The cry of the firebird is fierce, desperate, terrible. So Chrysom wrote of, he thought, a fabled bird."

"It sounds human," Meguet said simply, and Nyx looked at her, a colorless, dispassionate gaze. A line ran between her dark brows; she opened her mouth to answer, then turned her head as the guard, followed by curious guests, fanned across the tower yard. The bird cried again, wheeled at them, and they retreated beneath the archways of the tower wall. Fire washed through the archway at their heels, glazed the cobbles with opal. "Nyx, can you do something?" Meguet pleaded. "Before it gets hurt?"

Nyx glanced at her again. "You have a peculiar fondness for birds," she said drily. She lifted her hand as to a falcon; the bird circled the dark tower, circled again. Meguet, watching, thought she saw a thread form between Nyx's uplifted hand and the bird, a gossamer strand of air that shimmered faintly with light against the evening sky. The bird cried once again, spiralling down toward them. Onyx roses swayed on the vine, broke free. Something else flashed in the corner of Meguet's eye: Rush Yarr's blood-fox hair. She turned, running again across the yard as he crouched in an archway, following the bird with his arrow.

"Rush!"

She knew his aim; it was far better than the sorcery he was evidently breathing into his bow. Concentrating, he did not hear her. He shot. Behind Meguet, Nyx flung out another thread. It caught the arching arrow mid-flight; the bird, riding air to meet it, picked it up like prey and cried its fiery rage. The fall of red and gold streaked the dusk. Meguet, running headlong into it, felt a moment of complete astonishment before her eyes filled with gold and then with night.

The evening was suddenly very quiet. The bird flew up the black tower and disappeared. Rush's bow, dropping on the bespelled cobbles, seemed to echo within the tower ring. Nyx, motionless at the foot of the tower, met his stunned eyes. After a blank moment of shock, during which her brain seemed capable only of grappling with analogies, she regathered her attention and picked at the weavings of the force that had transformed Meguet. The spell, at first touch, seemed oddly seamless. Calyx, emerging breathlessly from the tower, bumped into Nyx; she stirred, blinking, overwhelmed again. As if the still emerald leaves had beckoned, they drew the three, along with guards and fascinated guests, to stand staring, speechless, trying to see Meguet among the leaves and roses.

"Oh, Rush," Calyx whispered reproachfully.

"I didn't—I swear I didn't even see her!" He touched a glassy leaf tentatively; his eyes sought Nyx's. "Can't you do something?"

"I was trying!" she flared, exasperated, and Rush flushed a dull red.

"I'm sorry. I am so clumsy with sorcery. It makes me blind and deaf and extremely stupid."

Nyx did not bother to answer. She touched the rose-tree here, there, with her mind. It was a great jewel of malachite and emerald, with ruby, garnet, amber and moonstone blossoming among closed buds of paler jade. Within the jewel was Meguet; seeking her, Nyx found veil after veil of fire, and, at last, the face of the bird.

It was masked, like a swan, with red plumage; its eyes were golden. Sensing her, it cried. The Cygnet in front of it, flying on a long triangle of night sky, melted into a strange vine with swan-shaped leaves.

The bird was on the tower roof. Nyx spun her thread again, flung it like a message: *I am the one you seek.* The bird landed a moment later, noiseless, glowing faintly, its white and fiery red bruising the dusk, clinging, with silver talons, to the malachite leaves.

The faces around Nyx resolved themselves again. The Gate-keeper's was among them, pale, expressionless, hard as the jewel he stared at.

"Apt," he commented. His hand slid among the leaves and silver thorns, closed gently around the stem. Nyx saw him swallow. "It was me put the idea into its head," he added, ten years of courtly smoothness swamped suddenly by his river-brat's accent. "Me shouting at her like that." Like Rush, he sought Nyx's eyes. She said slowly, her arms folded tightly,

"It's an intriguing spell. I can't seem to find her, only the bird. It should be simple, but it's not."

"I'll wait," the Gatekeeper said.

"The bird is waiting, too," Calyx said wonderingly. "It's not screaming now. Is it real? Or sorcery?"

"I can't tell yet," Nyx said. She held its eyes, looking, with her smudged, jewel-framed face, as fey as the firebird. Voices disturbed her; they all turned, saw the Holder and her oldest daughter, surrounded by household guard, half the Hold councilors and their assorted families.

"There it is!" someone cried, as they crossed the yard. They gathered in sudden, perplexed silence around what it clung to. The Holder, her hair nearly as dishevelled as her daughter's, studied the firebird grimly. The guard ringed it, arrows poised; Calyx cried in horror,

"Don't shoot it! You'll hit Meguet!"

"Meguet," the Holder exclaimed, then took in the truant Gatekeeper, his hand, and what he held. Her dark eyes widened; her voice, raised, caused even the firebird to shift. "Moro's eyeteeth! I'll wring its neck!"

"Mother," Nyx breathed.

"That's Meguet? Are you sure?"

"Magic seems to follow her in that shape," the Gatekeeper said.

"Why," Lauro Ro demanded of Nyx, "are you just standing there? Are you waiting for the roses to bloom?"

"I'm waiting," Nyx said tartly, "for some peace and quiet."

"After all that time in the bog, what you don't know about birds, inside and out, you could thread a bead with. How could you let this happen? Can she breathe in there? Is she even alive?"

Iris, her stately and practical eldest, glanced at Nyx's frozen face, and then at the guests fascinated by the sorcery and by the threat of explosion between the Holder and her unpredictable heir. Troubled, she touched her mother's arm. "Mother, Nyx knows what she needs to work with, and if it's peace and quiet, you could at least stop shouting. How could anything possibly be Nyx's fault? Do you think there is anything she wouldn't do for Meguet?"

The Holder looked at her dusty, barefoot heir, standing dark and still, with the first wash of light from the rising moon spilling over her shoulder. She gestured at the guard; they lowered their bows, but kept their tight, watchful circle. Nyx, her voice low, taut, said,

"There is no reason to think she isn't alive. But the bird's magic is random, uncalculated, and very strong. What I need to know is if the bird is the sorcerer or the sorcery. The maker of the magic, or simply its bewitched object. For some reason, it's difficult to tell. It shouldn't be this difficult, but it is. I can't find Meguet at all. You'll have to be patient. Please. If you startle the bird, it may scream again, and I'll have twice the mystery to undo."

The Holder sighed. Arms folded, pins dangling in her wild hair, she looked much like her magical daughter. "I'm sorry," she said. "All this sorcery makes me edgy. It's quiet, now. And not afraid of any of us. It didn't, most likely, fly into my house to turn Meguet into a rose-tree. Was it looking for you?"

"I think so."

"The guard say it snatches arrows out of midair."

"It caught mine," Rush said. "Meguet was running to stop me; she got tangled in its cry."

"There's a blacksmith in the yard with a silver hand," the Holder said grimly. "If this bird is the sorcerer, it has much to account for. May we watch? If it turns you into a black rose-tree, may I wring its neck then?"

Nyx smiled a little. "Please." The smile faded; her brows twitched together again. "What intrigues me most is something Meguet said. She has no power of sorcery, but sometimes she can make very complicated things very simple, by looking at them from an angle I miss. She said about the bird: It has a human cry. That, I think, must be what makes its cry so terrible."

The bird had not stirred since the Holder startled it; it clung like something carved of marble to its spell. A curve of moon rising behind the east tower caught in its silver talons; they flashed like blades. Its eyes, flooding with moonlight, turned milky. Nyx looked at it, leaving her mind open, still, tranquil, an invitation for whatever violence or enchantments or speech it might be moved to. It gazed back at her, as still as she. She tried again to find some thought of Meguet within its spell: Leaves moved through her eyes, endless leaves and petals of carnelian and beaten gold, as if she wandered through an enchanted garden.

Moonlight touched the jewelled leaves, spilled its cold fire over the bird. It roused abruptly, crying its fierce and terrible cry, but its fire only fell pale and spent, harmless as the risen moon's light. As it moved, leaves trembled. The Gatekeeper, still holding a stem, found his hand at Meguet's neck, her hair falling over his arm. For a moment her eyes were malachite, and then they were her own, blinking, surprised, at the Holder's face. The bird landed at her feet in a flood of light. The cry it gave, as it transformed itself, was fully human.

# CHAPTER
# 3

He looked without expression at the arrows aimed at him, as if he did not recognize them, or as if such things, in his peculiar life, were commonplace. Meguet, stooping instinctively for the sword she had dropped, started as it slunk away under her hand. No one else moved; his cry held them spellbound. But nothing of its raw fury and despair lingered in his face; he did not seem to realize he had made a sound.

He was oddly dressed, in a tattered dirty tunic of blue silk, and an embroidered belt of raw red silk. Beneath that he wore a close-fitting garment of gold thread or mail. His soft leather boots were torn and scuffed. He wore strange metal bands at his wrists, intricately fashioned, as if strands of molten metal had been poured over each other in a wide filigree. They looked fire-scorched, so blackened they might have been made of iron. His hair, thick, black, fell past his shoulders. The moon, striking his face at an angle, illumined half: a dark brow, long bones at cheek and jaw, skin drawn tightly across them. The other side of his face was dark.

He did not speak; he seemed resigned to whatever impulses his actions might have inspired. Nyx, connecting moonlight with the pale fire that had come out of the bird before it changed, asked abruptly,

"How long are you human?"

He seemed surprised that she had thought to ask. "Until midnight." His voice was nearly inaudible. "Then the bird hunts."

"What," the Holder asked sharply, "does it hunt?"

"I think mice."

"Who are you? What kind of outlandish place are you from, flying into my house, frightening my household, turning my niece into a rose-tree?"

Meguet, glancing around for the niece in question, took a step backward suddenly, found her own shape against the Gatekeeper.

"The bird cries. It changes things." His voice held a hollow, haunted weariness. "I cannot stop it. Are you the mage?"

"No. I am the Holder of Ro Holding."

"Ro Holding." The blankness in his voice was stunning. Then he added, "The realm of the Cygnet. I have seen the black swan flying on warships' sails. Or the bird has. One of us. Or perhaps it was only a picture. I don't remember."

"Do you remember your name?" Nyx asked. He looked at her for a long time before he answered.

"You are the mage."

"I am Nyx Ro. And mage, sorceress, bog-witch, something of everything." She was holding his eyes, speaking slowly, calmly, using words like tiny grappling hooks to draw and fix his attention. "You are ensorcelled. You came for help."

"Yes," he breathed. "The bird cries for help—it transforms its cries to jewels, gold, anything precious to catch the eye."

"How did you know to find help here?"

"The bird knew."

"You are the bird."

He opened his mouth, closed it. His face changed suddenly, like shifting flame: For a moment he was going to scream. And then it changed again, forgetting. "No. The bird is the sorcery."

"How long have you been ensorcelled?"

"I do not know. A week. A month. A century. I do not know."

"Where are you from?"

"I have forgotten."

"What is your name?"

"I have forgotten," he whispered. Nyx was silent; her own eyes, catching the moon's pale fire, turned misty, inhuman. Meguet, resigned to the expression in them, knew she had ensorcelled herself by her own curiosity. After a moment, Nyx loosed the man, turned her gaze to the Holder. Her brows crooked questioningly. The Holder, equally resigned, flung up a hand.

"All right. I am curious, too. But I will have no more sorcery from that bird. Keep it out of sight, and in Moro's name give the man something to eat besides mice."

The man slid to his knees. His head bowed; he held his arms together as if they were bound, elbow to upturned wrists that the strange, latticed metal protected. His fingers spread wide and flat, a gesture that riveted Nyx's attention. "This to the Cygnet," he said. "All the time I hold."

The Holder sent him, under guard, to be fed, washed, clothed and presented to Nyx's scrutiny in the mage's tower before the bell in the north tower changed night into morning. Nyx returned to what a hasty eye might have deemed the disaster in the library. So orderly was her chaos that she saw at a glance Calyx's futile attempts to straighten things. Musing, the stranger's gesture repeating itself in her mind, she stared into the eye of the Cygnet flying through black marble above the mantel. Beneath the Cygnet, things glinted in candle and torchlight: tiny opaque bottles, dark glass boxes that refused to open, mysterious things carved in amber, wood, gold, that had no openings yet when shaken moved from the liquid rolling within them. She fingered a seamless cobalt box; something buzzed in it like a furious insect. She still did not know, after years of wandering, study, work, what magic lay within that tiny box. What she had finally learned was why she was still ignorant.

The door opened; Meguet, about to enter, stopped in the doorway with an amazed face peering over her shoulder. She turned with barely a flicker of expression, and took the tray that had followed her up. The door closed; she stood, with more expression, looking for a place to set Nyx's supper.

"Just let it go," Nyx said. Meguet, who had been transformed into a rose-tree with less notice, yielded calmly to the whims of sorcery and left the tray hanging in midair. "Thank you."

"Your mother asked me to bring it. She said you hadn't eaten all day."

"How could she remember that? I didn't." She waved the tray across the room. Meguet, glancing around, caught sight of ancient weapons hanging like icicles above her head. She moved promptly, joined Nyx at the hearth, where nothing hung overhead but a faded tapestry. Nyx, bread in one hand, cold chicken in the other, asked,

"Where is he?"

"In a bath, I think. What is it in you that causes furniture to behave in such a peculiar fashion?"

"I prefer a world in a constant state of transmutation," Nyx said with her mouth full.

"Is that what you will tell the Holder?"

"Is she coming up?"

"She's hardly in the mood to leave you alone up here with a man who turns cart horses into trees by breathing."

"Oh."

"So she said."

Nyx shrugged. "The bird's spells wear away by moonlight. Luckily. You made a beautiful rose-tree."

"A rose-tree," Meguet said with feeling. "In front of half the household. Why did you wait for the moon to rescue me? You could have spared me some dignity."

"I couldn't."

"Why not?"

"I don't know."

Meguet gazed at her. She folded her arms, leaned against the mantel. She rarely made unnecessary movements; the heel of her boot ticked uneasy questions against the hearthstones. "You mean you couldn't."

"I couldn't." She put down a chicken bone, eyed it with a bog-witch's speculation, then licked a finger. "That's what fascinates me so. To break a spell, you simply unweave it, strand by strand, until the spell does not exist. Of course, doing this, you are liable to catch the attention of the sorcerer who cast the spell, who may look askance at your meddling. I couldn't undo the spell over you because I couldn't find a single strand. It was of a piece, that magic, like a single jewel. Very beautiful."

"You mean if the moon hadn't risen—"

"Eventually I would have worked it through. There is always a way. Always. But the moon worked faster."

Meguet was silent. A night breeze drifted through the windows, scented with roses; she saw in memory the rose on her shadow. She asked slowly, her fingers gripping hard on her arms, "Is there a connection between the mage and the firebird?"

"I don't know." Nyx poured wine, stared into it without drinking, her dark brows knit. "Is there a connection between a mage looking for a key and a firebird flying over a wall? If the mage had come a month ago and the firebird tomorrow, I would say no. But they came one after another, and both from lands beyond Ro Holding."

"He spoke of warships."

"Then the spell may be very old and the mage dead. Which may make it easier for me. Or more difficult, if the spell is archaic. How long has it been since warships sailed under the Cygnet on Wolfe Sea?"

"Centuries." Meguet shivered suddenly, envisioning time. "Ensorcelled so long, no wonder he cries like that. But will the mage or sorcerer be dead? Didn't Chrysom live for centuries before he even built this house for Moro Ro?"

"Legend says."

"What did he say?"

"Chrysom said very little about himself; he hid his life behind his spells. And apparently he hid a few spells as well, locked away in a secret place. . . . Meguet, if you had something to hide in this room, where would you hide it?"

"Up the chimney. Under a hearthstone. In a table leg. Unless I were a mage. Then—" She shook her head helplessly, blind to sorcery. "I don't know how mages think."

"I do. I want to know what you think."

"What am I hiding?"

"A spellbook. It may not look like a book; it may look like a doorknob. It might even be a book within a book, lines hidden between lines, words within words, but I've searched every book in here that was made before Chrysom died."

"Someone took it."

"No."

"How do you know?"

"Because the spells would have become common knowledge by now. I've suspected for some time that a book had been lost or hidden. What gave the visiting mage a clue to look for the key, I have no idea. Perhaps he will come back and I can ask him. Perhaps he realized what I did: that Chrysom hints now and then at spells which are unknown, even to the mage Diu, for he never told me."

Meguet nodded blankly. The ancient mage Diu, a descendant of Chrysom's, was such a legendary figure it was difficult to conceive of him still alive and swapping spells. "Why? What made you suspect?"

"These," Nyx said, touching the mysteries on the mantel. "He never makes use of them in any book I've ever seen, and I thought I had all his books. And because I came across an odd mark now and then at random, in the margins of his spellbook: a C or a crescent moon holding an M in its arms. The key has the same design on its handle. I've always thought the spells he marked with that sign were incomplete, or so old they are little more than curiosities. But now I know he completed them in another place. A secret place, locked by the key he hid."

"But why would he hide them?"

"That," Nyx said softly, "intrigues me most of all. What kinds of spells did he feel compelled to hide?"

Meguet recognized the gleam of compulsion in her eye: the sorceress in pursuit of the unknown. It had led her most recently into a morass, and the house into turmoil. Meguet said resignedly,

"So you tore the room apart searching for this secret book that may or may not exist."

Nyx nodded, unperturbed, chewing again. "Every crack, every glass rose, every stone and every stone bird in this hearth. I've searched as a mage searches, and I've searched with nothing more than my eyes and my bare hands."

"Then it's not here."

"I think it is here. . . . Chrysom kept everything he used in this room. He lived here; his bones are still here, buried beneath this tower. Even after a thousand years, these old stones are saturated with his magic. They send a signal like a beacon, a ghostly signal, but visible to those who can see the imprint of power. . . ."

"Like the bird? Is that what drew it?"

Nyx was silent, her eyes on Meguet while she mused, using the calm in her cousin's face to focus her thoughts. "I still don't know," she said at last, "where that bird's sorcery comes from. Perhaps it was simply made to find this place. Or any place of power."

"For yet another mage?" Meguet looked shaken. "Nyx, how many mages will we have to contend with?"

Nyx shrugged. "It's only speculation. I'll worry when I find something to worry about." She paused, listening, the wine half-way to her lips. She put it down abruptly. "Like now. My mother is coming."

The room composed itself in an eye-blink, as if, Meguet thought, its tidy self had been simply waiting in abeyance around the moment of time Nyx searched through. Carpets and skins lay underfoot, weapons and tapestries hung on the walls, books surrounded them on shelves and pedestals. The account books Calyx had been studying lay open on a table, her pen angled on a page to mark a place. The mound of chairs that had been balanced in an impossible pyramid on the wine table fanned around the hearth; not a shadow or a flame had been misplaced. Nyx picked her supper out of the air and set it on a table. The door opened.

The Holder entered, followed by her two older daughters, and Rush Yarr; a pair of armed guards flanked the stranger. Even dressed in more civilized fashion, he looked formidable, tall and muscular, something of the bird's wildness about him. Meguet, remembering the rage and desolation in his cry, wished she had thought to arm herself, for he was a man unaware of his own anger. The bird's fury shaped itself into jewelled leaves; what form the man's might take was as yet unknown, perhaps even to himself.

But, entering, he seemed quiet enough. He barely glanced around himself; his eyes found Nyx and clung. Nyx gestured at a chair; he sat hesitantly, as if he had forgotten how. Meguet moved unobtrusively to a table near him, leaned against it. Rush joined her. The guards stood behind the Holder and her daughters, silent, watchful. Nyx, at the hearth, studied him, fingering a strand of tiny pearls sliding down over one ear.

"Is there a name I can call you?" she asked. "One you might remember to answer to?"

He was silent, dredging unknown fathoms of memory. He said finally, "Every name I reach for eludes me. It might be anything. Or nothing."

His face formed suddenly, clearly, under Nyx's absent gaze, as if, until then, she had only seen the firebird. His eyes reminded her of something. She slid the strand of pearls behind her ear and remembered what: the little cobalt box on the mantel behind her. She blinked; the entire room was still, everyone fascinated, it seemed, by her silence. She gathered her thoughts, which had been fragmented by a color. "Two things I must do first. I want the bird's fire and I want its cry."

His lips parted; he whispered, "How?"

"I'll tell you how after I have done it. I don't want to be turned into a gaudy pile of leaves every time it looks at me. And the cry that bird makes is like the crying of every bird I have ever tormented in my sorcery. It would wear me to the heart."

He was staring at her, transfixed, as if she had just changed shape, or taken shape, in his eyes. He made a sudden movement, muscles gathering, his hands closing on the chair arms. The cry came and went like lightning in his face. Silver flashed from behind the Holder as one of the guards moved. Meguet caught his eyes, held him still. Nyx continued, her voice grim but deliberate, "Mages find themselves sometimes on strange roads, in strange places. You can trust me, but you don't know that. My past casts a shadow. If you want a mage without a shadow, you must fly farther north, to a mage called Diu, who is very old and tired, but would do a favor for me if I asked. You must—"

"The bird found you," the man said. He was still gripping his chair, but he had made no other movement. Nyx waited; he added, some feeling breaking into his low voice, "I don't know how long the bird flew to find you. But, entering this house, it cried its magic until you listened. You must do what you can. What you want. The bird will choose to stay or go. It's no question of trust. Or of choice, for me. I have no choice."

The Holder opened her mouth, closed it as the sorceress's eyes flicked at her. Nyx said, answering her unspoken question, "I cannot know how the bird found me, or why, or if it was sent until I begin to work. I suspect that the spell was cast very long ago, and that the bird came here simply because it sensed a thousand years of magic in this tower. So I will assume that, for now, all I have to do is remove a spell."

"And if the bird was sent?" the Holder asked. "Perhaps by the mage who appeared yesterday? You may put the entire house in danger."

"Well," Nyx said softly, "it won't be the first time."

"But—"

"You have heard that bird cry. Is there anything you would not do to stop it, if you could?" The Holder was silent; jewels sparked on her hands as they clasped, containing a mute argument. Nyx added, "I can stop it. I can help. If I bring down sorcery on this house, then we will find a way to deal with that. But now, the bird is here and the sorcerer is only a possibility. I must begin with the magic I see, not with the ghosts and shadows conjured up by fear." She looked at the man again. He had not moved a muscle or an eyelash while she spoke; still she was not certain how much he understood besides hope. "So," she said, toying with an earring, a circle of amber ringed with pearls, "we will wait for the bird to return. Tell me what you remember of your wanderings."

"I remember sea. I remember the bird flying through a storm of burning arrows. I remember the face of a small boy just before he was caught in the bird's fire. I remember waking in snow, in mud, sometimes in trees, sometimes falling out of the air and running from hunters."

"And before you were spellbound?" The earring fell off; she caught it in her palm. She dropped her other hand toward the metal on his wrist, but did not touch it. "What are these?"

He gazed at them without a flicker of recognition. "Armor, of some kind, I think."

"May I see?"

"They don't come off."

"Do you remember any place? A city? A house?"

He paused, made an effort. "I remember a doorway."

"A doorway?"

He shrugged slightly. "Nothing more. A marble doorway, with a marble pot of flowers beside it."

"What was inside the door?"

"A noonday shadow. That's all I remember, except that I saw it, not the bird, because I remember the scent of the flowers and the soft air. It could be any door, anywhere. It means nothing."

"What did you mean when you said to the Holder, 'All the time I hold'?"

He was on his feet, then, with no warning. Meguet, pushing away from the table, saw the cry beginning in his face. Then she heard the midnight bells, and saw the fiery plumage streak his back. She checked her instinctive movement to Nyx's side, having no desire to be caught in the enchanted fire. The bird finished the cry in midair. Fire swarmed at Nyx; Meguet heard Calyx cry out behind the silken, red-gold wall. Nyx opened her hand, held up her defense: an amber earring.

Fire kindled in the amber, a reflection of the onslaught of flame. It kindled in Nyx's misty eyes, washed them with color. For a time her mind was an amber, fire-filled jewel guiding the magic, inviting more, expanding endlessly as it flooded into her, while, to watching eyes, the small jewel in her hand focused and ate the fire. The gorgeous and magical imagery of the bird's enchantments changed and changed again in her mind as it tried to change her: black roses, emerald leaves, snowflakes of silver latticed like the odd armor, birds with sapphire wings and eyes, golden lilies, bird-eggs of topaz and diamond. The threads of the spell were a tapestry of tiny detail worked by a skilled hand. Dimly, as she dragged the fire and rich images endlessly out of it, she heard the bird's ceaseless cry.

Then there was only pale moonlight in her mind, a final rose the color of mist. She could see again; she dropped her hand, blinking. The bird, perched on the chair, was silent. The air darkened slowly, candlelight and shadow. The faces gazing at her looked haunted, exhausted by the cry. She lifted the amber, red-gold now and cracked like glass, and put it back in her ear; her hand trembled slightly.

"So the bird knows where it is," she said.

"Nyx," the Holder breathed, and nothing more. Beside her, Calyx lifted her face from her hands; tears slid between her fingers. Rush, stunned by the sorcery, moved behind her, put his hands on her shoulders. The guards' faces looked pinched, as if they had been standing in a freezing wind. Iris had gone. Nyx's eyes moved to Meguet. Her face was composed, watchful, as always, but so white it might have been carved of snow.

"That must have wakened the house," Meguet commented. Her voice shook suddenly; she put her hand to her mouth, hearing an echo of the fury and the sorrow. "Can you find a jewel hard enough to hold its cry?"

"Maybe," Nyx said softly. Her eyes were wide, luminous; they seemed to look through Meguet. "Maybe one." Meguet, recognizing that expression, felt herself grow very still; she seemed to pick out of Nyx's mind the jewel that hung there. "You do it so easily, Meguet, when you need to, but I have never tried. Yet I saw it all within the Cygnet's eye. . . ."

"What?" Calyx and the Holder asked together.

"All the fractured moments within the whole, like light fractured within the prism . . . a moment shifting into all its layers. If I could throw the bird's cries into another layer of time, we would not hear them and it would still have its voice. I have taken its fire. That cry is its heart and the only word it knows. I will not take its heart." She paused, her eyes clinging to Meguet in lieu of the great dark prism beneath the tower that was the Cygnet's eye. "I looked into the Cygnet's eye, and saw its power. But did it only show me things I could never know? Or did I take that power?" Meguet, transfixed, birdlike, could not look away. The room was soundless. "You wander through the walls of time at need; so did I, that one time, flying faster than thought. But can I wander at will? I am the Cygnet's heir: Did it give me only what I needed, or what I wanted? I wanted everything I saw. . . . For that one moment, I flew within time, but did I fly? Or did the Cygnet?" The black tower walls wrapped around her like the small, circular chamber at the heart of Chrysom's maze. Concentrating, her gaze still on Meguet, she saw the black prism, the faceted eye of power, hanging in the still darkness within a triple ring of time. "You could cry into that silence," she told the bird. "I did."

The bird cried. She heard it standing once again beneath the great prism, which was no longer dark, but fire-white, sculpted with planes of light. The cry filled the chamber, buried deep where only the Cygnet would hear it. It cried, and cried again; the stone walls echoed with its tale, as if it had found the safe and secret place to tell it. Nyx, gazing into the prism, listening for one familiar word, saw Meguet's face reflected in every plane. Then she saw Meguet, in the shadows on the other side of the prism, caught in the tangle of cries, as if Nyx, using her face to open memory, had pulled her into the fractured time.

She blinked; the prism faded, and she saw Meguet's face again, a stillness in it like the stillness of stone. The mage's tower circled them again, with its triple ring of stone and night and time. Color flooded suddenly into Meguet's face; she stared, incredulously, at Nyx. The bird cried, but its cries were soundless now, its story hidden.

The Holder and Calyx were both on their feet.

"Where did you go?" Calyx demanded, astonished. "You both vanished."

"I sent the bird cry into the heart of the maze," Nyx said. She ran her hands through her hair wearily, scattering jewels, her eyes on Meguet. "I seem to have pulled us both along with it."

"That's not possible," the Holder said. She appealed to Meguet. "Is it?"

"No." She drew breath, shivering slightly. "There was no need for me there."

"I needed you," Nyx said. "You took me there in memory. Who knows which of us guided whom? The bird is crying to the Cygnet instead of to us, which means we can all sleep soundly." She dropped her hand on Meguet's shoulder, and smiled a little, tightly. "Maybe that's all we did: walk back into memory, and leave, appropriately, a bird cry there."

Meguet, still standing tensely, shook her head. "You shifted time," she said simply, "not memory." She paused, listening to her words, or to other words echoing under the moonlight. The Holder said softly, her dark, troubled eyes on the sorceress's face,

" 'All the time I hold.' "

# CHAPTER
## 4

Meguet watched the dawn unfurl like a wing of fire across the Delta. She had wakened early, anticipating a summons, and had seen the Gatekeeper, anticipating dawn, extinguish the torches beside the gate. Beyond the wall, the waves picked up light, rolled it into scrolls and unrolled it again, like a spell in some forgotten language across the sand. She dressed quickly, without waking her attendants, pulling swans down her wrists and across her shoulders, for despite the mysteries and magic, there was yet another prosaic day of council ahead of them, if they could dodge the sorcery falling headlong out of the air. She braided her hair as she went down. Crossing the yard, she caught a breath of the moist, dank sweetness of the inner swamps, lily and mud and still, secret waters. The Gatekeeper's face turned toward it; she wondered if he had smelled it, too, if he were breathing in memories. And then he saw her.

His breakfast followed close behind her. He shared it with her, the tray balanced between them in the tiny turret. He buttered hot bread for her, offered pale, spiced wine from his cup, peeled quail's eggs. She nibbled, weary and absent-minded, listening, in some deep part of her, for the Holder's voice.

He said, "I saw light all night from the mage's tower."

Her eyes, following the white thread of a gull's flight, flicked to his face. "Then you were awake all night."

"I thought it best," he said wryly, "the way things have been getting past me." He cut wafer-thin strips of melon and passed her one. "I don't know what to expect next."

She saw then the familiar shadows under his eyes, that came when he saw too little or too much in the small lonely hours of the night. She set the tray aside abruptly, shifted to sit beside him.

"Nobody knows," she said, and told him what the firebird had said, what Nyx had done. When she finished, her head in the hollow of his shoulder to dodge the flood of morning light, he commented,

"She has a way with birds."

Meguet lifted her head, eyed him narrowly. He let her see the faintest line of a smile beside his mouth. "You had better be smiling," she said dourly.

He smoothed her hair. "It's not so long ago that she had us all dancing at shadows because of birds. Now here's another over the gate so fast it left the Gatekeeper of Ro House standing with his mouth open in a wake of pinfeathers. I might as well row myself back to the swamp."

"Take me with you," she sighed. "I'm housebound with this council. I want to pick lilies in a bog and have you braid them in my hair."

"They must be getting edgy, the Hold Councils."

"They're curious. I'm edgy. The Holder looks as if she swallowed a thunderbolt. Her house was spellbound by a mage with no good intentions who may or may not return, and her heir is up in Chrysom's tower with a bird who may be trouble or may not, but most likely has trouble on its tail. In the middle of this, she has to sit through speeches about sheep."

"What kind of trouble does she look for from the firebird?"

"The mage who cast the spell."

He made a soft sound, stirring. "Another one? How many mages are we looking at?"

"Maybe this one will knock on the gate."

"They don't seem in the habit of knocking. Why would a mage

twist a man out of his shape for all but a few moonlit hours? Only to make him remember that he's human?"

"That's all he does remember."

"Not what he did to get himself turned into a bird?"

Meguet was silent, thinking of the cries that came and went across the man's face like lightning across a barren landscape. She said, "The bird remembers."

"But not the man." His eyes strayed seaward. "So. I must watch for a dangerous and cold-blooded mage."

"If he's still alive. And if—" She paused again, her brows crooked uncertainly, her eyes on another bird: the Cygnet, flying across the mantle of the bell ringer entering the north tower to summon the councilors together.

"And if what? What do you see, Meguet?"

She blinked, her thoughts clearing. "I see that I must leave you."

"If what?" he asked insistently, holding her with nothing more than the tone of his voice, his eyes. She gazed back at him, perplexed, hearing again the terrible, desperate cry of the firebird.

"If," she said, "the bird is innocent."

Nyx, present to the outward eye during the council that day, was so preoccupied that Calyx touched her once or twice, wondering obviously if she were still breathing. All her attention was focused in the high tower room, where the mage might return. He would want the key. He would guess that she had hidden it in a different place. She had spent some time before dawn trying to turn it invisible, or change its shape into one of Calyx's hoary household records, or a rose among the hundreds on the tower vines. It resisted all enchantment. She gave up finally and put it in her pocket, a solution which would have horrified the Holder. Nyx did not approve of it herself, but she had run out of ideas by morning. The mage might disrupt the council, demanding the key, but the worst he would most likely do would be to give everyone something to talk about besides border tolls. The bird, she suspected with no particular evidence, might fare differently.

So she had separated them, the key and the bird, in hope that the strange, ruthless mage, seeking one mystery, would ignore the other.

She carried the key with her to the great hall in the third tower, where the councilors ate savory delicacies with their fingers, drank wine, and continued their endless debates while families and guests slowly gathered from woods and gardens, city shops and neighbors' houses, for supper. She had promised the Holder that for one evening at least, she would not shut herself up behind another locked door with yet another bird. But birds and rumors shadowed her, it seemed. As she bit into melted cheese wrapped in butter pastry, young Darl Kell of Hunter Hold, who had eyes like some of the frogs she had used in her fires, asked with a bluntness he meant to be charming,

"Is it one of yours?"

She raised a brow mutely, her tongue busy dodging hot cheese.

"The great bird in the tower. A bit of your leftover magic from the swamp?"

She coughed on a pastry crumb. "No," she said when she could speak. "If nothing else, I'm tidy. If I transform something, it stays transformed, and I don't leave it a voice to complain with."

Darl Kell flushed to his broad ears. "You're not like your sisters," he said, and stalked off to gaze at Calyx. Nyx brushed crumbs off her silk and wished she could be as tidy in life as she was in art. Someone pushed wine into her hand and said, his voice too close to her ear,

"He could stand some room for improvement, if you're in the mood to transform."

She looked up, into the smiling eyes of Urbin Dacey, whose father led the Withy Hold Council. He was tall and black-haired and amber-eyed. She had noticed those eyes several times during the council, and had wondered what perversity they watched for. She took a sip of wine, and answered equably,

"I don't transform by whim. And I don't practice such sorcery on humans."

"Pity. His ears could stand some." He turned deftly, lifted a plate of stuffed mushrooms as she opened her mouth. "What sorcery do you allow yourself to practice on humans?"

"As little as poss—"

"You have been practicing some on me."

"What?"

"I've felt it in the council chamber. You meet my eyes with your pale moon eyes. You draw at me. Calyx is very beautiful, but she is day, and you are night, secret, beautiful, mysterious, perhaps dangerous. Are you dangerous at night?"

Nyx gazed at him, a mushroom halted midway to her mouth. "What in Moro's name are you talking about?"

His smile never faltered. "I believe I make myself clear. I am falling a little in love with you."

"Oh, don't be ridiculous." She bit into the mushroom, added, chewing, "Love is the last thing on your mind."

He was silent, looking down at her so long that she wondered if she had left mushroom in some unsightly place. "It's a game," he said lightly. "You should learn to play it. It gives the world grace."

He slid the glass from her hand, took a sip of wine, and slipped it back between her fingers. She said softly, "And how well you play it. You must practice often."

"I'll teach you."

"Unfortunately, I lack grace." She set the glass on the table and stood quietly, not moving or speaking, simply looking at him until his smile finally faltered and he turned away.

She picked up the glass again, took a hefty swallow. Someone else stepped to her side and marvelled, "You made Urbin Dacey blush."

She lowered the glass with some relief. "Rush."

He brushed a crumb off her sleeve. "It takes a complex sorcery to discomfit Urbin. He won't give up easily, though. I've seen him watching you. He plays a game he hates to lose."

"I have no time for games," she said, feeling the weight of the key in her pocket. Rush looked at her silently a moment; she glimpsed a familiar curiosity in his eyes and wondered what

realm she had neglected to explore. He asked the question in
his eyes.

"Does sorcery preclude love?"

"I wouldn't know. It's not in Chrysom's books."

"Is that all you—" he began, then saw he was being teased. He
smiled a little, still curious, while she helped herself to a plate of
tiny biscuits rolled in poppy seeds and spices. She said, because
he wanted to know,

"I take after my mother, who roamed Ro Holding when she
was young and found three fathers for three daughters. Sorcery
does not preclude curiosity, and I have satisfied my curiosity at
times. But—"

"With whom?"

Like her mother, she ignored the question. "But you have to
stand still for love. I could never stand still."

"Like Urbin," he said, then flushed a little. But she mulled that
over calmly.

"Maybe. But at least I'm honest."

"Yes," he said, not looking at her, but she saw the memories
in his eyes. "Urbin has a thousand ways of saying one thing. You
don't hide behind language, which is why he can't find, among
his thousand ways, the one way to make you listen. Neither could
I," he added, but lightly, and she smiled, seeing no bitterness in
his eyes.

"Now," she said, "we listen to one another." She touched his
arm and turned, to find Arlen Hunter in her path, who had come
to tell her what he believed about her, and what he didn't, feeling
it was important for her to know. She extracted herself abruptly
from his muddle of awe and prurience, deciding that no effort
to please her mother was worth becoming civilized for this. She
slipped away to wait for moonrise.

Across the hall, Meguet, disarmed, dressed in red silk and gold,
found siege laid against her own patience. Tur Hunter, blue-eyed,
golden-haired, heir to Hunter Hold, had lost, he said, his heart to
her green eyes. He was smiling, but relentless, burning hot and
cold, and willing to fight a slight to his pride. She said carefully,

"My own heart is bound to this house; my eyes are not free to stray."

"Not from the gate?" he said, his smile thinning, and she felt the blood rise in her face. "Your whims are your business, but you should have some respect for your own heritage. What in Moro's name can you do with a Gatekeeper?"

"Love him," she said simply, with no tact whatsoever. Tur Hunter snorted, flushing.

"What will you do? Marry him and live among the cottagers?"

She shrugged slightly. "I hadn't thought. If past is status, some among the cottagers can trace their families back a thousand years, when Moro Ro's status in Ro Holding was that he had a bigger cottage than anyone else and a bloodier sword."

"And what does your Gatekeeper have?" he retorted. "Born among tortoises and river rats, he still has the swamp in his voice. You'll tire of that soon enough."

"Then," she said, keeping her voice steady with an effort, "it is not worth your breath to interfere, since I will cast him aside eventually over the cadence of lilies and slow dark water and small birds in his voice."

Tur was silent a breath, then changed weapons. "Now," he said solicitously, and took her hand in his, "I have put you in the position of having to defend him. I have made you angry. That was hardly my intention. If the Holder hasn't interfered in your infatuation with the murkier side of the Delta, it must be because she is wiser than I am, and knows it is like the elusive, colorful swamp lights, of little substance and will burn itself out. Tell me what I can do to persuade you to forgive me."

She almost suggested something. But the Holder was beside her suddenly, as if summoned by the swamp lights smoldering in the air between them.

"Tur," she said, fixing a dark eye upon him, "stop trying to lure my niece to Hunter Hold; I need her here. She is one of the foundation stones of this house, like my Gatekeeper, and I won't free her for all the gold in Hunter Hold. Go and get me wine and

take it outside and drink it." She took Meguet's arm, forcing Tur
to loose her hand, and led her to the hearth. It was cold, unoccu-
pied, and offered a moment of privacy within the crowded hall.

Meguet said softly, "I can fight my own battles. Though I
didn't think I would have to."

The Holder, who loved fires, eyed the empty grate wistfully.
She said, "Neither did I, but then I never admitted to anything
I had to defend. Anyway, I wanted to talk to you. When you are
not guarding the Holding Council, I want you with Nyx."

Meguet, startled, said, "There's not much I can do for her."

"I know that and I don't care. I don't want her alone with
that stranger, and you're the only one in the house she would
put up with." She kicked the grate moodily, and turned, gazing
at the placid, murmuring hall as if mages were concealed in the
hangings or underfoot beneath the carpets. "I want you with her
in those night hours when the bird becomes human."

Meguet was silent, seeing again the rich and stunning shapes
the bird's cry had taken in the yard. "I wonder where he came
from . . . I wonder if anyone is alive to miss him or search for
him."

"I'm wondering who cast that spell and when Nyx's meddling
will bring yet another mage to my door."

"If that mage is still alive."

"There are too many mages." Her fingers lifted to her hair,
searching for pins to pull, but they were too well hidden. She
folded her arms instead, frowning at her shadow in the torchlight.
"Nyx assumes the mage is dead. I assume otherwise, for the sake
of my house. That is why I want you with her. She trusts you,
and you have more common sense than she does."

"Only for an ordinary world."

"That's the one I want to keep her alive in," the Holder said
grimly. "She has so much power, and she has hardly scrubbed
the mud off her feet from that morass she trapped herself in."

"The power was given to her freely."

"It's not her heart that worries me now, it's her magpie curiosity that picks at anything glittering of magic. She's facing a

twisted sorcery unfamiliar even to her. She may have terrorized the population of birds in the swamp, but she never made anything human cry so desperately. And all she can see of the sorcery is something she can't do herself—she's blind to danger. Even the young man seems dangerous to me."

"Yes."

"I don't think he's just an innocent under a spell. He looks powerful and unpredictable."

"Like Nyx, not long ago."

The Holder's brooding attached itself to her. "Meguet Vervaine, are you counseling compassion over common sense?"

"Never," Meguet said flatly, "where Nyx is concerned. But given the murkier sorcery she has dabbled in, she may have more success with a bird with a questionable past than a mage with a tidier history would."

The Holder made an undignified sound. "Let's hope his past is tidier than hers. Wherever his past is. Or was."

"Perhaps he is from Ro Holding and he simply can't remember. He does remember the Cygnet flying on warships."

"He'd have to be a very old bird."

"Or a young man trapped outside of his time."

The Holder touched her eyes. "That is something Nyx would find irresistible. But how much does she know about time? Is that common knowledge among mages?"

"She pulled me within time to stand beneath the Cygnet's eye. For all I know she may have all the Cygnet's power."

The Holder drew breath. "Moro's bones. It's unprecedented." Her eyes moved over the hall, searching. "Where is she? I asked her to stay through supper."

"I saw her talking to Rush. And then to Arlen Hunter."

"I don't see her."

"She must be here," Meguet said, failing to find her. "She doesn't forget things."

"She forgets unimportant things," the Holder said darkly. "Supper, her shoes, sleep, time. Maybe that mage returned without our knowing, ensorcelled us all again between a bite and a swallow.

Maybe," she added, with some hope, "he has found the book himself and vanished back into his own secret country."

"It can't be all that secret," Meguet pointed out, "if he has heard of Chrysom."

The Holder closed her eyes. "Don't raise side issues," she said tersely. "Find Nyx before the moon rises and I lose her again to that demented bird."

The bird's eye reflected a sorceress within its golden iris. It perched on a window ledge; its shadow, cast long and black by the torch beside the window, cut across the sorceress's path to take shape against the hearth: a faceless dark beneath the stone Cygnet. Nyx was aware of the bird's scrutiny and its shadow. She moved imperturbably through both, continuing her search for the missing book and waiting for moonrise. She had explored everything but the oddments on the mantel. There, she reasoned, it must be: the mage's voice buzzing inside the cobalt box, the barely perceptible shift of weighty thought within the emerald bottle.

The bird opened its beak. No cry came out of it, no fire, but the sorceress turned to face it.

"Be patient," she said. "I haven't forgotten you."

She folded her arms, leaned against the mantel, frowning slightly, studying the bird. The red on its folded wingtips made an elaborate chessboard pattern against the white. Its longer plumes trailed down the stone, delicate puffs of white that stirred at a breath. Its sharp talons caught light like metal; the mask of fiery feathers around its eyes gave it a fierce and secretive expression. Nyx, slowly dissolving within an amber eye, saw only herself in its thoughts. Whatever language it spoke—bird or human—was hidden.

"You are well guarded," she commented, returned to herself on the hearth. The bird did not shift a feather, as motionless as if it had become one of its own enchantments. The fire still hung in Nyx's ear. She toyed with it absently. The bird opened its beak soundlessly, in recognition.

Red the color of the bird's mask snagged her eye. She turned her head, studied a tiny red clay jar on the mantel. It was shaped like a hazelnut with a flat bottom and a cap of gold. The clay was seamed with minute cracks, as if whatever it held had seeped out centuries before. Nyx picked it up, weighed it in her hand. Chrysom, who had, centuries after his death, gotten suddenly more complex, might have left an empty bottle on his mantel, or a mage's trap. A day or two ago she had known how he thought. Now, she was not so sure.

"Well," she said, and met the bird's intent golden stare. "Better sorry than safe."

She gazed down at the jar, letting her thoughts flow like air or water into the spider web of cracks. The rough, dry edges permitted her only so far, no farther, into their tiny crevices. What stopped her, she couldn't tell; it had no substance. The gold cap, molded into the clay by the slow shift of particles of metal, seemed solid; touching it, her thoughts turned into gold.

It was of a piece, like the bird, like the bird's enchantments: a weave of magic so fine she could not isolate a single thread. Baffled, she withdrew from it, fascinated by her ignorance.

She put it back on the mantel, picked up a round bottle of opaque, swamp-green glass, no bigger than her palm. Its neck was short, slender, and had no opening. But it was not empty. Something within it shifted against the glass sides; the bottle tilted sluggishly in her hand, then rolled upright. Her thoughts grew crystal, rounded, green, then eased inward, dropped away from the glass into the tiny pool of magic it enclosed.

She fell into a great pool of nothing. The world lost hold of her, sent her tumbling headlong into an endless mist. Startled, she nearly withdrew; then, curious, she continued falling, seeing nothing, hearing nothing, moving toward nothing until she realized she could fall forever in that tiny bottle and never reach the bottom.

She withdrew slowly, finding stone walls beyond the mist, books, the bird's unblinking eyes. It took some effort; she rested a moment, wary now, but still intrigued, before she explored farther. She chose something black: glass or stone carved into a little block of shadow. It was wrapped in a web of silver filaments that wound around one another and parted and crossed again in an endless, intricate pattern. Concentrating on a single filament, she found herself on a silver road.

She did not need to move; it moved beneath her, swift as wind. Darkness dropped away from the road on both sides, as if the small block enmeshed in the silver had no reality itself. The silver turned and coiled, looked back, crossed itself, moving so fast she felt she had left her thoughts at some forgotten crossroad. The road went everywhere and nowhere, it seemed. On impulse, she dropped off the rushing silver into the darkness within it.

She found herself in a cube of night, with the silver running in front of her, behind her, underfoot and overhead, like a net. She tried to withdraw, but she could not reach past the silver. It was too intricate, it moved too quickly; catching hold of it was like trying to hold water pouring down a cliff.

*So I am caught,* she thought, *like a fish in Chrysom's net. But what is the net made of?*

The way out of the trap was to become the trap. . . .

She could not hold a single, wild thread; she might, leaping out of the dark, out of herself, hold the entire moving, glowing web. Unthinking, forgetting even her own name, she expanded into the darkness, and then, at all points and loops and crossroads, into the rushing current of silver.

The flowing pattern froze. Suspended, her mind the intricate net of filament, she saw what the dark had hidden: cubes within cubes of patterned silver, each a completely different weave, growing smaller and smaller but never vanishing. If she could move between them from one cube to the next, if she could walk each pattern . . . But what were they?

And then she remembered the filaments, blackened with age and fire, on the wrists of the stranger. His hands opened wide, as if to loose some lost power within the patterns. He spoke . . .

She whispered, "Time."

She was suspended within tantalizing spells for time. But what spell opened the paths to use? How could she get here, there, or anywhere on those fantastic silver roads that led nowhere outside the box? How, she wondered more practically, could she get herself outside the box?

*I got in,* she reminded herself. *I can get out.*

But if she had flung herself down a deep, dry well, that would be easy to say and not so easy to do. She swallowed, for the second time in her life, the little, cold, pebble-hard fact that all her will and all the knowledge she possessed might not be enough to find her way back to the world.

*I am looking into Chrysom's eye,* she thought. *Into his mind, which until now I thought I knew. This is one of the puzzles in the missing book, which is why I cannot solve it. Yet.*

Later, after she had contemplated the frozen, glowing paths without inspiration, she felt again the feathery touch of fear.

*They will find me,* she thought, *in the library, silent, blind, motionless, holding the box in my hand. Will they have the sense to leave me with it? Rush wouldn't. He would smash it, to set me free. I could be trapped in its broken shards forever . . . I should have taught Rush more sorcery. But I never had the patience. And he would never stop to think.*

She quieted her unruly thoughts, focused them again. Nothing to do, it seemed, but pick a path again, see if her thoughts might lead somewhere, if the path wouldn't. She narrowed her vision, dropped onto the nearest pattern. Instantly she felt it move, dividing, looping, flowing everywhere and nowhere, as it had before, and she was powerless to control it.

*Time,* she thought. *What is it? A word. To endow a word with power, you must understand it.*

Settling into that one place to begin to understand Chrysom's spell, she saw a man in the distance ahead of her.

His head was bent slightly; he did not turn or speak. He simply walked, his eyes on the flow and weave of silver as if, out of the endless twists and turns, he fashioned a solid path and followed it.

She found the path he left, a stillness in the wild flow, a single strand of silver frozen among the rushing patterns. Amazed, she followed it, wondering if Chrysom had set a shadow of himself within the paths to guide the unwary mage. The road beyond the guide began to blur into darkness. Nyx quickened her pace; as if he felt her sudden fear, he slowed. Closing the distance between them, she recognized him.

She caught her breath, stunned at the sight of the long black hair, the warrior's straight line of shoulder. Turning, he met her eyes, held them. She blinked, and the tower stones formed around them, the moon hanging in the black sky beyond a window. Gazing at her, still caught, perhaps, in some twist of past, for an instant he recognized himself.

"My name is Brand."

# CHAPTER
# 5

With the name came memory. He flinched away from it as from fire; for an instant his human face became the firebird's cry. Then his eyes emptied of expression: the dreamer waking, the dream forgotten. She whispered,

"You were with me in Chrysom's box. You led me out."

He only gazed at her blankly. "I don't remember."

"Brand." She added, at his silence, "That is your name. You just told me."

"I don't remember."

The door opened. Preoccupied, she did not loose his eyes, just help up a hand for silence. She received it, so completely she wondered if she had thrown a spell across the room. "You remember," she said. "Your eyes remember. The bird remembers."

"The bird—" He paused, bewildered. "The bird is sorcery."

"It cries your sorrow."

"It cries jewels as well as sorrow. Are those mine also?"

"Perhaps. If you are a mage."

He was silent again, throwing a net into the still black waters of memory. The net came up empty. "Why would I be that?"

"Only another mage could have rescued me from Chrysom's spell." She heard something from the door then, not sound so much as a rearrangement of disturbed air. She asked, because it had to be asked, not because she had much hope of answer, "Do you know the mage who wears a white dragon on his breast?"

His head lifted slightly; he gazed beyond her, as if dragons were gathering soundlessly in the shadows just beyond the candlelight. For an instant he seemed to see what lay beyond the light: the country where he had been named. The memory faded; he shook his head. "I cannot see that dragon."

"The mage?"

"What?"

"Do you know the mage?"

He started to speak, stopped. All color left his face then; his hands clenched. Nyx saw the firebird cry in his eyes, of grief and rage and danger.

Red shimmered in the corner of her eye. She turned her head, saw Meguet, dressed for supper, slide a blade noiselessly off the wall. Whether she wanted it to fight mages or dragons, Nyx wasn't sure; either, it seemed suddenly, might blow in unexpectedly on the night wind. She turned back to Brand, touched the metal patterns on his wrists lightly. When he made no protest, she lifted his hands in hers.

"Is this the path of time you followed here?" He looked at them, mute. "All Chrysom's paths are silver. How did these get so black?"

He shook his head, seeing nothing of mage or time or color in the blackened metal. "I don't understand. The bird brought me here. Not these."

"You are the bird," she reminded him patiently, and as patiently he replied,

"The bird is sorcery."

Meguet tugged at Nyx's attention. She still stood silently at the door, but her face was pale and her eyes flicked at every breeze-strewn shadow. She met Nyx's glance, asked softly, "Is the mage looking for him?"

"Probably."

"Nyx—"

"It's an interesting problem," Nyx admitted. "It's hard enough to hide the key, let alone the bird."

"Where did you put the key?"

"In my pocket." She added, at Meguet's expression, "It refused to change its shape, and I couldn't think what else to do with it."

"So you took it to the council hall?"

"Well, I could hardly slide it under a carpet. If the mage returned, I wanted to be there."

"I didn't," Meguet said succinctly. She made a move toward a chair, then drew back to the door, looking, Nyx thought, with the gold threading through her loose hair, and the ancient sword, almost as tarnished as the metal on Brand's wrists, half-hidden in the silken folds of her skirt, unlikely enough to startle even the mage again. Nyx said,

"You might as well sit. I doubt that either dragon or mage will use the door."

Meguet did so, but reluctantly, still holding the sword. "Dragon," she said, "being the little winged animal made of thread."

"According to Chrysom, who must have roamed farther than I ever realized, dragons are made of flesh and blood and fire, and most are not small."

"How big," Meguet asked after a moment, "is not small?"

"Huge. So Chrysom said."

Meguet shifted uneasily, hearing dragon wings in the rustling wind. "Well," she sighed, "at least they can't come through the windows. Did Chrysom happen to say where there might be dragons?"

Nyx shook her head. "Like the firebird, he considered them fable. Or he wrote as if he did. Now, after coming out of that black box, I'm not sure what he knew, where he travelled, or when. He—"

"What black box?" Meguet's eyes fell to what Nyx still held in her hand, and widened. "That? You were in there?"

"My mind was."

"Moro's name. Why?"

"It seemed a good idea at the time. Not," she admitted, "one of my better ones. I wanted to see if any of those odd things were the missing book. This is full of paths, twisting, turning, looping strands of silver. I think they lead to different times, moments within moments, perhaps the sorcery the mage used to slow time. But I don't know how to use them, and I think the knowledge is in the missing book, as well as in the firebird's memory."

"That was the spell he rescued you from?"

"Brand. Coming out, he remembered his name. But nothing more, not even that he had walked a path of time with me in that box, and led me out."

Meguet closed her eyes, dropped a cold hand over them. "I don't know why your mother bothered to send me up here."

"I don't know, either. Why did she?"

"I'm supposed to guard you. At best a futile notion, at worst laughable."

Nyx turned, set the box carefully back on the mantel. "My mother worries too much."

"How can you say that? The mage is not only looking for the key you are carrying around in your pocket, but for the firebird, both of which are in the place he will obviously return to, unless you spun him into thread so thoroughly he is still trying to untangle himself." There was a tap at the door; she nearly jumped, then rose with more dignity. "That will be Brand's supper. The Holder requested your presence in the hall."

"I can't go now," Nyx said absently. "I'm thinking." She sat down, slipped her shoes off and propped her feet up. Arms folded, she frowned at midair. A wide-eyed page set the supper tray on a table, seemed inclined to linger to watch the firebird eat, and encountered Nyx's eye. Meguet, left between the pensive sorceress and the ravenous man, sat tensely, watching for a thread of white dragon-wing, a dust-gold face in the shadows, and wondering what raw deed the firebird's jewelled enchantments hid. She murmured,

"There are too many mages."

Nyx's eyes rose, fixed on Brand. She nodded, still frowning. "He could have ensorcelled himself."

"And the other mage is following to free him?"

"It's possible. There is a way to find out."

"How?" Then she leaned forward, gripping the sword hilt. "No."

Nyx shrugged. "I don't see how we are to get closer to the truth this way. The man retreats constantly into the firebird. If we let the mage find him, Brand might remember himself along with the mage."

"Not here. Not in this tower, in the middle of the Holding Council. They may be bitter enemies. The entire house would be in danger. I think you should hide the firebird—"

"Where?" Nyx asked. "In the maze beneath the tower?"

"Of course not."

"Then where?"

"In the thousand-year-old wood. Not even the mage would find him among the shifting trees."

"I could find him easily there. What I can do, I must assume the mage can do."

"Then somewhere in the city, or in the swamp—"

Nyx's mouth crooked. "I can't disappear into the swamp with a bird. My mother would spit lightning. I would prefer to face the mage."

"I'll leave," Brand said abruptly. They both looked at him, startled, as if they had forgotten he could speak. Disturbed, he pushed away his food. He came to stand before Nyx. "I didn't know the bird would endanger you."

Nyx checked her immediate response, said patiently, "You might walk out of here, but the bird would return. It's you who must learn to cry jewels. To cry sorrow. Or the bird will never set you free."

He shook his head at her obtuseness. "All I know," he said, "is that the bird came to you, sorcery to sorceress. First you must deal with the sorcery. Then I will be able to remember."

She drew breath. His eyes held some of the bird's fierceness, but it was the fierceness of desire, of determination. "All right," she said at last, wondering that he had guided her so skillfully out of one maze, only to be so blind in another. "I will work with the spell awhile, instead of your human memory. One can't be more difficult than the other. But I have already tried to find my way into the spell, and gotten nowhere."

"Try again," he pleaded and sat down on the window ledge where the bird had waited for the rising moon.

She found the bird's face within his thoughts; its spellbound mind yielded nothing to her of memory or enchantment. When the bird itself reappeared, Nyx slipped within its mind, as easily as she had dropped into Chrysom's tiny box. For a time, she wandered among the bird's enchantments that bloomed cease-lessly behind its eyes, and faded again without the fire that fashioned them. They formed like dreams around her, thought-less, intangible, with nothing of either mage or Brand in them. She found her way out again, and said, studying the bird with some perplexity,

"This is exasperating. The bird won't give me a path into the man; the man won't give me a path into the bird. It's as if they exist in separate worlds. I might as well be back in Chrysom's black box for all the sense I can make of this."

"There is always a way," Meguet said sleepily. "You told me that." She received no answer; Nyx had disappeared again. To Meguet's eye, she looked pensive, very still, as if she were chasing the tag-end of some sudden, imperative notion in her head. She did not move; she scarcely seemed to breathe. Meguet sighed noiselessly, and settled back in her chair. Just before her eyes closed, she saw the white dragon's golden eye in the shad-ows beside the hearth.

She was on her feet almost before she had opened her eyes. The dragon was gone; Nyx had not moved.

"Nyx," she whispered, shifting toward her, the blade poised in her hands. "Nyx."

Nyx did not answer. Meguet, glancing at her, saw her frowning at the bird, her arms folded. She did not move, she did not blink. Meguet raised her voice. "Nyx!"

"She won't hear you," the mage said. He was still invisible, though she caught the flick of a dragon's wing, the shift of a claw here and there, as he moved noiselessly, restively, in front of the mantel. Listening, she heard faint music, soft laughter on the parapet wall. He read her mind. "I didn't meddle with your time. I didn't come for trouble. I came only for the key."

Meguet screamed Nyx's name. Nyx remained oblivious, but through a south window Meguet saw one of the turret-torches raised aloft, as if the Gatekeeper had felt her desperate need. She heard voices within the tower, guards and pages tossing alarms down the stairwell, a flurry of running in the outer yard.

"I sealed the door," the mage said. "They won't get through. Where is the key? Just tell me that. I'll find it and go." He spoke softly, as if not to disturb Nyx, but Meguet heard the strain in his voice. She wondered if he hid himself from Nyx or from the firebird.

"She put it somewhere."

"Where?"

"I think in a book. One of the household records over there, I don't remember which—"

"You're lying." He sounded amazed. "I didn't think you could lie. Where is it really?"

"Among the roses on the vines."

The dragon eye came closer; she shifted a step or two toward Nyx. "A good place to hide it. One rose among a thousand roses. But even if I picked them all, I'd never find it there. Where is it really hidden?"

"The firebird changed it with its cry," she said desperately, and he was silent, as if at last he believed her. Fists battered at the door; voices, impatient and furious, made improbable suggestions about makeshift battering rams, and Rush's makeshift sorcery.

"Meguet," said the air, startling her with her name. "I can't wait for tomorrow's moonrise. Where is the key? If you don't tell me, I will turn this household, one by one, into screaming firebirds. Beginning with the Gatekeeper."

"So," she whispered, her mouth dry, "this is your spell."

"So it seems."

Nyx turned abruptly, pulling amber from her ear lobe. She held it up. The bird, freed from her mind, cried soundlessly. Its enchanted fire leaped from the amber, illumined the mage for a breath. He vanished before the fire struck him, but not before the firebird had seen his face.

The bird cried. Its noiseless cry became the man's cry, of such fury and agony that it froze both Nyx and Meguet and silenced the crowd outside the door. Brand moved under their amazed eyes, tore swords off the wall. The white dragon leaped to fly. The blades in Brand's hands spun and flashed in a whirling, singing dance of death too quick to follow. Meguet, mesmerized by its glittering intricacy, moved a fraction too late to intercept the dragon in its deadly flight. The blades soared upward, turned again, came down so fast at the dragon that when the mage halted them in midair, Brand lost his balance, stumbled against them. He was instantly surrounded by a ring of swords, shear-edged, gleaming like ice. The white dragon slipped under his blades and flew headlong into the amber fire. A swirl of leaves the color of bone and pearl scattered to the floor.

Brand, his face white, set with fury, was thwarted only for a moment by the blades. He changed himself; the firebird cried within the ring. It caught air, flew above them. Nyx's searching amber found the mage again: a flickering just visible beside the windows. He shifted. The fire continued out a window; Meguet heard an outraged shout from the yard. The firebird circled, its wings brushing wall and torch fire, silver talons outstretched to tear the mage out of the air and hold his shape. The fire swept over him again. He moved, fading, but not quickly enough; the bird's claws raked his outstretched arm before he vanished. Nyx, sweeping the amber fire across the dark, following his movements with a mage's eye, nearly transformed Meguet as he reappeared beside her.

"Give me the key," he said to Nyx. "Or I'll take her with me." His voice shook; Meguet saw the blood under his tattered sleeve.

"Take the spell off Brand," Nyx said with disconcerting control, "and we'll discuss the key."

"He is fighting his own way out of it," the mage answered. "If I take your cousin, you'll never find her."

"Brand is fighting you," Nyx said evenly. "He is still spellbound. Remove the spell."

Meguet, disinclined to being haggled over, slid smoothly out of the mage's grip, whirled away from him. He vanished again; this time he threw up a mist to scatter Nyx's fire. Meguet, swinging her blade, attacked a sudden shower of rose petals as the fire hit the mist. The bird snatched at them as futilely; she ducked as one of its claws tangled in her hair.

"Moro's eyes," she breathed. The bird became man, desperate, furious, bewildered, and then bird again, taking wing. Gold fire flared, limned the mage, and encased half the household records in amber. The bird swooped at random, swooped again, then cried noiselessly as its talons snagged the mage and dragged most of him into light. The mage spun away; the bird's claws scored his shoulders just before he vanished.

Someone cried: Brand or the mage. Brand appeared again, blurred, half-bird, half-man; blood dripped from his fingers. The bird wrenched him out of shape, took wing, and Meguet saw its broken, bloody talon. She cried, a sudden, helpless pity snagging at her voice,

"Nyx, stop this! Can you stop this?"

Nyx cast her a glance, frowning slightly. The color had come into her eyes. "This makes no sense," she murmured, and the amber flared again. Something flew through the window, shadow-dark, as graceful as the dragon. Meguet, expecting dragons, saw it in the corner of her eye and turned her head. The fire transformed it instantly: A black swan circled in golden flame became a white rose falling through the fire into shadow.

Tears pricked her eyes, for no reason, she insisted to herself: Everything was enchanted, even the air. The mage was at her side again, and then the firebird overhead, swooping, talons open, descending toward him.

He seemed to slow the bird; Meguet saw its movements over-lapping, image fanning out from image in the air. But he could not stop it entirely. In that charmed moment gold turned and turned through the air, clinked finally at the mage's feet. Bending, he eluded the bird's grasp; its talons flashed, scarred empty air just above him. He could not seem to balance himself; he gripped Meguet, dragged at her until she stumbled. The stones rose like water around her; a key floated on them into her hand. Then whispering air and fire slashed down again at the mage. He gasped, reaching for the key as for a spar in the shifting world. His hand locked around Meguet's wrist. She gave one terrified cry and then he pulled her into stone.

Nyx, staring at the stones where Meguet had vanished, found her nowhere. The firebird, searching as futilely for its prey, gave a soundless cry and glided to the window, with Brand as lost inside it as Meguet was inside the mage's time. She whispered, "Meguet."

A deep, rhythmic thumping began at the door; they had brought up something for a battering ram. Nyx lifted her head, her face mist-white in the candlelight. The floor was littered with the fire's enchantments. She checked her first, absent impulse to open the door to the battering ram, which would have proceeded across the room and out a window, taking the bird with it. She raised her voice instead.

"Stop—" Her voice caught; she cleared her throat. "Stop pounding! I'll open the door."

"Quiet!" the Holder said sharply, and the din outside the door ceased. Nyx broke the mage's spell; the door opened, spilling guards into the room. They stared at the glittering debris from the fire: pearl leaves, rose petals, books sealed in amber. Then they saw the blood on the firebird, and a whispering began.

The Holder tugged at the pearls at her breast, her eyes, wide and dark, reflecting something of Nyx's expression. "What happened?"

"The mage came back," Nyx said. "The firebird attacked him. They seem to know one another." She stopped, pulling at a strand of sapphires in her hair. She frowned, searching for words, her eyes going back to the stones. The Holder read her mind.

"Where is Meguet?"

"The mage took her."

"Took her! Moro's bones, took her where?"

"Somewhere. Some time. Some place."

"Why?"

"She was attached to the key I threw him." The strand of sapphires came loose, dropped to the floor. She touched her eyes and added, "He'll be back. Probably to exchange Meguet for the key."

"Moro's bones," the Holder breathed again. "How many keys does he want?"

"Just one. I gave him a false key to make him leave." She paused, feeling the weight of the Holder's still, black gaze. "There are things that are not making sense—"

"You," the Holder said succinctly.

"I mean, other than that."

"What in Moro's name possessed you to put either of your lives in danger for the sake of some moldy sorcery no one has paid attention to in a thousand years?"

"It's not—"

"Why didn't you give the mage the key the moment he came back for it?"

"Because—"

"Instead of jeopardizing the house and losing Meguet in some time beyond memory and some place without a name? And why is that bird still a bird? You've been immersed in sorcery since you learned to read—what's so difficult about turning a bird back into a man? Surely you've done more complex things with birds. How do I know this one won't attack you next?"

"Because, I don't think—"

"And where in Moro's name is my Gatekeeper?"

Nyx glanced around the room. "I saw him come in. I think it was him."

"If that mage stole him as well as Meguet—"

"No, it was my fault. I was fighting with the bird's fire. I must have changed him into something."

The Holder closed her eyes, pushed her hands through her hair. Pins flew. "You're a sorceress. Do some sorcery. Disenchant that bird. And my Gatekeeper. Find Meguet. And if that mage returns, give him whatever he wants, including the bird, if he wants that. I want no more bloodshed, mage's battles, stopped time or misplaced people. I want to end this council in even less excitement than it began. I want it to be a dull reference in the history of Ro Holding, not an entire flamboyant chapter."

"Yes." Nyx's voice came with effort. "I am sorry."

"And do it by dawn."

She did not quite slam the door. Nyx sat down, blinking, her face stiff. She stirred a couple of garnet rose petals with her foot, trying to think; her mind only filled, like the tower room, with enchantments. The door opened softly. She lifted her head. Calyx entered, side-stepping spells.

"I'm sorry about the books," Nyx said wearily. "They'll change back at moonrise tomorrow."

"Never mind the books." She touched Nyx's hair gently, removed a dangling pin. "I only wanted to tell you that the Gatekeeper is at the gate."

She straightened a little, blinking. "Is he?"

"He could never have gotten through the door. You only thought you saw him."

"Most likely."

"Should someone tell him about Meguet?"

"He knows." She added, at Calyx's puzzled expression, "Rumor is faster than thought in this house."

"Besides," Calyx said comfortingly, "you'll find her by dawn."

"Only if the mage brings her back from wherever he went. I don't even know the names of places beyond Ro Holding. Do you?"

"Just what Cado the Peculiar mentions."

"Who?"

"He was the fourth son of Irial Ro. He was called Cado the

Restless when he was young. He signed on a merchant ship, disappeared for eleven years and then came back to astonish his family with tales of one-legged giants, women made of gold, flowers with eyes, sorcerers with tails. According to the historian Blaconnes, it is most likely that Cado went ashore at Hunter Hold, lived an obscure and happy life digging for gold in the Junil Mountains, until the woman he lived with ran away with a rich miner. Then he shipped himself back home, whereupon, meeting his wife again, he thought it prudent to invent a few marvellous lands."

"Oh." Nyx's eyes strayed to the firebird, its eyes hooded in the torchlight. "The firebird would know where the mage went."

"The bird can't speak."

"And the man can't remember." Nyx sat silently, contemplating the pair, then touched Calyx, who was working the pins back into her hair. "You'd better go. If I lose you as well as Meguet to the mage, I'd be better off living an obscure and happy life as a swamp toad."

"Our mother ordered supper sent up to you."

"She's still feeding me. That's a good sign."

"You're too much alike, that's all." Calyx bent, kissed Nyx's cheek. "Be careful."

Alone, Nyx studied the sleeping firebird. Her supper came; she ate a few bites, pacing, her eyes, colorless and heavy, focused on the bird, while her mind drew constant, fraying patterns between the firebird, the man, the mage, the blackened weavings of metal on Brand's wrists, the silver paths within Chrysom's box.

"You know," she whispered to the bird, who had tucked its head under its wing. "You know where they have gone."

But all its memories were enchanted.

She sat down finally in a chair beside the firebird, waiting for the mage to return. He would know the difference between a key made by Chrysom's hand, and one by hers; he might have felt it, her mind instead of Chrysom's as he fell back through time, if Meguet hadn't been holding the key. He hadn't been too hurt to work a spell; most likely he could heal a scratch or two. And his white dragon lay in a pile of pearl leaves; if it were more than thread, he might return for that. And where was the book he so desperately wanted? He must have it already, she reasoned, since he wasn't contorting time to look for that, too. A book without a key was far more valuable than a key without a book. . . .

Her eyes closed. The key floated behind her eyes: gold, with an ivory-and-gold haft, a C or a crescent moon holding an M in its arms. Mage Chrysom. Chrysom's Magic . . . the key . . .

She woke at the sound of the council bells. The sun was up; it flung the bird's shadow over her and glittered in amber, garnet, as if its own fire might wake the things frozen in time, waiting for the moon. She felt the key in her pocket, heard the bird pecking water from a bowl. There was no sign of the mage or Meguet.

She slumped in the chair, feeling the tear in the tidy fabric of household life where Meguet should have been. The mage must return for the key. If he did not bring Meguet with him, there would be a mages' war in the dark tower, despite the Holder's wishes. It was inconceivable that he would not bring Meguet. But why had he not returned? Was he afraid of the firebird? Would he return at moonrise, when the bird changed? Would Brand remember him? Would the Holder wait patiently through another moonrise?

"She has no choice," Nyx murmured. "All she has is me."

She pulled the key out of her pocket, baiting the air with it, in case the mage lurked in some moment where a flash of magic from Chrysom's tower would snag his attention. She turned it over in her palm; the gold caught a fiery tear of light. The crescent moon arched over the upside-down Mage.

Her lips parted. She felt a stirring deep in her, as if small birds had suddenly scattered through her into light.

Chrysom's Work.

She whispered, "The key is the book."

# CHAPTER
# 6

Meguet watched the sun rise over a nameless land.

She had been sitting for hours on bare ground, thoughtless and stunned, under a sky full of unfamiliar constellations. There was some protection in the night. Unless she looked up, her eye did not have to acknowledge that she had travelled beyond Ro Holding: the dark might have belonged anywhere. She sat quite still where she had fallen, waiting for Nyx to rescue her, while the night stirred constantly around her, winds roaring and subsiding, hissing sometimes, the warm, malodorous breath of something she refused to imagine. Now and then the mage murmured, moving restlessly, but he never woke. She did not try to rouse him. Nyx would find her, take the key, and they would vanish before she caught a glimpse of this strange place somewhere beyond the Cygnet's wing.

But the morning light seared the land's image into her mind. It unfolded desert, vast, barren, gold as a hawk's eye, with juttings of bare stone like fantastic towers and crazed palaces. It was noisy; the winds blew unexpected notes through those stones. It smelled of sulphur and something charred; it hissed and steamed, in the distance, from boiling underground waters.

She drew against herself, feeling dangerously exposed, as if the stones had eyes. They might, in that weird place: the ground itself had mouths. Mages might be riding the air above her head. And there she sat, dressed for last night's supper in a gown as red as fire that flowed like fire on every passing breeze. Her thin velvet slippers would have sailed away in the wind; her sword had vanished somewhere between here and there. And even shod and armed and fitted for a journey, she could not have chosen here instead of there: Ro Holding might lie beyond the distant, shimmering peaks or, as easily, within the winds.

Light sparked everywhere in this hard, bright place, finding flecks of gold in the sandstone, turning silvery in the steam. It snagged under the mage's shoulder, and from there, leaped painfully into Meguet's eyes. She blinked, saw the gold key half-hidden under him. He had that, she told herself; he had no use for her. But would he bother to send her back? She could take the key, hide it from him, bargain with him . . . But he had seen the key across time itself; it seemed unlikely that his mage's eye would miss it under a rock. Both eyes were still closed; not even the sun had wakened him. She reached for the key quickly, slid it into her pocket. He did not move. She shifted closer after a moment, touched him.

She heard his breathing then, shallow and erratic, saw the chalky whiteness beneath the sweat and dust on his face. Pain clawed furrows between his brows. He stirred a little, as if he felt her gaze; he murmured something, wincing, and lay still again, while the dust drifted over him.

Horror, fine and dry as the dust, prickled over Meguet: that he might die and leave her alone in a strange land which might as well have been on some distant star. She stood up, panicked, searching the plain for a blue thread of water, a dark thread of wood smoke, symmetrical shapes of houses or a village among the broken tumbled towers of stone. They might have been the only living things in the world, she and the mage, and he was only half-alive. What water there was bubbled and stank; shadows on bare ground provided the only shelter she could see. She knelt again, trying to calm herself. The mage might have broken a bone, falling. But, running her hands over him, she felt nothing out of place. He didn't seem to notice her, not even when, with some effort, she rolled him on his side to study the marks the firebird had scored across his shoulders.

The weals were long but shallow; they looked irritating but hardly deadly, unless the bird carried some unexpected venom in its talons. The thought panicked her again; she closed her eyes, felt the desert sand in her throat, the hot sun melting into her skin. She must find shelter, water to clean his wounds. The nearest shadow, flung by a jagged and oddly folded stone, she could reach in a dozen steps. But the distance between shadow and mage seemed insurmountable. She rolled him gently on his back again, and slid her hands under his arms. It was only when she tried to lift him that he came alive, jerking out of her hold, crying odd words, names out of dreams or nightmares.

She let him lie and knelt beside him, wondering what he might have inadvertently summoned. She stroked his hair, murmuring. She had missed something; the bird had hurt him in some deep, subtle way. She contemplated the problem, her eyes wide, gritty, her thoughts stark as light, while she drew her fingers across his cheek, his hair, until he quieted again. Then, slowly, carefully, she coaxed his boots off.

They were fine leather, scuffed and scratched, big enough to fit over her feet and her shoes. He lay still, in the safe, private place where he sheltered against his pain. He did not stir even when she checked his robe for pockets. She found one in a side seam, and rifled it. She drew out a worn, jagged triangle of crystal or glass larger than her palm, the broken leaves of some dried herb, a tiny cube of gold etched on all sides with a delicate pattern not even the heavy crystal battering it had scarred. She sniffed the leaves: something pungent, unfamiliar. She could start a fire with the crystal and the dried leaves, though there was nothing to feed it. The sun had already burned everything. As she returned his odd possessions, the mage murmured again, frowning at the light; already it had become fierce, heavy, burning brass. She had to move him, find water, or she would die there beside a stranger under a strange sky. She stood up, blocked the sun on his face with her own shadow, scanning the land for one place more likely than another.

Above her, a shadow blocked the sun.

She looked up. The sun had vanished; an odd mass of air had swallowed a piece of sky overhead. She could not see what hovered; it was nothing, of no substance, but it cast a shadow all around her. She forced her eyes down finally, not wanting to look, but seeing it, black and clean-lined in the light: the shape of the little white-winged dragon of thread, but huge enough to swallow the sun.

Winds flew across the plain; blowing between cracks and towers of stone, they sounded deep, wild notes. Other voices bellowed among them from beyond the edge of the world. Meguet heard her own voice making an unfamiliar sound. She dropped, huddled against the mage, hiding her face from all the hidden eyes around her.

"Don't die," she pleaded numbly, scarcely hearing herself. "Don't die. I can spin hope for us out of a stone's shadow, but I cannot deal with dragons. Please wake. Please."

The mage did not answer. Shadow peeled away from the ground, left her to the sun. The winds blew dust and great stone flutes, but the otherworldly voices had sunk to a distant murmur. Steam shot a feathery plume out of the ground. The earth shook a little, as if something enormous, invisible, had walked across it. The steam dwindled; earth settled itself. Meguet straightened cautiously, wondering what other sorcery to expect from that exuberant, deadly place.

It seemed for the moment quiet. She rose, went in search of water.

She found, not far from the boiling pools, great thin crescents of something as darkly iridescent as beetles' wings. Upright, they were nearly as tall as she, but they were light enough to drag. She took four of them, made her way slowly, doggedly, through the heat back to the mage. She looked back once; the crescents trailing from under her arms grooved the earth behind her like some great claw. She closed her eyes against the sight, trudged on, awkwardly, her footsteps echoing hollowly in the mage's boots.

She dug shallow holes with the sharp end of one claw, balanced the claws on either side of the mage's body like four bedposts. Then she tore her skirt loose from the bodice, and picked apart a side seam. She dragged the length of silk across the claws, forced it down the sharp ends so that it stretched like a rippling canopy above the mage. He stirred, his face easing. She tore the sleeves from her bodice and wiped the sweat from his face. She rose again, as oddly dressed as she had ever been in her life, in tattered red silk bodice, long white linen shift and oversized boots, to look for water.

There was water everywhere, it seemed, but it boiled and stank and grew crusts of oddly colored crystals where it splashed. She wandered in a wasteland of heat and steam and bubbling mud-holes, her hair plastered down her back, her mouth so dry she would have drunk what steamed in the rifts and crevices of rock if it had not been too hot to touch. She sat wearily on a sandstone ledge, searching for green in a parched land, while her eyes teared at the smell, and behind her, she heard the sudden hiss of jetting water and steam. She leaned back, resting in the shadow, and felt a drift of cold on one cheek.

She found a cave of ice.

It was small, dark, and it steamed like the water holes. Its mouth was rimmed with icy teeth; the threshold was solid ice. Beyond the threshold lay shadow so black she guessed the earth had fallen away there into some deep chasm of time. From the chasm, icy air blew constantly. There were noises, too, shifts like stone against stone, a kind of subdued, rhythmic bellowing, as if a mountain were snoring. She broke off a piece of ice, sucked it. It tasted of earth rather than rotten eggs. She stepped out of one boot and used it to knock down a fat icicle. Limping, the ground burning through her slipper, she made her way back to the mage, carrying a boot full of ice.

She bathed his face with ice, forced it between his lips. Then she turned him over, washed the dirt and dried blood and torn cloth out of his wounds. He scarcely stirred until she touched a corner of one ragged cut above his shoulder blade. Then he stiffened, crying sorcery and dreams carelessly into the wind. She looked more closely, saw something the color of silver trapped there.

She drew it out: a broken piece of the firebird's talon.

She was trembling and nearly in tears when she finished; the mage, having wakened every snoring dragon in the world, finally subsided when she put ice against his back. On impulse, she felt in his pocket again, drew out the broken leaves. She lay one on the ground, caught the sun in the crystal, and focused it until the dry leaf smoldered. She held it under the mage's nose.

His eyes opened. He stared at her expressionlessly, then at the silken canopy, the dark curved spikes that held it up, the icicle melting in his boot. He tested his back, wincing a little. He gazed at her again, this time with amazement.

"Did you do all this?"

She sat back on her heels, answered wearily, "No, of course not. I summoned my attendants."

"You did this without sorcery?"

She closed her eyes briefly, looked at him again. His face was pale as old ivory; he carried his voice from word to word with an effort. She asked, "What else was I to do? You dragged me into this wasteland dressed for supper. You refused to help me. I could have sat here and wept, I suppose. But you only would have died, and I need you to take me home. Why in Moro's name did you pick the middle of a desert to fall into?"

"It's my home," he said simply. He drifted a moment, asked, when she thought he had fallen asleep again, "Where is the key?"

"I have it."

He held up a hand, his eyes still closed, and murmured, "Let me see it."

She did not move. "Swear to take me back to Ro Holding. What I've done for you, I can undo. This time I have a weapon." His eyes opened; she held up the little shard of silver. "I will use it."

She heard his breath stop. Then he drew air deeply, blinking. "Of course I will take you home."

"How can I trust you?"

"I don't know. Maybe you can't. But it's hard for me to believe you would put that sorcery back where you found it. It would be a bloody and noisy piece of work. And you would still be forced to keep me alive. Unless you want to wait here alone, hoping that someone will rescue you. If you choose to do that, remember that the only thing you'll want to eat are the rock lizards. The smaller black ones, not the yellow. You can boil them in the steam pools. They're less tough that way, than if you roast them. There's not much to burn, anyway. But if you do want a fire—" He stopped, shifting ground a little. Meguet, still clinging to the shard, her only argument, said tautly,

"What do I burn?"

"I'll make you something, before you kill me."

"I don't want—"

"You will, with that. It is a dark magic that goes straight to the marrow." He added, at her silence, "I'm trying to persuade you to trust me."

She ran one hand over her face, felt the fine dust clinging to her everywhere, even beneath her eyelids. "How can I?" she demanded. "You attacked my cousin and stole from her. You cast a spell over the Holder's house. You did such terrible things to Brand that he can't speak of them, he can't even remember them. He can only cry the firebird's rage. I don't trust you. The only reason I did all this for you is so that you will stay alive to take me back to Ro Holding."

He stirred again, wincing, his eyes straying to the bare, distant crags. He said tiredly, "I doubt that your cousin tossed the real key to me. She just wanted me out of the tower. So, you see, I may be forced to return to Ro Holding for the true key."

"You dragged me into this crazed, dragon-haunted place because of a fake key?"

He lifted one hand, touched her arm, speechless a moment. "You've seen dragons?" he asked huskily.

"I saw a shadow. You cried out such strange things when I tried to move you. I thought you summoned it. It hovered above us, hiding the sun. It was invisible and yet it cast a shadow."

"A shadow."

"It looked like a shadow your white dragon might have cast. Only a hundred times bigger. I was afraid—I was afraid it might attack."

"Oh, no. They never do."

"Your white dragon did."

"That's sorcery. I made it from a petrified dragon's heart. I'm not sure how real it is. But I've grown fond of it. I left it there, didn't I," he added, remembering. "In the tower, with the firebird."

"It is, I think, a pile of white leaves."

"Until moonrise. And then it will change and Brand will see it."

"Who is he?"

"Brand Saphier. His father, Draken, rules Saphier. This is the Luxour Desert in south Saphier. The edge of the world, some call it. I was born here."

That explained his coloring, she thought. "And why," she asked steadily, "did you turn Brand Saphier into a firebird?"

He moved abruptly, as if the tiny blade of talon in her hand had touched his back again. He answered, his eyes shadowed, heavy, "If I had made the firebird, the magic would be part of me. It could do no more harm to me than my reflection could. The spell that enchanted the firebird is deadly to me."

She was silent, weighing his words against every inflection in his voice, every change of expression in his face. "Assuming it's not yours," she said tautly, "then who cast the spell?"

His brows drew together hard; his eyes shifted away from her, toward some memory. "It's not a thing," he whispered, "I want even the wind to know."

"Then why did the firebird attack you?"

"I think it was made to kill me."

Meguet stood up. Standing brought her into the stifling light, but movement helped her think. In this case, thinking proved futile. She dropped her face in her hands, saw the fierce light behind her eyes. "I don't know how to believe you." She lifted her head, blinking the mage's face clear again. "I don't know what's truth and what's lie, between you and the firebird."

"You don't have to trust me," he said simply. "You're entirely at my mercy. No one knows where you are. Brand would guess his father's court. If he remembers Saphier at all. You can threaten me with that sorcery, but if you hurt me you will only be forced to care for me so that I won't die, so that I can take you home. . . ."

"And if the key is the real one?" she demanded, torn. "You'll vanish with it, leave me stranded here among the dragons. Why should you take the trouble to return me, and face my cousin and the firebird again?"

"It can't be the true key." He turned his face restlessly away from her. "Your cousin is too shrewd."

She knelt, chipped a piece of ice with the crystal, and put it to his lips. There was color in his face now, a feverish glitter in his eyes. "Why," she asked abruptly, frowning down at him, "did you pick that rose for me?"

"Because," he said softly, "you made me remember what words like honor and courage mean. Why did you pick up the rose instead of the sword?"

She sighed, defeated. "I wish I knew." She turned, lifted the dripping icicle out of his boot. She held the boot upside-down; the key dropped out onto the ground.

He picked it up, studied it curiously. He traced the crescent moon of ivory with his forefinger, and then the letter that clung in gold to the dark of the moon. She watched his face.

"Which is it?"

He shook his head. "Every spell carries somewhere in it the mage's signature. It may be the order in which things are done. Or the favorite spellbook used. Or some familiar element. Chrysom liked riddles. Unexpected images. Your cousin had no time for that. This has no centuries clinging to it. No riddles except for its shape. Nothing of Chrysom's; something of a mage I wouldn't have recognized."

"How do you know so much about Chrysom? Is Saphier in another time? Or are you a thousand years old?"

"I like to wander . . . sometimes I wander in and out of time. I learned things, watching Chrysom. I would go and build his fires, fetch things—"

"You spoke to him?"

"He never asked where I was from. But we spoke of time, how it turns and loops. . . . He knew I didn't belong there. He spoke of a spellbook of time he had written. He had hidden it, but he gave me hints, from time to time, when I came. From time to time." He smiled a little, holding the key one way, and then another. His smile faded; he saw the shadow behind the key. "So you see I must return to Ro Holding."

"Why?" she asked wearily. "What more do you need to know of time? You and Nyx will only fight each other."

"I must have the key. I need it. Your cousin only wants it out of curiosity. I need it for my life."

"Tell her that," she said, startled. "She'll help you."

"Mages don't help one another."

"In Ro Holding—"

"Not in Saphier. And I can't tell her why. I can't even whisper it to air. Not in Saphier. And most certainly not in that tower in front of the firebird."

"Why? What are you to the firebird?"

He kindled a tiny flame out of nothing, set the crescent moon on fire. "Once," he said, "we were friends." He let the flame devour moon and letter and shaft, like a candle, until the flame danced on a tear of gold on his palm. He blew it out, let the tear melt into the ground, and buried it. "Now," he explained, "there is only that much of your cousin to be found in Saphier. What is her name?"

"Nyx Ro."

His brows went up. "She is—"

"The Holder's heir."

"And you, Meguet Vervaine?"

"Her cousin."

"And?" He smiled a little at her silence. "The woman who sees into time. You saw the dragon's shadow. It takes a great, complex power to find the dragon." His eyes wandered to the jagged, barren thrusts of rock, the varying hues of gold and dust, the plumes of steam. "That's why I love these deserts. From the time I was young, I could catch glimpses of the dragons. A shadow. A wing folded into a rock. A roar that is not wind. Light that is not sun. If you saw an entire shadow, it is more than most see in a lifetime. I dream of seeing them emerge from stone and air and light. . . ."

"Are they ghosts?" she asked, entranced.

"No. I think they shift in and out of time. Which is why," he added obscurely, "I need that key."

"Can't you open the book without it? If you know Chrysom's ways?"

"I do know Chrysom's ways," he said, but no more. He slid his hand into his pocket, brought out the little cube of gold. "You used a dragon's tooth to start that fire," he commented. Her eyes widened, going to the crystal. "And claws for the canopy. They leave pieces of themselves around."

"I heard one snoring, I think, in the ice cave."

"I tried to see that one. No light will shine in that dark, not even fire. It lives in some black plane so cold its breath freezes even in this heat. It must look like its own shadow, to the human eye." He set the cube down on the ground.

"What is that?"

"Supplies. For when I travel." He murmured something. One side of the cube opened; he shook a water skin out of it. "Size," he said, as Meguet's eye tried to fit the full skin back into the tiny cube, "is illusion. I didn't want to frighten you before, with my sorcery." He shifted to hand her the skin, then sagged back wearily, settling himself into the ground as if he drew some deep, healing comfort from it. "I have a house in a village on the edge of the desert. I can take us both that far. I need to rest before I return to Ro Holding. You saved my life, but there wasn't much of it left. If I hadn't taken you with me, I would be lying here dreaming while the sun and the sand and the carrion snakes worked their magic on me."

She brought the skin down incredulously, splashing herself. "You deliberately brought me with you? To help you?"

"I hoped you would. I was desperate. But I didn't expect—" He shifted again, his eyes on the dark spikes holding up her billowing skirt above his head. "I didn't expect you to find ice in the desert. I didn't expect you to see the dragon's shadow."

She looked at him, frowning again, but feeling the strange desert working its magic of light and illusion into her bones. She said abruptly, "Do you have a name?"

"Yes," he sighed. "I thought you'd never ask. My name in Draken Saphier's court is something he gave me, and that only mages use. In this place I love, where I was born, my name is Rad Ilex."

# CHAPTER
# 7

In the black tower, Nyx waited for the mage and the moon.

The Gatekeeper came before either one of them, at evening when the household had gathered for supper and the yard was calm. Nyx, deep in contemplation of Chrysom's key, which opened nothing in itself that she could find, scarcely heard him knock. She lifted her eyes to find him in front of her, an occurrence so rare that for a moment she wondered if the tower were the gate and the Gatekeeper watched them both. Then she remembered why he had come.

"Hew." She pulled her bare feet off the nearest chair. "Sit down."

He shook his head. "I came to ask you—"

"About Meguet." She was silent a moment, studying him, her eyes luminous with sleeplessness. Gatekeepers of Ro House were rooted like stone and vine to the house. When they grew old, they wandered away looking for an heir to some peculiar power which Nyx had never explored. The Gatekeeper, his own face set and shadowed with weariness, did not look accessible to exploration. But a part of him had gotten tangled in the fire's enchantments, the night before; she was aware he had been there, though in what form she was not quite certain. Instead of waiting, like the mage's dragon, for moonlight to free him, he was on his feet in front of her, looking perplexed. If, as she suspected, he saw everything that came and went in and out of Ro House, including ghosts and portents and the Cygnet itself, he would have known Meguet had gone. But not where.

"I thought," he said, "the bird might have told you something by now about where it came from."

"It's a good guess that's where the mage took Meguet," Nyx said. "But where is still a mystery. He left something here; he may still return."

"With Meguet?"

"If not," she said grimly, "I'll search for her."

He sat down then, his head bowed, his eyes on the floor where it had opened like a mist to Meguet's falling. Would it, Nyx wondered suddenly, open also to the Gatekeeper who opened and closed every door? But he did not seem inclined to dive headlong into solid stone. He asked, "Where would you look? Or would you just fling yourself blind into time beyond Ro Holding? Did the bird or mage give you a word to guide you?"

"Not yet. Why? Do you know of places beyond Ro Holding?"

"Me? No. I know the gate and the house and the back swamps of the Delta. The winds don't blow me names of other places. And even so, what name would mean more than another? Unless you could tell me."

"And what would it be worth then? Would you leave the gate for Meguet?"

He lifted his head, met her eyes, his own colored like the silvery bog-mosses and about as transparent. "You would leave the house for her."

"My mother told me to find Meguet. I have no intention of finding out what life is like with my mother and without Meguet." He said nothing, still waiting for an answer; she added, "I'll find her. If the mage brings her back, I'll do what I must. If I have to search for her, I do have the means and I'll discover how and where any way I can. It's only a question of time."

"I have more than enough of that, during the night at the gate."

She was silent again. Something vital hovered beyond her memory: He had been in the tower, seen the mage and Meguet, but in what shape? Had she seen his face? Or only something she recognized as Gatekeeper that had entered a mage-locked room, and had been transformed by the bird's fire just long enough to have known what became of Meguet? She eased back in her chair. Meguet would remember. She said softly, "What time you have is counted by the movement of the Cygnet's stars. I'll find Meguet. If you leave the gate, my mother will only have me searching for you as well."

He stirred a little. "And if you leave? Who will search for you? How far beyond the Cygnet's eye can you go, before you come to a gate without a Gatekeeper to open it?" She stared at him; he met her eyes again and said more plainly, "There is only one gate in this house and everything enters and leaves by it. Including the odd mage. It's bad enough losing Meguet to a place with no name. But you are more than mage, and if you vanish from this house without the Holder's knowledge, if you leave the named world, then you must either find yourself another Gatekeeper, or pay the one you've got with a time and a place to find you in. Gatekeepers grow old at the gate; they don't get thrown out of it before their time. Which is what will likely happen to me if I let you out under strange stars."

"You let Meguet go. And the mage." He said nothing; she straightened, frowning. "Hew, what are you seeing that I missed?"

"I only want to know where you go when you go. That's all I'm asking."

"You're not asking. You're making demands. You're only asking what little you're asking so that you can search for Meguet if I fail."

"Both," he said softly. "Both of you."

"How? If you cannot leave the gate?"

"It's not a question anyone will bother asking if the Holder loses you. Least of all me." His face eased a little, at her expression. "It's only what you didn't notice, following Chrysom's path into sorcery. A little household magic. It's an ancient house, and it has its ways and means. I'm one of them. That's all."

"Is it?" she breathed. "Is that all you are? A little household magic?"

"You know that. It's why you've been talking to me, instead of telling me politely to mind my business and let you mind yours."

"You could stop me from using all the power of Chrysom's sorcery to go where I want?"

He shook his head. "It's a power with a singular purpose. To protect the Cygnet. Only that. Tell me where you are going, beyond the Cygnet's eye, and you are free to go."

"But why you?" she asked, fascinated. "Why must it be you who will come searching for us? You are bound by household magic to the gate."

"And by other magics to Meguet," he said softly. "That's why it must be me. How is what I'll figure out later." He rose; she watched him, wordless. His eyes flicked at the firebird, then back to her. "You must make him remember. Or time, for you, will begin and end at the gate to Ro House. It's the way of the house, to protect."

"Will I know these things when I am Holder? All the household magics? Or should I begin to ferret them out now?"

He smiled his tight, wry smile. "I don't know. It's my guess that whatever you want the house will give you. There's never been a mage-Holder of Ro Holding. Once you start looking, who knows what you'll find?" He bent his head and left her staring at the door he closed behind him.

After a time, she transferred her gaze to the firebird. It was nearing moonrise; the sky at the bird's back had grown milky. "You," she said, "must find a way to remember."

The bird cried its silent cry, then was still again, waiting for the moon. Moonlight touched it. The bird spread its white wings, dropped down from the ledge. As it reached stone, it changed: Brand stood in a mingling of moonlight and candlelight. Other enchantments changed: The amber-sealed books were free; garnet and opal petals swirled together to form a glittering mist that slowly dispersed. Beside the hearth, leaves of pearl and bone drew together, formed the mage's dragon. Hovering in the shadow of the wrong world, it seemed both real and unreal. Fire picked out a scallop of thread along one unfurled wing, turned it into a delicate layering of flesh and bone.

Nyx, marvelling at it, froze it with a word before it could fly. She heard Brand move and turned quickly, but he had only stepped closer to see the dragon. Memories struggled into his face. He whispered,

"Where is he?"

"Who?"

"Rad Ilex. The mage I fought last night."

"He hasn't come back yet. Why do you want to kill him?"

"Because—" He stopped, linked his fingers over his eyes. His voice came harsh with pain. "He betrayed my father. He betrayed me. He trapped me in the firebird's shape. His face is the last thing I remember, the first thing the firebird saw."

"Why?" She stood as motionless as the dragon, scarcely daring to ask questions, lest the sound of her voice disturb the fragile cob-weave of his remembering. "Why did he put you under that spell?"

He was silent a long time; his shoulders dragged. "I don't remember," he said bitterly.

"Do you remember who you are?"

"I am Brand Saphier." His hands slid away from his eyes; he turned. His face looked ashen, haunted, but his past had etched expression back into it. "My father is Draken, Lord of Saphier."

Nyx's eyes flicked, at the name, to the dragon at his feet. "Draken?"

"His father was a dragon."

Wordless, Nyx found herself staring at him, searching for the dragon. She found the firebird instead, its beautiful, proud, ruthless face within Brand's face, as if some boundary between enchantment and truth had grown strangely fluid. She said finally, softly, "Sit down." She sat at the table, still studying him, wondering if the spellbound man would prove even more exotic than the spell.

She said, "In Ro Holding, there are no tales of dragons. You could walk the four Holds and find maybe four people who even know the word. Setting aside physical complications, is that customary behavior in Saphier, humans mating with dragons?"

He shook his head. "Some say there are no dragons in Saphier, only the memories of dragons. But my father's mother went to the desert in south Saphier and came back with child. She ruled Saphier, and if she said her child was dragon-seed, no one would argue. The dragon was a great mage, she said, capable of changing shape. My father—" His voice caught. He gripped the arms of his chair, his eyes widening, as other memories shifted into place. "My father." He rose, paced, the tower room no longer a haven but a cage. "I wonder how long I have been gone. If he knows what happened to me."

"He must be searching for you."

"He may be mourning me, for all I know." He added savagely, "With Rad Ilex beside him."

"Is Rad Ilex your father's mage?"

He looked perplexed by the question. "My father's court is full of mages. My father is very powerful; he trains mages, those with special gifts, like Rad. It's not like this house. You seem to be the only mage. And you have little sense of order." She drew a breath, but found no argument. "Or manners."

"What?"

"No mage would speak to my father the way you speak to the Holder."

"She's my mother," Nyx protested.

"Perhaps it is because you have all the power in this house." He turned, pacing again; she stared at his back. "The mage would be stripped of power."

Nyx's brows lifted. She picked up a wine cup, blew the dust out of it and filled it. She took a sip, watched him turn, pace back. "Is that where Rad Ilex took Meguet? To your father's court?"

"I don't know. Perhaps, if my father still trusts him."

She took another swallow, set the cup down. "Fortunately, Meguet's manners are better than mine. Who is this Rad Ilex? Do you remember?"

"Yes." He stopped, turned his face away. Nyx saw him tremble, in rage or grief, she couldn't tell. "He was born in the Luxour Desert, and he came to my father when he was a boy and said there were dragons everywhere in south Saphier. There have always been rumors of dragons. Crystals that look like dragon's teeth. Spiky plants that die and turn black and look like claws. My father always wanted to see dragons. He wanted to become one, like his father. He wanted to find his father, be taught by him. He says that a mage-fire like no other power runs through the blood of dragons and he wants that power. So when Rad said he saw dragons, my father took him into the house to train."

The door opened. Servants summoned by moonlight entered, bearing supper. Brand roamed again; Nyx watched him, wondering if he had come to the end of his memories, or the heart of them. He came back to the table, stood gazing down at the trays. "That's what I can't remember," he said at last, tightly. "That's where the wall is. I can remember loving Rad. And now I hate him. I would kill him as quickly as I tried to destroy his dragon. But I don't remember why."

"The firebird remembers."

He looked at her, his eyes dark, bruised, but he did not answer. Nyx pushed a tray toward him. "Eat something. If Rad Ilex wants the key and his dragon, he'll return here. But I want no blood shed in this tower. My mother forbade it."

He made no response to that, either. Nyx broke into an elaborate crust, found duckling flavored with orange and rosemary. She ate hungrily a few minutes, then asked, "Did your father find his father among the dragons?"

"No. He went with Rad to south Saphier. Rad was able to show him something—I don't know what. Enough to give my father some hope, whether it was truth or lie. In the Luxour, some villagers collect big, iridescent lumps of stone they say are dragon's hearts, and sell them. Those who buy them call them one thing, those who don't, another. Rad said he knew a way to draw the dragons into time, but that he had to find something. A key."

Nyx made a sound. "Not a book."

"He said key."

"How could he have known to find it in Ro Holding?" she breathed. "He knows too much, this Rad Ilex."

Brand stirred edgily. "And where is he, if he wants this key so badly?"

"Being cautious, I suppose. Coming here, he must face you or the firebird. Perhaps—"

"I have remembered," he interrupted. "He will face me, not the bird."

"You have not remembered everything. We'll know at midnight."

His knife hit the edge of his plate; he pushed away from the table and rose, his shoulders bowed as if the firebird clung to his back. "What kind of a mage are you that you can't break a simple spell?"

She picked a bone out of a bite, watching him. "I suppose, by the standards of Saphier, not very apt. But I am considered adequate in Ro Holding."

He came back to her, head bowed. "Forgive me. You took me in, tried to help. It's not your fault you are pitted against the most devious mage in my father's court."

She frowned, thinking again of Meguet. "Where is Saphier? Do you cross a sea to get to it? Mountains? Maybe, if you could get home, your father could help you."

"Saphier is the world," he said absently. "I never looked beyond it." Then his eyes widened, and she saw the sudden flare of hope in them. She pushed back her chair, rose.

"What do you remember?"

"These." He turned his wrists up, spread his fingers, as if the tarnished metal wove through blood and bone into his fingertips. "They are all the paths to Saphier."

"Paths of time." She drew her finger down a weave lightly. "I thought so. But are they always so tarnished?"

"No," he said, puzzled. "They should be silver, like the paths inside your tiny box. You need to know the path before you travel it; that's why you couldn't find your own way out."

"You led me out," she said abruptly. "You are also a mage."

He shook his head. "I am a warrior. I don't have mage's gifts."

"But you wear these. You can use them."

"Yes." He hesitated, still perplexed by them. "It is something my father taught me."

"Do you always wear them?"

"I don't think so."

"Then why are you wearing them now? As if you know you might need them? Or you were working a time-spell, or travelling a path when you were transformed?" She saw his face change, as he veered dangerously close to memory. He said quickly,

"I don't remember."

"Do you remember," she asked after a moment, "how to use these?"

"Yes." He rubbed at one, trying to polish it with his thumb. "They are so dark. As if some enormous power ran through them." He looked at her; she saw Saphier in his eyes, future instead of past. "I can go home."

"Yes."

"Tonight. Now. Before I change."

"Yes," she said, breathless at the thought. "But if you leave, and Rad Ilex does not return with Meguet, how will I ever know where to look for her? Can you wait a little longer for them?"

He gave her a distant, masked glance: the firebird's eyes. "I forgot he must come here."

"I will give him the key and his dragon for Meguet," she said. "I will not give you to him, or him to you. If you fight him, it must be in Saphier, or my mother will never forgive me for that as well as for a few other things she won't forgive me for by now. Please," she added, at his weary, desolate expression. "Only a little longer."

"And then what? If he does not come?"

"Then," she said steadily, "you will teach me the path to Saphier and I will look for her myself."

He was silent, studying her, as if she had flung some peculiar spell over herself. "You would walk into a strange land to search for her?"

"She searched for me once in a strange place. She is part of Ro Holding, part of this house. It's inconceivable that she is wandering around lost in some other country."

"You are eccentric."

"Even," she said drily, "in Ro Holding."

"My father's court is structured according to precise law. Within that law, nothing disorderly exists for long. Either it shapes itself to law or it is destroyed."

Her brows rose. "Does that include guests?"

"It is my father's working philosophy," he answered simply. "Out of order comes art. The art of government, the mage's art, the art of poetry, the art of war. We do not give ourselves the luxury of eccentricity."

"Perhaps freedom is a luxury," she said. "But that aside, there must be someone you would wander through a stranger's land to find."

She saw it again in his face: the sudden, desperate aching shadow of memory, the firebird's cry. He whispered, "No one has come searching for me."

She blinked, shaken by a glimpse into something more complex than she could unweave, or even imagine. She touched him; he looked at her, mute again, unable to give her either dragon heart or stone.

"We'll go to Saphier now," she said abruptly, and felt her own heartbeat. "It's cruel to keep you." And safer, she thought, remembering the spinning swords, than another battle in the tower. "Take me to your father's house. If Meguet is not there, then teach me the paths so that I can return to look for her if I have to. Will you do that?"

"My father can, easily. And he will, in gratitude. The Holder will not even know you have been gone. Thank you." He took her hands, dropped his face against them. "You took me in when no one in the world recognized me as human. Whatever else the bird knows, it knew enough to come to you."

And not, she observed with a certain grimness, to Saphier.

The word, spoken aloud in the tower, would find its way to the Gatekeeper, following its own peculiar path within the house's time. Brand held out his hands, spread his fingers as if to channel the flow of light from the silver. The bands remained black. He closed his eyes, walking the path in his mind. After a while, he put the bands against his eyes. Nyx felt pity well up from some deep place within her, as if hidden water had broken through layers of earth and hoary stone and old leaves. She put her hand gently on his shoulder.

He whispered, "I am half man, half bird, and I am lost, with no way home."

"There is always a way," she said. "Always."

He looked at her, read the promise in her eyes. After a while he moved to his place at the window, and waited silently for oblivion and the firebird.

# CHAPTER
# 8

Meguet sat rapt beneath the risen moon.

In its light silver feathers of steam or dragon-fire glittered and faded. The high, jagged towers of stone transformed themselves. Here a great wing unfolded against the stars almost as slowly as the stars behind it moved. There an eye shone, moon-white or darker than the night. A craggy head lifted, or had just lifted before she saw it. A moon shadow, massive and curved, lay across the ground, cast by nothing visible. Crystal flashed. Vague, dark, iridescent colors swam against the stars and vanished.

Beside her, the mage lay watching with her. Sometimes he watched her; she felt his eyes. "You see," he murmured now and then. "Did you see that?" His voice, worn, fading, sounded tranquil; he was lost in some fever-dream of dragons that he had pulled her into. She saw through his eyes, she thought, most likely. But still she watched, as he dreamed dragons and set them free into the night.

"We should go," she said now and then, for he shivered, though warm wind or dragon-breath sighed over them. She had taken down her canopy to see the sky. Things that had come out of his cube—wine, salted fish, bread, dried apples and figs—littered her skirt.

"Yes," he said, but made no effort to move. "I wanted you to see this, if you could."

"I see," she said softly. "But I don't know what I see."

"Time shifting. Dragon-paths. Chrysom saw this. He made the key to unlock their paths into time."

"Can they see us?"

"Oh, yes. Oh, yes. Far better than we see them. We glimpse them indirectly, and with the heart more than the eye."

She looked at him. An odd, heavy, nameless feeling pushed through her; she scarcely knew what to call it. Hunger? Sorrow? Desire? "I wish," she whispered. "I wish."

"What?"

"I don't know . . . I wish I could watch you free them with that key."

"You can. Stay here until you have seen the dragons fly. Until I draw them out of stars and stone, until bone and blood cast shadows instead of dreams. Stay until you have seen the dragons' fire."

She dragged her eyes from the stars, still heavy with the strange, impossible yearning. "I cannot. The white dragon waiting for you in Chrysom's tower must be enough for me. I was not born to see dragons."

"They get into your blood. They call you in some secret language spoken by stones. They show you a shadow, they leave a bone behind. And so you spend your life searching for them . . . Stay until I free them."

"I don't dare," she whispered. "You were born under the dragon's eye. I was born under the Cygnet. I have never in my life come so close to forgetting that."

"The Luxour will make you forget."

She was silent, remembering the desert by day, hot and golden as some vast wing stretched taut to catch the light, the massive framework of its bones visible just beneath the surface of the stones.

"We must go," she said, but did not move, still riding the dragon that was the Luxour through the stars. Finally she felt his hand, and saw her skirt attach itself to her again. Everything had vanished back into the little cube. Only the dragon claws, scattered in the sand, told where they had been.

"We must go," he said, and the stars blurred together to form their path.

Night, where the path ended, was unexpectedly still. Here and there a light that was not a star burned, illumining a circular window or a door. Even the winds were silent. Pebbles shifting under Meguet's feet as she turned sounded loud enough to wake the sleepers within the small stone houses. The handful of them, huddled together in the vast dark, seemed an unlikely place for a mage to dwell.

The mage, rising, lost his balance; Meguet caught him. He dropped an arm over her shoulders, and was still a moment while the earth settled. She whispered, "Where are we?"

"On the south edge of the Luxour." He added obscurely, "Safe. Even mages have trouble crossing the Luxour. This is my house."

She helped him toward one of the simple wooden doors. It had no latch. He placed his hand flat against it and it opened. Sudden light spilled over them. Within, the little house was bare and tidy as the desert. The sandstone walls were unpainted; a single rough-woven rug lay on the stone floor. His table held none of the disorder of magic and mundane—books, apple cores, crystals, bones, assorted nameless things—that Meguet had come to expect of mages. Except for a layer of dust, it held nothing at all. Another door opened to a tiny chamber that held a wooden chest and a pile of skins and neatly folded blankets. Only the collection of colored desert rocks on the stone ledge above the hearth was unnecessary. Other things, a couple of copper pots, a clay water jar, oil lamps, sat neatly in their niches and, like the table, gathered dust.

She said, helping him sit on one of the unpainted benches beside the table, "You don't come here often."

"Not as often as I want." He smiled at her as she moved through the lamplight. "There are some clothes in that chest. People will think I conjured you out of gold and fire and ivory, the way you are now."

She eyed him. He did not seem in much pain, but his eyes were bright with fever and he moved and spoke slowly, as if air were too heavy to shift aside, too heavy to breathe. Worried, she asked, "What will heal you? Are there desert plants I can find?"

"No. I need to rest."

"How long?"

"I don't know. I've never been attacked by an enchantment before. I'm sorry," he added, at her expression. "You'll have to wait. I'll take care of myself if you don't want to look at me."

She sat down on the opposite bench, dropped her face in her hands, felt the desert grit behind her eyes. "Nyx will be waiting for you to bring me back. In exchange for the true key. She'll wonder when you don't come."

"Most likely, she'll assume I died."

"And left me stranded. Moro's eyes. What does that key open?"

"Stone. Sky." She looked up at the longing in his voice. "It opens time itself to reveal the dragon's face."

She felt again a touch of his desire to wake dreams, to step into them. But she said only, "There are no dragons in Ro Holding. Nyx only wants the key because she does not know what it is. When she finds out, perhaps she won't want it anymore."

"Some say there are no dragons in Saphier, either."

"There are no tales of dragons in Ro Holding. Why would she want a key to unbind dragons in Saphier?"

"Because it exists?" he guessed. She was silent at that, knowing Nyx.

"But if you told her what danger you are in—"

"I can't speak of it," he said. He didn't; she was left listening to the silence. It took on an eerie quality then, as if the sandstone walls were paper-thin and something crouched beyond them, listening to her listen. She stirred finally.

"Tell me what to do for you."

"Mages," he said, with a faint grimace as a memory clawed his back, "are easy to care for." He glanced into the other room: Skins and blankets had sorted themselves into a bed on the floor. Another formed beside the hearth. A thought struck her; he looked at her, reading her expression, or her thoughts. "Water. There is a river behind the house. It's slow and warm even at night. If you want to bathe in that, I'll set something on the bank to guard you."

"I'll guard myself," she said, uneasy at what guardian he might conjure up. But he sent one anyway, she noticed later, as she stood in dark water that mirrored a silvery stream of stars. An upright bar of light, elusive as color in moonlight, stood near her clothes. Exactly what it might do, she never knew; nothing disturbed the night. She emerged finally, dried herself with a blanket, and dressed in long, thin, flowing garments the colors of the desert. She sat on the blanket, combing her hair with her fingers and letting it dry, thinking helplessly of Nyx and the Holder, and the Gatekeeper, who had opened the gate for her into a stranger's country. She lay back on the blanket, wanting the river to speak with his voice, the night to curve itself in his shape against her. *Hew,* she said without sound, wanting to protect even his name from the vast, dangerous, magic-riddled land.

After a while, she went in, found Rad Ilex asleep at the table. She touched him; he vanished so abruptly that horror flashed through her: He had not been real at all, only some sending of himself. Then he reappeared, looking dazed.

"Meguet. I forgot you. You frightened me. I was dreaming of the firebird. Only it had a human face."

"Whose face?" she asked, wondering what faceless mage he feared. But he said nothing more. She helped him rise; the bed, it seemed, was too far for his strength. He walked two steps and sagged into the pile beside the hearth, so deeply asleep he did not feel her undress him and wash his wounds with something besides the ice of dragon's breath.

At dawn she stood at the open door, watching the village wake. A patch of stone houses beside a river's bend, it seemed little more than a scattering of pebbles between two planes of earth and sky. The south Luxour was flat as water, but she could see far in the distance the tiny, fantastic shapes of stonework among which dragons, or tales of dragons, dwelled. Along the river, in patches of green, sheep and goats grazed. People bringing buckets to the village fountain looked at her curiously. They did not speak, but their eyes said: *The mage is back.* Their faces looked brown and tranquil, like the desert stones. One old woman driving a cart stopped in front of Meguet, handed her a stone that had been rolling among some sacks in the cart.

"For Rad," she said. She had a broken tooth, and a face as wrinkled as a root. "For healing my donkey, last year."

"But what is it?"

The woman's sparse brows and the reins flicked up at the same time. "A dragon's heart." The reins came down, the cart lurched forward. "I'm going out again for stones. Tell him to stay home, this time. There's nothing good beyond the Luxour."

"How do you know?" Meguet asked curiously. "How does news find its way here?"

"People come and go. And they come back again, for they leave their hearts in the Luxour and they wander back all hollow looking for them. Sometimes," she added with a half-smile, "I find them first. I keep them safe on my shelves until they're claimed." She ticked to the donkey; Meguet stared after her. The dragon's heart, big as a cabbage, crystal under a thin, worn layer of stone, weighed heavily in her hands. She wondered if the ghosts of dragons came back through time, searching for the hearts that the strange old woman harvested in her cart. Most likely, she thought, taking another look, it was just a rock.

She turned to go in, and coax breakfast out of the sleeping mage. Something blocked her way.

It was as if the shadow in the doorway had become a sheet of night with a constellation flying across it, and once she stepped into that night there was no way out of it, no book of time, no gate, just the icy outline of a great dragon with eyes and teeth and talons of stars, breathing a pale, glittering cloud of stars into the dark. She stood transfixed, staring into the dragon's fierce and empty eye, until, with terror and astonishment, she recognized the challenge.

She made some noise. She was aware that, beyond the dark, something fought towards her. A hand reached through the stars where the dragon's heart blazed, a furious, white-hot jewel pulsing with the fires it breathed. The hand caught her, pulled her into the dragon, and then into light.

"Meguet?"

She dropped the dragon's heart. It shattered on the stone floor, shards of crystal flying everywhere. She stared down at it, sorrow for the old woman's simple gift knotting the back of her throat.

"I'm sorry," she whispered. "She left it for you."

"Meguet."

She looked up finally, to meet the mage's eyes. They were lucent as the morning sky, vast as the desert. She blinked, and was suddenly no longer in his hold, but on the other side of the room, watching expression break into his face. He seemed to hold himself upright with an effort, as if, caught in the wake of her movement, he had lost his balance. He looked less feverish, but the weariness dragged at his shoulders. He said finally, "You are a mage."

"No."

"There's a power stirring in you. I can feel it. You hid your thoughts from me. You folded time as you moved." He waited, then pleaded tiredly, "Trust me. Please."

She was silent, feeling the warnings of her heritage wash over her like a slow, endless tide. *The Dragon hunts,* the tide said. *The Dragon hunts the Cygnet.* Then the warnings passed and she could speak again. She said with rare bitterness, "All you care about is power. All of you."

He made a soft sound, shaking his head, the shadows deepening on his face as if she had somehow hurt him. "That's not true. But I can sense it in you—something unusual, unnamed. The power that permitted you to see me when I cast the spell over Ro House. The power that forced you to guard the tower, to see through sorcery. But you aren't a mage. What is the power?"

She was silent, backed against the wall, splinters of the dragon's heart glistening, sunlit, at her feet. He sat down finally, listening to her silence. He said to the table top, "It's my fault. I have a mage's habits. I wander where I have no business going. I won't trouble you with my curiosity. You don't have to be afraid of me. But you're afraid of something, in a land that never even existed for you before yesterday."

It was a long time before she answered, and then because she had no other hope of understanding what she feared except for the mage she was afraid to trust. She whispered, "A dragon made of stars, hunting through the stars. A threat to Ro Holding. To the Cygnet."

His head went back; his face, stone-still, was white as bone. "How could you—" he breathed. "How could you know that?"

She moved then in sudden fury, leaning over the table, her hands coming down flat, hard on the wood. "You knew."

"Listen to me." He gripped her wrist. "Listen."

"You talk too much, Rad Ilex. You make me see dragons among the stars, but you don't show me what they hunt. You say you want a key, only a key, just a small key to unlock the gate to an unarmed land that doesn't even know the word dragon. You drag me here and I can't even warn—" She lifted her hands again, let them fall helplessly, beating at her own futility. "I can't even warn. But I can fight. This is where the danger begins. Where there are dragons."

"Meguet—the dragon—"

"How far is Draken Saphier's court? Is it close? If you won't tell me, the villagers will. I'll walk across the Luxour if I must. I'll ride in that old woman's cart."

"Gara. Her name is Gara." He stopped to catch his breath. "Walk out of the door. I won't stop you. The Luxour may stop you, or it may not; I won't. But when you get to Draken Saphier's court, the dragon there will stop you. He will sense the power in you, and he will test you and test you until you can't call your own bones private. The Dragon of Saphier is dragon-born, a mage who trains mages. He trained me. What he wants more than anything is to find the path to the power within the dragon's heart. His father's power. For that he needs a certain key."

Meguet gazed at him. She began to tremble suddenly. She sat, her face hidden behind her unbound hair, behind her hands. "Nyx," she whispered, so softly that not even the dragon's heart broken at her feet could hear. The mage heard; his own voice was feather-soft.

"Yes."

"You must get the key from Nyx. Then, with the key in Saphier, the danger to Ro Holding will no longer exist."

"The danger will still exist. And it may well be insurmountable."

She lifted her head, stared at him again, her own face pale, stunned with shock. "Then I will go to Draken Saphier's court. If the danger must be fought there."

"You cannot fight Draken Saphier," he said flatly. "Your power comes and goes apparently, and from what I've seen, when it goes you can't even fight a dragon made of thread."

"If I must go there, I will be there."

"How—"

"I will be there." She linked her hands tightly, dropped her face against them, avoiding his curious, questioning eyes. "You must go back to Ro Holding and get that key."

"She won't give it to me without you."

"And the Holder will never let me return if I go back now. The danger showed its face to me here, not there. If I leave Saphier, how will I recognize danger when it reaches Ro Holding?" She paused, trying to think. "I'll give you a message for Nyx."

"You'll trust me with a message?"

She shook her head a little, wearily. "I trust you to get that key you want. Little more. Tell Nyx—"

"She'll never believe you chose to stay. She'll think I coerced you. I did once before."

She frowned at the dust on the table, brushing at it, as if to find some message hidden in the wood. She felt drained, hollow, as if she had left her heart somewhere in Saphier and could not return home until she found it. Her finger shaped a swan's wing in the dust; she saw the black swan flying through the tower window, just before she vanished into Saphier. She said abruptly, "Tell her to tell the Gatekeeper of Ro House that he is about to find a dragon at his gate and only the key she has will lock the gate."

He looked dubious. "You want me to give her a message for the Gatekeeper?"

"He is no ordinary Gatekeeper."

"Is that so." He leaned forward a little, caught her eyes, curious again. "A Gatekeeper," he mused, and she felt her face warm. "And this will persuade Nyx not to fight me."

"I don't know. I do know you'll get the key any way you can. Tell her I had a vision of what the dragon is hunting."

"Come with me," he said insistently. "Home to Ro Holding. It's Saphier's dragon. I'll fight it."

"If that were true," she said sharply, "I would not be seeing visions in your doorway. You love Saphier's dragons too much to fight them."

He swallowed, said heavily, "Then promise me you will wait here for me. You will not cross the Luxour without me."

"I will go where I must," she said. "I cannot promise anything."

He opened his mouth, closed it. He stood up, holding her eyes, as if the path to Ro Holding lay there, not within his memories. He closed his eyes at last, his face white as tallow, his shoulders straining against some enormous burden. She saw him vanish finally. And then he was back, no longer standing but fallen among the glittering fragments of the dragon's heart.

She made a sound, staring at him, for he seemed, amid the light and stone and scattered crystals, another vision, a foretelling. But, touching him, she felt his weight, and heard his ragged breathing. He lifted one hand weakly, dropped it over his eyes.

"I'm sorry, Meguet. It was too far . . ." He fell asleep there within the broken heart. She closed her eyes, felt the long, dark tide of dread and warning well through her. Its ancient voices finally ebbed and she could move again. She picked shards of crystal from beneath the mage, and saw the Cygnet's eye in every shattered piece.

# CHAPTER
# 9

In Chrysom's tower, Nyx stood spellbound, exploring the gold key she held. The sunlight had faded some time ago; the long summer dusk had filled the tower room and darkened. She scarcely noticed light or lack of it; her mind had become the size and shape of the key. The key was the book; the book, she suspected, was the key to the paths of time in the little black-and-silver box. It would teach her how to pick one path, control its speed, follow its turns, focus its end. She could find a path to match the twists of time on Brand's wrists, if she could find the spell, if she could open the book . . . The book remained stubbornly a key.

Her thoughts turned around themselves, like the graceful lines of gold. *The key is the book, the book is the key. The key is the key to itself, it unlocks itself.*

It might unlock a path to Saphier, she knew, for Chrysom had seen dragons. Had they been the elusive dreams of Saphier, becoming real as he looked at them?

*The key is the key. The key opens itself.* Her mind roamed within its gold and ivory. *Chrysom,* it said at every touch. Power was implicit in it, like the power in a tuned, silent string. There was a way to touch it, make it sound. . . .

*Chrysom,* she said within it, but the name did not change it. She tried other words from his ancient spells; none revealed the book. She tried her own name, and then Moro Ro's name; the

**105**

key ignored both of them. *Time,* she guessed. *Book. Open. Mage. Unlock.* Finally, she told it what it was, and what it must become. *Key,* she said within it, and the key blossomed like a flower in her mind.

It remained a key in her hand; she was aware, in some distant place, of its shape and weight. But the spells, written in Chrysom's clear, precise writing, turned slowly, page after page, in her mind. Some were labelled incomprehensibly; others dealt directly with the oddments that still survived after a thousand years to be recognized. The pages slowed under her scrutiny, stopped when she studied them, turned easily when she wished to go on. She found the box finally: the drawing of a dark cube scrolled on all sides with silver ink.

*Time-Paths,* the spell said. Pages of miniscule explanation followed. Nyx, engrossed, wandered down path after path of spells, and found at last the one she wanted.

*Saphier,* it said. *Here Be Dragons.* She followed it, memorizing its patterns. Other spells and paths, labelled strangely, wandered through Saphier; Chrysom, evidently, had found something there to fascinate him. But she concentrated on the path that ended at the ruler's court, hoping that, after so long, it was still there, or that Chrysom's journeys had led him into a time more recent in Saphier's history than his own.

She became aware, dimly, that stars had been burning in the dark around her for some time, a curiosity which coaxed her out of the key finally to investigate. She found candles lit throughout the room. Brand, his supper finished, sat in a window waiting for her.

A moon-paring hung over his shoulder, high above the swamp. She slipped the key back into her pocket, rubbed her eyes tiredly. Movement felt strange; she tried to remember how long she had been standing there, bewitched with Chrysom's knowledge. His taut, uneasy face told her: long enough.

"What were you doing?" he asked. "You didn't move, you wouldn't speak. I thought some spell had been cast over you by that key."

"No." She drifted to the table, her thoughts inlaid with winding paths of silver. She ate bits of cold peppered meat, and bread and a stew of mushrooms and leeks, until she felt she had climbed out of the little black cube into her own time again. She poured wine, drank a mouthful, then turned. In the candlelight her eyes held a trace of lavender. "I found Chrysom's path to Saphier."

She heard his breath catch. He moved away from the window, relinquishing the bird's familiar place. "I can go home?"

"I'll take you."

"How?" His fingers twisted the blackened path on one wrist. "How?"

"The black cube. You came into it once, to rescue me. Do you remember?"

"No." Then he shook his head a little. "Perhaps. It's like a dream—"

"It was real," she said soberly. "I was lost and you led me out. That's when you remembered your name."

"I don't remember," he said, but for once with regret. He added, "I would like to remember that I did something for you."

"You will." She nibbled pieces of slivered carrots and almonds with her fingers, thinking. "Where would Rad Ilex most likely have taken Meguet?"

His face tightened at the name, but he did not retreat from it. "My father's court," he said after a moment. "It's where he lives."

"He'd go there even after casting a spell over you?"

"He wouldn't expect to see me. He is still free to come and go from Saphier; my father must not suspect him."

"Well," she said, "it's a place to start."

"My father will help you. He can send his mages searching across Saphier, even across the Luxour if need be. Not every mage can cross the Luxour. So I've heard. They say ancient magics, old as the beginning of the world, blow across it like wind. But some mages learn to anticipate the winds."

"Rad Ilex?"

He was silent, struggled again; he nodded briefly. "Yes. And my father. And some others."

"It sounds fascinating."

"Perhaps. I never understood his love of the Luxour."

"Your father's?"

"Rad." Blood streaked his face suddenly; he turned away from her, but she saw him tremble. She wondered uneasily what jagged edge of truth waited for him in Saphier. She dipped her fingers in orange-scented water, wiped them on a napkin, then pinned up a stray coil of hair. She said slowly,

"I should tell my mother that I'm going."

"Will she let you go to a strange land?"

"Most likely she'll be so amazed I told her that she won't ask where. But I don't know how long it will take me to find Meguet, and I don't want her thinking I'm in danger."

"My father will protect you," he said swiftly. "Nothing will harm you in Saphier."

Absently she looked for her shoes, found them on her feet. She brushed a crumb off her skirt. "I'd better change. I can't wear silk shoes across a desert, if it forces me to walk."

"There will be no need for you to go. The mages will search the Luxour."

She stared at him. "A desert full of magic, and you expect me to sit in your father's house trying to watch my manners?"

He blinked. "I forget," he said, "how much freedom you have. You choose to come and go; my father's mages do his bidding. You also do things for love." His face closed abruptly, before she could question him. She said to his set profile,

"I'll be back as soon as I speak to my mother."

His brow crooked anxiously. "It's late," he reminded her.

"I'll hurry. If Rad Ilex comes—"

"Do you expect—"

"No," she said quickly. "Though it would be worth this key and more to find Meguet here instead of there. If he comes, tell him to wait for me. Don't touch him. Don't let the firebird break out of you."

"How can I stop the bird?" he demanded.

"Find a way. Do anything to keep Rad Ilex here. The heart of sorcery is the clear and patient mind. So Chrysom says. I am trying to be patient and clear-headed, for once in my life. But if the mage vanishes again with Meguet, I am liable to lose my temper and do something impulsive."

"My father says the heart of sorcery is the fire that forges the dragon's heart."

"He does."

"So he teaches."

"Moro's eyes. Just don't fight."

She summoned one of the tower pages, sent him running to the Holder's chambers to request a few moments' privacy. Then she vanished, reappeared in front of her startled attendants, picking jewels out of her hair. She changed quickly, packed a few oddments of her own. She felt for the amber at her ear lobe, and tossed everything—earring and key and cloak, comb and little jewelled mirror, a few dried herbs—into an ivory ball so tiny it seemed invisible in her pocket. The key, now that she understood it, had consented, to her relief, to fit itself inside the ball.

She didn't bother with stairs and towers; she simply appeared in front of her mother. The Holder had dismissed her attendants and was pacing; seeing Nyx she barely changed expression, as if what she frowned at were only an extension of her thoughts. She said,

"Where is Meguet?"

"I believe, in a land called Saphier."

"Where is that?"

"I have no idea. It's not on any map I can find."

The Holder was silent. Her arms were folded tightly; she seemed too disturbed even to throw hairpins. "You said the mage would return for the key."

"So I thought," Nyx said.

"Then where is he?"

"I don't know."

"I have told the Holding Council that Meguet is guarding you, and that you are guarding Ro House against the return of the mage. Rumors are already—" She stopped, touched her eyes. "Rumors."

"They follow me, don't they?" Nyx said softly. "The bog-witch alone in the tower with a bird . . ." Her own arms were folded; she was frowning, reflecting her mother, but pensively, at the problem itself. "The mage slowed time and fought me for that key. It seemed most reasonable to think he would return for it."

"Then where is he? Surely he didn't find Meguet an adequate substitute!"

"I think—" Nyx hesitated, received the full brunt of the Holder's troubled, angry gaze. Her brows lifted a little; she said patiently, "If you are going to shout at me, shout. I'll listen."

"What I think," the Holder said tersely, "is that my youngest daughter and heir stays alone in that ancient, magic-riddled tower with a dangerous bird, waiting for the return of a very dangerous mage, and that my niece is lost in a country that exists on no map, and at the mercy of that mage. Shouting would hardly satisfy. Reducing the hearthstones to rubble with a poker might. Now. Tell me what you think."

"I think I can find my way to Saphier."

The Holder shouted, "What?"

"And I think I know why the mage has not returned."

"You are not going to Saphier."

"I might have to search for Meguet."

"No. Absolutely not."

"Mother, I may have no choice. From what Brand has said, Saphier is not the most hospitable place in the world. It sounds fierce, violent, power-ridden. The mage may be the least of Meguet's problems."

The Holder's tight grip of herself loosened suddenly; she pulled a net of gold thread and emeralds from her hair, flung it to the floor. She stared at Nyx, hair tumbling around her shoulders, her eyes night-dark, lined with pain. She said harshly, "I forbid you to leave this house. You said the mage will return. Wait for him.

I will not lose both you and Meguet to some barbaric land beyond Ro Holding. Meguet is resourceful; she may be able to find her way back—"

"No." She gazed at her mother, her throat tight. Her face had lost color. "I won't let you sacrifice Meguet for me."

"You sacrificed her for a key."

"I—" She swallowed, unable to speak, then steadied her voice. "I make mistakes. Yes."

The Holder closed her eyes. "I'm sorry."

"I was careless." Nyx spoke carefully, her eyes wide, colorless as cloud. "But I'm not entirely without resources myself. Meguet fought for me. I owe her. I think I can find a way into Saphier."

"But why?" The Holder's voice rose again, dangerously. "Why must you go there if you expect the mage to come here?"

"I think he can't."

"Can't what?"

"Return. I think he was injured by the firebird."

"Moro's eyes," the Holder breathed. "Badly?"

"It's not a question of degree—"

"Do you think he's dead?"

"I have no idea."

"You saw him before he disappeared. What had the bird done to him?"

"It was enough," Nyx said slowly, "that the bird had done anything at all to him. If he had made the firebird, with all his formidable power he should have been able to control it. He never tried to harm it; it was trying to kill him. It drew blood; it lost a talon. That may have been enough to kill the mage."

"A bird claw? I don't understand."

"The spell itself. The sorcery that transformed the firebird. It might have been deadly to the mage."

The Holder stared at her. "I thought it was his spell."

"So did I, until I saw him wounded. I think Meguet may be somewhere in Saphier with an injured mage on her hands."

The Holder was silent. She turned abruptly, found the nearest chair and sat. "Then whose spell is it? Are we to expect yet another mage who won't bother to use the gate?"

"I don't—" Nyx's voice shook suddenly with worry. "I don't know what to expect next." She leaned against the massive fireplace, gazing down at her mother, and finding some comfort from the solid stones. "I've never asked your permission to leave the house before."

"I know."

"I've rarely even told you where I was going. I'm your heir, yes, but I'm also all you've got for a mage, and I must be free to work. Though I realize I've hardly given you much, these past months, to have faith in." The Holder shifted, gestured wordlessly, her ringed hands flashing, falling. "All you've seen me do here is turn the Hold Signs back into embroidery and silence a bird, which rumor already told you I could do."

"Nyx—"

"All I seem to do with the firebird in the tower is to fail. It does seem a simple thing to do: change a bird back into a man, something any mage could do."

"It must," the Holder said, "be a very subtle sorcery."

"Oh, it is. Very subtle. And so stubborn, it seems to me at times that Brand himself cast the spell, masked himself behind the firebird, and refuses to relinquish it."

The Holder made a noise, staring at her daughter. "He enchanted himself?"

"I don't think so. But I am beginning to think he has some very powerful reasons to avoid becoming himself again. And I think the truth of the matter lies in Saphier. He cannot return on his own; the time-paths on his wrists have been damaged. I must take him."

"I don't like this," the Holder said. "A ruler's son, ensorcelled and exiled—it sounds dangerous. It's not your business to solve Saphier's problems."

"No. But Brand has given me no reason to believe his father won't want him back. If I were missing in a strange land, you would be grateful if someone brought me home."

"Yes, but—"

"Also, there is Meguet. I can't leave her there."

"No. But—"

"But, why me? Because you have no one else who can do these things."

"You are my heir."

"I am your mage. This is what mages do."

"I don't like it." The Holder rose abruptly to pace again, down a woven path of flowers and ivy to its edge and then back again. "You are too much like me," she said abruptly. "Strong-willed and prone to wander. What if I lose you to Saphier? Where will I go to look for you? You can't even tell me where this land is, assuming it exists now, at this moment and not some other, which occurs to me to wonder about since it doesn't exist on any map."

"The problem," Nyx said carefully, wondering herself, "may not exist either. It's not something to worry about until we must."

"That," the Holder said explosively, "is the kind of muddy thinking that has led you into trouble before."

"Perhaps. But I've always found my way home. Somehow." She put her hand on her mother's arm. "Please," she said softly. "I didn't run away nine years for nothing. I am a sorceress. Let me do some sorcery."

The Holder came with her to the tower. The midnight bells had not yet rung; Brand, whirling mid-pace as the door opened, was still human. Nyx cast a glance around the room; he answered her unspoken question.

"No one came. No one that I could see."

"All right," she said tautly. "We'll go there." She turned, looked at the Holder a moment, wordlessly. She said with wonder, "I've never said goodbye to you before."

"Don't say it now," the Holder said fiercely. She touched an errant strand of Nyx's hair, then dropped her hand, stepped back. "Just go. Return Brand to his father, find Meguet, and come home. Nothing more complicated than that. Promise me."

"I'll come back as soon as I can." She drew the ivory ball out of her pocket, gazed into it. She could see the key float-ing in the dark; she touched it with her mind. Pages turned, time-paths wandered through them, through her thoughts, into the room itself. She was vaguely aware that Brand had knelt at the Holder's feet. He said something, rose again through a misty net of silver. Something else happened as he stepped to Nyx's side and the room itself wavered, dreamlike, beyond the widening silver filigree: There were unexpected sounds, sudden movements. A door opened; faces appeared, then faded into a soft darkness that grew so deep it swallowed even the bright stars of candlelight. Nyx, paths rushing everywhere around her, struggled a moment to remember the faces. Not Meguet, though one had her hair. Not the mage. She was aware of Brand with her, a presence and a name, though he had moved behind her. *Saphier,* she said, and all the glowing paths around them froze and vanished. All but one . . . She stepped onto it; it began to move. As she shifted the path to form the pattern that led to Saphier, elusive sounds, faces, drew urgently at her attention, demanding to be named. She pushed them away, concentrating, intent on accurately shaping the whorls and crooks of time and distance so that the path would end in Saphier and not in the middle of some sea. It was not until she had formed the final turn and something vast began to shape itself beyond the dark, that she relinquished her attention to memory, and the sounds, the faces, came suddenly clear.

A knock . . . The Holder turned, and the bells began to ring. The door opened . . . The Gatekeeper, his face hard, white, as it was when he swallowed fear whole and tried to hide it in some private place . . . The face beside him was so unexpected that for a moment she felt only amazement: dark-skinned, pale-haired, eyes as dark as the first night of the world. It was Meguet's kin, her unlikely shadow, as powerful and as powerless, standing under a roof that was not stars or light. And then she saw the warning in his eyes.

She felt the blood startle out of her face. The darkness ebbed, revealing a quiet, shadowy hall, a house at night, some time after, she guessed, the midnight bells had rung.

The firebird flew ahead of her toward a moving circle of light.

# CHAPTER
# 10

Meguet picked her way across a dragon's spine. It pushed itself in a sharp, uneven ridge of red stone out of dry, weathered earth; it was not high, but too long to walk around and almost too steep to climb. Nothing grew on it. On the other side of it lay more of what she had already crossed: the Luxour with no perceptible horizon, shimmering with heat or with air disturbed by the flicker of dragon wings.

She had left Rad's village at dawn, sitting beside a young, straw-haired man on his cart. He was going to cut salt blocks, he had told her when she stopped him. There was a place he knew in the desert, a white pool of salt. She needed to get to Draken Saphier's court, she said. He looked surprised, but offered her a ride as far as the first wall of stone.

"I go due north," he said, "to the dragon's backbone. Then I go west along that to the end, and there's the salt pond. You'll want to keep going north." He eyed her askance as she climbed onto the cart seat; an answer presented itself. "You'll be a mage, too, then. We were all wondering. Only mages cross the Luxour on foot."

"How do others get across?" she asked. He urged his donkeys forward.

"They ride. Mostly they go around to the east, then follow the

river. Others come in caravans, on carts, well-supplied. Those
who hunger after dragons. Most buy a heart and go home again."
He ticked at the donkeys; his voice was good-humored, unhurried.
"Some stay along the river, spend their lives looking for crystal
bones. A handful stay on the Luxour itself."

"In the desert?" she said, startled.

"A half-dozen, maybe, I've seen; there must be others. They
find their places in the rocks, their underground streams. They see
their private dreams of dragons to live near—a shape of stone, a
hot spring, an odd configuration of shadows at sunset—and there
they stay. They find me or they find the salt, eventually. That's
how I know them."

She looked at him, at the crook of his mouth, his eyes that
expected no surprises. "You don't believe in the dragons."

He shook his head, surprised again. "But I love the desert. It's
enough for me, just the way it is, without suppositions. Most born
around here never leave. Or like Rad, they come back. He never
stays long, though. He believes in dragons, Rad. He's seen them
since we were small, running barefoot into the desert after lizards.
'Look,' he'd say, 'look.' But I'd never see. So I wasn't surprised
when he left for Draken Saphier's court. All mages go there. Is
that where you were born?"

"No."

He waited, then flicked the reins idly. "I thought maybe so,
because you came with him and you're going back there. But they
say the mages come from all over Saphier, to Draken Saphier's
court."

She opened her mouth to ask a question, closed it again.
Mages, she thought, and wondered if they were all as powerful
as Nyx. She felt a familiar, terrible impatience, wanting to be
there instead of here with a desert to find her way across, at
least until urgency loosed her powers, pleated time and desert
to take her where she was needed. Whether or not Rad Ilex
would search for her after he took the key from Nyx, she had
no idea. She could do nothing for Ro Holding, staying in that
village at the edge of nowhere. Nyx, she had reasoned starkly,

would not sit still in Chrysom's tower wondering where Meguet was, if she could find her way to Saphier. And if she came, she would not bother with a desert; she would go straight to Draken Saphier. . . .

"There," the young man beside her said. "The dragon's back-bone."

The sun had risen above the distant blue mountains, begun its arc across the sky. It peeled shadow away from the dragon bone, left a low, jagged ridge cutting across the landscape, beginning and ending nowhere. He pointed.

"Salt's there, at that end." He looked at her a moment, silently; perhaps, Meguet thought, he did not believe in mages either, and saw only a woman, unprotected and ignorant, about to wander into a place abandoned by everything but light. He said only, "Rad's doings taught me never to question mages; not even their answers make much sense. If you need me again for something, I'll be at the west end for two days."

At the top of the ridge, she could still see his cart, lumbering and patient as a beetle, crawling along the bone. She rested a moment. Ahead lay the odd, crazed towers and palaces and dragons' wings of stone. Wind roused suddenly, pushed at her hard; she smelled sulphur, and a darker, sweeter scent, as if in some deep, moldering cave something huge had shifted, disturbing earth. She started down the slope.

Sometime later, she walked along shallow furrows, straight lines raked long ago across the ground as if by some giant claw. The scars had weathered, but never closed. She glanced up uneasily, wondering at the size of such a thing. A fierce, golden eye left an imprint of fire in hers. She looked down, blinking, and continued doggedly, wondering if she would become like the desert dwellers, seeing dragons everywhere. Her shadow fluttered like black fire in the wind: the loose, flowing garments she had taken from Rad. He had worked some magic into her velvet shoes, during one of his waking moments, so she could walk, he said, if she got restless while he mended himself. Wearing them, she would feel neither heat nor cold nor water nor stone;

she would walk on air. Dust did not cling to them either, she noticed, though dust clung to her sweating face and wove itself into her hair. She carried a water skin and a pouch with some bread and fruit and goat cheese. She would find lizards when she ran out of food. She would find the water that the desert dwellers drank. She would cross the desert somehow; even the Luxour came to an end eventually.

Her shadow shrank; the eye overhead blazed at her. She felt even her bones shrink under its cruel gaze, as if the weight of light pouring down over her pushed her closer to the earth. She reached one of the strange ruins, steep upthrusts of stone that had weathered and sheared pieces of itself away. From a distance it had doors, broken towers, and fallen walls, empty windows framing sky. Close, it was simply a pile of rock, within which she found shade, a resting place. She ate and drank sparingly, then leaned against a slab of warm stone and closed her eyes.

She woke with a start at a sound, and found a woman watching her.

"Are you mage?" the woman asked. "Or dragon?" Her eyes were blue desert sky, split with streaks of silver lightning; she peered at Meguet, blinking. Her long hair was white, her hands slender and delicate. She wore a black robe and magic shoes; there was no dust on them. "I hear you breathing. I cannot see so clearly now; everything breathes now, everything has wings. Which are you?"

"Neither," Meguet said. She straightened slowly, stiff. The woman, perched on stone like a butterfly sunning, smiled, her smooth brown face breaking suddenly into a spider web of wrinkles.

"A riddle!"

"No. Only a woman crossing a desert."

"You are not a mage."

"No."

"Then," the woman said, "you have a chance of getting out."

Meguet was silent, puzzled. She found her water skin, drank a mouthful, and held it out. "Are you thirsty?"

"No. But thank you. I have learned to smell clean water, after so many years here. I never go thirsty."

"Years." Meguet swallowed, staring at the ancient, beautiful, half-blind face. "How many years?"

"I can't remember. I only remember how old I was when I got lost here; after I decided to stay I started counting dragons instead of years." She smiled again. "In dragon years, I might be five. Or a thousand. Or I may not even be born. They are that elusive. . . ."

"Are you a mage?"

"I was. Maybe I still am. I never think about it."

"I thought that's all mages thought about."

"Being mages?" She nodded, her hair drifting in the wind, a long cobweb cloak. "You've been around them, to know that."

"A couple of them. But how did you get lost? All you have to do is follow the sun or cross it, to find your directions."

"Mages," the woman said, "tend to get distracted in the Luxour. There's such a tangled magic here. It lures you this way, that. It tantalizes, it whispers." She put her hand on a jagged tower of rock. "It lies. It says: *Once I was this, search me, find who built me.* So you search, and once you begin to see one fine, lost palace, you begin to see entire kingdoms lost; you wander from ruin to ruin, trying to find a memory."

"A memory of what?"

"Of those who might have lived here among the dragons. Or, dragon-born, built them." She patted the stone fondly. "Oh, they're like the dragons, these old stones. They never say yes or no, but always maybe. *Maybe I'm stone. Maybe more than stone.*"

"Then why did you never turn your back on them and leave?"

"Because by then you yourself live within the ruined palaces; you have inherited the forgotten kingdoms." She stood up on the rock, let her hair flow on the wild currents. She held out her hand. There was a blood-red jewel on her forefinger: a dragon's eye. "Come with me. I'll show you where I live, among the lizards and the sand beetles and the blue-eyed snakes. There's a well of water beneath the rocks, so deep I never touch the bottom when I bathe in it. A dragon sleeps at the bottom of the well. Sometimes at noon when sunlight pours between the rocks, I glimpse it, coiled, golden as the light. Come. I'll show you."

"I cannot," Meguet said gently. "I must cross the Luxour. I dare not be distracted by it."

"So I felt, when I was much younger. That a hundred reasons compelled me across the desert. But after a time, I realized there was no reason for me not to stay. No reason at all. What compels you?"

"I must get to Draken Saphier's court."

"Draken Saphier." The woman's face smoothed, as if she barely remembered the name. Then she gave a sudden laugh. It held memory, ambiguity, a touch of rue. "The Dragon of Saphier. I was in Saphier when his mother ruled." She was silent a little, her silver-blue eyes looking inward. "Perhaps that's why I lost myself in the Luxour so long ago. I, too, wanted the dragon's child. But—" She tossed her hands lightly, freeing memory. "I could never find the dragon. If you stay long enough, Draken Saphier will come here. The Luxour will call him home." She waited; when Meguet did not answer, she turned, slipped away among the ruins, as swiftly and easily as a desert animal. Her voice drifted back. "The world beyond the Luxour is the dream. Stay here."

Meguet rose. As she stepped out of shadow, light pressed down at her again, trying to melt her, reshape her into something shrunken and flat that huddled close against the earth. She drew long scarves around her face, her head, and marked a path from stone to stone, shadow to shadow. Water, the desert-mage had said. A well. Deep water. But perhaps that was also a dream, for nothing grew out of the ground but rocks. Still, she remembered the ice cave, the dragon's cold breath. The memory itself cooled her until she reached another shadow. *Stay*, the desert said. *Sit. Wait. There is no end to me, I am everywhere, and you will never find your way beyond me. There is no path out of me. Stop here. Stay. Rest.* But she refused to listen, even when the light pressed her head down, her eyelids closed as she walked. The light was dragon's breath; the Dragon hunted the Cygnet . . . She walked across the face of the sun itself, and she told the desert: *I have fought the sun and lived.* She stumbled into shadow and back into endless fire, and again into shadow until both sun and shadow weighed her down, and time and the sun seemed to have stopped.

Finally the hot black cooled; the sun loosed its grip of the desert. A lavender sky began to darken, reveal the first faint stars. She heard water bubbling around her, smelled sulphur. Her mouth felt stuffed with sand, her body worn like old stone. She sat, felt for the water skin, took a few sips of warm water. Her eyes burned suddenly, though she had nothing left for tears; her body shook in a sudden, noiseless sob of fear and despair. She calmed herself, watching the night deepen, the stars grow huge, impossibly close. She saw no shimmering wings, no shadows unfolding to block the stars. Perhaps all she had ever seen were Rad Ilex's dreams. The vast, warm dark, the star-shot silence comforted her. *Others have been lost here and lived,* she thought. *And I'm not lost yet.* She ate fruit that had fermented in the heat, cheese that would not last another day. She lay back again, above the ground along a ledge of stone, feeling the stone pull at her bones as if to draw her into itself. *Tomorrow,* she thought, *I'll walk before dawn.* Just before she fell asleep, she saw the stars flow together against the dark, shape themselves into the dragon's face.

The next day she walked into the dragon's heart.

It was vast, golden, seething with hidden fires that blazed within stone, sand, shadow. Plumes of steam blurred the landscape, were snatched up and shredded by winds that blasted from the dragon's mouth. Mud bubbled and belched; the ground hissed. Even the air she breathed burned, rank and fiery with steam. Sometimes she could barely see to cross the sun's path; other times sun was everywhere, glowing in water, leaping out of raw crystals or dragon's eyes. Steam or dragon's breath trailed through the ruins, shaped ghostly faces where windows might have been. The ruins gave some shelter from the light, and the hot, stinging winds, but even their shadows burned. She made some attempt to capture lizards, shards of sun or shadow that scattered at her footfall and darted among the rocks. But they were too quick, and she couldn't remember which Rad had told her not to eat. She ate dried, crumbled bread, a withering apple. Her eyes closed. She forced herself to rise, find her direction. She could barely see the dragon's backbone pointing east and west behind her; the great towers, the roiling steam, half-hid it. At least it was still behind her; she hadn't begun drifting in circles. The broken fragments of the lost kingdom rose everywhere in front of her. She could only sketch a path from one shadow to the next, and hope they did not shift themselves from place to place, stones and memories of stone, like some moving labyrinth, to trap her there. She walked until she turned gold with dust, and her thoughts under the violent heat were distilled to vapor, blown away before she could grasp them. Finally, a dragon-claw of light raked through her eyes, into her mind, and, between one step and another, she fell into her shadow.

She tasted water, impossibly sweet and cold. She tried to speak, and choked. A hand cradled her head, raised it. She opened her eyes, trying again to speak, and saw a stranger turned away from her as he set the water skin down. Behind him stood a great dragon the color of twilight. Its eyes were stars, its wings, opening, spread purple-grey across the sky. She tried to rise, managed to lift one hand. The stranger turned to her. The dragon breathed; night swirled around her, a blinding dark without a star.

When she woke again, a vast, silvery tide had swept across the sky. The dragon, looming against the night, was a shadow limned by stars. One star had fallen near her, giving out a soft, unwavering glow in spite of the restless winds. The stranger sat outside the circle of its light; she saw his loose, pale desert garb straying in the wind. He might have been dreaming or watching dragons, but he sensed her waking. She saw a flash of silver beneath his sleeve as he reached out to touch the fallen star.

It burned brighter, sent its soft light washing over her face; his was still in shadow.

She asked, "Is the dragon yours?" Her voice sounded thin, far-away, as if she were dreaming it. But he heard her; he had risen suddenly, noiselessly, to scan the dark.

"What dragon?"

"The one there against the stars."

He saw it; she heard his breath. Then he settled himself again. "It's stone." His voice was low, dispassionate. "Sometimes I think these great stones change shape at night, wander where they will. . . ." He passed her the water skin. "Hungry?"

"No."

"You will be." He passed her another skin, of honey wine. She drank a little, and closed her eyes. She saw dragon wings, sheer and delicate as moth wings, dusted with stars. She remembered then where she was going and why, and dragged her eyes open.

"I must go." But she could barely lift her head. He took something out of a pouch, began peeling it; the wind brought her the impossible scent of oranges. He passed her a section, ate one himself. "It's easy to get lost at night, even for a mage."

The desert, it seemed, abounded with mages. "How many dragon years have you been here?"

He was silent; she felt him study her. "Not long enough," he said at last, "to be unsurprised by everything. Have you taken to dwelling in the desert?"

"No."

"Then you came to see dragons."

"No."

He handed her another piece of orange. "Then why are you walking through the heart of the Luxour?"

"I'm travelling north."

"From where?"

She did not, she realized, even know the name of Rad's village. "South."

"Most people," he commented after a moment, "would have followed the river around the desert."

"I'm in a hurry."

"The Luxour slows time for those who hurry; it elongates itself. It hides itself from the curious; it shows itself to the innocent, and the unwary. It works its own magic." His voice sounded detached, as if his attention were roaming the desert around them, peering into moon-shadows, listening to the winds. "It is a place of enormous power, and when you reach for that power, it slips away to return when you have stopped looking for it."

Scanning the night for intimations of such power, she saw only a great, sinuous spiral of stars following the moon's path, that reminded her of Rad's white dragon. She thought of him, drugged by some deep, healing sleep, and of the white dragon in Chrysom's tower, and then of Nyx, finding the key in Ro Holding that would unleash the dragons of Saphier, and she moved abruptly, murmuring in frustration, blinking dust out of her eyes.

"Do these winds never stop?"

"Never," he answered. "They are dragons' breath, fire and ice."

"I saw the ice-dragon."

He leaned forward slightly, his voice less distant. "Did you."

"Not the dragon itself—"

"No."

"But the cave where it sleeps. Like a hole in the night."

"Yes."

"I heard it breathe."

"And what else have you seen?"

"A shadow. But nothing that cast the shadow."

He said, "Ah," very softly. "And what else?"

"Nothing more. A heart, maybe. A bone. The mage I saw yesterday said there was a golden dragon at the bottom of a well. A dragon of light."

"Mage." His voice went flat on the single word; she sensed all his attention then, pulled back out of the night to focus on her.

"The one who lives among the rocks."

"Does this mage have a name?"

"I didn't ask. She is quite old and somewhat blind."

He made a soft sound; his attention strayed again. "She may see better, then, on the Luxour, where nothing is quite as it seems."

"She had lost, she said, all interest in magic long ago. How is that possible? To stop being a mage?"

"To stop being compelled," he answered; his face was turned away from her again, to the dark, singing distances. He added after a moment, "I don't know if that in itself is possible."

"She seemed compelled by dragons."

"On the Luxour everyone is compelled by dragons."

She was silent: A dragon had compelled her into the hot, unbearable eye of the sun. She said, "It was kind of you to help me."

"You're not the first I've found overwhelmed by the Luxour," he said. "It happens. People come looking for wonders, for the dragon's claw, the dragon's fire. They never stop to think that they might find what they are looking for. They see crystal bones, a piece of petrified fire, fragments of some long forgotten age. They never see the living fire that breathes over them out of a passing moment. I find them and they wake and tell me they were struck by sun. Then they stumble to the nearest village and buy a dragon heart and go home, never knowing they have worn dragon's fire, they have stood within the dragon's eye."

She was silent, compelled, by something in his voice, to search the winds and stars for their reflections. "I thought it was the sun myself," she admitted.

"I thought you must be a mage when I saw you," he said a little drily. "With enchanted shoes and no food. No one has less common sense than a mage on the Luxour. But I didn't recognize you, and I know all the mages of Saphier."

"I'm not a mage," she said. "A mage I met put the spell into my shoes."

"Yes." His voice went soft, very thin; he might have been listening to the sound of a shadow shifting across sand. "I recognized his spell. Mages leave fingerprints that the skilled can read. How well do you know him?"

She was silent, thinking of Rad with a dragon across his doorway, telling her what to fear. "Not well," she said finally.

"Is he in his village now?"

"I don't know," she said truthfully. "He comes and goes." He moved. The mage-light flashed suddenly in her eyes. She winced, catching dust again, her vision blurring.

"I know those river villages," he said. "Everyone knows everyone and everything."

"It's true." She wiped tears from her eyes, shielding her face from the light. "I've lost track of time, here. It seems so long ago, now, that I walked out of the village. I don't even know where I am; how can I know where a mage might be? Mages—except you—don't pay attention to you unless they need you."

"And did he?"

"Did he what?"

"Need you?"

She looked at him, her eyes finally clear, wondering at this stranger pushing her gently, question by question, into lies, and why she felt compelled to hide the sleeping mage within her thoughts. In the wider cast of light she finally saw his face.

She remembered to breathe after a time. It was the firebird's face, older, passionate, controlled. She recognized the black brows slashing over cobalt eyes, the hard, clean-lined warrior's face, weathered by experience. His long hair was varying shades of black and smoke and ash, tied back with braided ribbons of leather. The flash of silver at his wrists were the woven strands of time.

She swallowed drily. He said curiously, "You know me. I don't know you."

"You wouldn't," she said. She felt her body trying to grow small, push into the ground away from his eyes. "You wouldn't," she said again, desperately. "I'm just another face in those river villages you know."

He held her eyes for a long time until it seemed she began to hear the secret voices of his dragons, and to see their wings moving in his eyes. Then his expression changed, lines deepening

between his brows, beside his mouth. He said, "Rad Ilex sent you
into the Luxour leaving the track of his sorcery in every step you
take. Are you running away from him? You won't elude him
wearing those. He put some thought into your shoes, but into
little else." She did not answer. He touched the light again; it
dimmed, throwing a welcome shadow over her eyes. "You are
protecting him." His voice was suddenly husky, edged with pain,
his face so like Brand's it startled her. "It doesn't matter. I will
find him."

"Why?" she whispered. He set the pouch near her, along with
skins of water and wine. He sat still again, as she had first seen
him, but his hands were tightly closed, his face taut.

"He injured my son." His hands opened, closed again; he stared
into the mage-light. "Brand," he whispered. "My only child. He
is lost somewhere in time, crying fire like a dragon, unable to
speak anything but strange, jewelled spells. Rad forced him out
of Saphier, and destroyed his only path back."

"Why?" The word hurt, coming out, as if it were a strange,
hard jewel.

"I don't know. They had been friends. Rad Ilex had discovered
something, I think, something of enormous power, dangerous to
Saphier. Brand tried to warn me, Rad silenced him. I have been
searching for them both. I have sent my mages searching for
them. But Rad Ilex is elusive and my son is—anywhere. You
have been with Rad in his village. Is he there, still? You do not
know. He comes and goes. So he came and went in my son's
life and twisted him out of shape, and tore time itself apart to
fling him beyond Saphier. Beyond even my sight." He paused;
she saw him swallow. "I taught Rad to do those things."

She started to speak, couldn't. She heard Rad's voice: *The Dragon of Saphier will test you and test you until you can't call your
own bones private* . . . The dragon of night and stars had been on
Rad's own threshold, had filled his own doorway. It was Rad who
searched for the key, Rad whom the firebird attacked, Rad who
had tested her himself . . . Rad who lay helpless against Draken
Saphier, alone and dreaming, recovering from Brand's fury.

Or was he? Had he lied to her, gone in secret to Ro Holding to trade her warnings for a key? Was he on the desert now, coming to find her, or had he sent her on an impossible journey to Draken Saphier's court, simply to lose her and her suspicions to the Luxour?

"I can't help you." Her voice trembled badly, torn as she was between truth and lie, recognizing neither. She felt something like wind glide over her feet, and Draken Saphier rose, holding her shoes.

"You can help me," he said simply. "You can stay here until Rad follows the path of his sorcery to you. Not even the whims of the Luxour can hide your steps from him. When he finds you, I will find him." She stared at him, stunned. "Keep the food and water," he said. "I'll take the light." He added, "Don't try to walk in the dark. Things that are afraid of light, that bury themselves against the heat by day, dig out at night to feed. They are small, vicious, and can feel the vibrations of a falling pebble. As long as you stay still, you'll be safe. And I'll be here, watching."

The light went out. He was silent. He had, she realized, faded into the desert: a dark streak of wind, a thinking stone. She lay still, scarcely daring to breathe, trying to remember why, in another time, in another country, she had not picked up a sword instead of a rose.

# CHAPTER
# 11

Nyx sat in a white room, contemplating three black leaves floating in a bowl of water. The bowl was white; the table it stood on was white. Thin white curtains caught light before it spilled a hint of color across the white floor. Nyx wore a fine, flowing, complex assortment of garments, all of white silk. In the entire room, only her eyes had color, the lavender in them so deep it seemed, when she caught her reflection, a comment on her surroundings.

She was alone in the small chamber, whatever alone meant in a house full of mages. She had been treated with impeccable courtesy from the moment she appeared: a sorceress from a strange land walking a path of time into a ruler's house, with a firebird she claimed was his missing son. This she explained to more mages than she had ever counted even among the dead in the history of Ro Holding. There was not a shadow of disbelief in their expressions, as the firebird cried noiselessly, constantly overhead. Of course this was Draken Saphier's son, this wild bird trying impotently to turn them all into jewelled trees. Unfortunately, Draken Saphier was not there to thank her himself. Neither were Rad Ilex and Meguet, her eye told her, among this grave and attentive gathering. She must wait, of course, for Draken Saphier's return. She had, she explained, urgent business elsewhere. No, they persuaded her, she must wait. Draken Saphier

**129**

would want to question her more fully about his son's enchantment, perhaps seek her advice. This, she had to admit, seemed reasonable, considering the state in which his son had returned. Draken Saphier's arrival, they told her, was imminent.

It remained imminent. She had been given pristine quarters, three leaves in a bowl to contemplate, attendants of exquisite tact and skill who were all, she realized, mages of varying degree. Draken Saphier had not yet returned, but would soon. Soon became three days, and in three days she had been shown extraordinary things in the vast, white, light-filled palace. But she had seen nothing of the firebird.

She kept an eye out for him, as mages led her through the palace. It seemed an irregular assortment of cubes piled at varying heights, the whole house formed around a great square which was separated into formal gardens, and, at the center, a broad square of red and white stone. From the highest windows in the house she could see the pattern in the stones: the emblem of Saphier, an intricate, stylized weave of lines coiling, locking, parting, meeting. She wondered, if she walked that path, where it would end. It held, she realized after a time, the only curved lines in the palace. The palace had no round towers, no turrets, no spirals or circles, only a series of arched windows now and then, open to air and light, overlooking the gardens. The chambers and halls, corridors, stairways, all carried continuous straight lines from angle to angle as the palace turned at the corners of the square. Nothing was jumbled, labyrinthine, untidy with past. Past had been relegated to memory, or it was framed in orderly fashion within the present. For a house full of mages of varying powers the space and pale walls and light would be calming, and the strict lines the eye perceived might order the mind. So much Nyx conjectured, though, within those lines, she was shown fascinating deviations.

"This wall is very old," a very old mage named Magior Ilel, who was Brand's great-aunt, told her. She was quite tall and thin, with hands that seemed all bone, translucent with age, and eyes as dark and still as the new moon. The wall, a great slab of pale wood at one end of a white room, was so completely and intricately carved with tiny figures that it seemed to move. It was a battle, Nyx realized, taking a closer look, depicted with ruthless and startling detail: Not even the cart horses seemed exempt from slaughter. Only birds, picking out an eye or a bloody heart, eluded arrow, spear, fire, club, stone. The carving of the devastation was elegant, skilled. She studied it, curiously; such fury seemed remote in the peaceful house.

"Where are the mages?" she asked, turning to Magior. She surprised a fleeting expression on the ancient, composed face.

"A mage witnessed it," she answered. "He carved it, as an example of power he thought beyond the control even of sorcery. There were few mages then, and magic seemed a force as raw and random as lightning."

"Then he didn't connect sorcery with savagery," Nyx commented. She turned away from the silent, frozen carnage, to a more tranquil tapestry hanging on a side wall. At first glance it seemed a tree full of birds and flowers, bright, varied blooms growing along the same bough, with small, vivid birds fluttering among the leaves. As she gazed at it, odd dark shapes intruded: broken pieces of shadow, faces, perhaps, half-revealed behind the leaves, or even within a flower, as if some other work were embroidering itself through this one. She looked closer, intrigued, trying to piece the darkness together, but it remained elusive.

"It makes me want to frighten the birds out of the tapestry, part the leaves," she said, "to see what the tree is hiding." She looked at Magior. "What is it? What do you see?"

"I am too old," Magior said in her slow, dry voice, "to see anything. Flower and shadow, dark and light, in the end they are what they are. There is no resolution. You are unconvinced. What do you see?"

"A mystery," Nyx answered simply. "What I would like to see, unless you have some objection, is the firebird." Magior looked at her silently; she added, "It flew to me for help. I've grown—accustomed to it. To Brand. I've left work unfinished, which worries me, and will worry me until I see it completed.

Or has he remembered everything? Is the spell broken?"

Lines moved across the aged face, undecipherable expressions. "The firebird is resting. It has several—roosts, I suppose we must call them. We thought it best to surround him with familiar faces, so that he could more easily remember his past. The past he remembers with you is intricately bound with the spell."

"I see."

"Please do not be offended."

"No."

"If he looks at you, he will only remember himself as the firebird, needing help."

"And is he remembering himself?"

"It is," Magior said after a pause, "an exasperating piece of sorcery." Her face worked again. "When we follow his memories back, there is a point at which all we find, inevitably, is the bird's face. The bird's silent cry."

"You go into his mind?" Nyx asked, startled.

"You didn't?"

"Only to find the bird's mind. And that was like entering some hard, polished jewel, where every part is like every other part. And yet Brand kept insisting that all he lost of time and memory could be found in that enchanted bird."

Magior nodded. "So he still insists," she murmured. "All we can do is wait for Draken Saphier." She paused again, her eyes on Nyx's face. "We wondered," she said at last, "what you did with the bird's fire and its voice."

"I trapped them outside of the bird. I didn't want to dodge its fire while I worked, and I couldn't bear hearing its cry. No one in the house could. Have you heard it?"

"Once." Magior closed her eyes briefly. "In the middle of the night. Its first cry. Before it vanished. A terrible, terrible sound."

"The spell was cast here, then."

"Yes. By a mage who also vanished."

"Brand remembered something of that . . . He was afraid the mage had deceived his father, and was still here."

"No," Magior said a trifle harshly. "He has not been seen here since. He would not dare return."

"I see." Nyx kept her face and her voice calm, but still the dark eyes lifted, at some disturbance her impatience caused in the air between them. She asked quickly, "Something I wondered about: the time paths on Brand's wrists. How did they get so black?"

"We assume the mage destroyed them, when Brand tried to escape him."

"Would that be simple to do?"

"No. It would take enormous power. The paths are nearly indestructible. They must be so, or people might be left stranded in odd places, in strange times."

"Who made them?"

"Draken. He fashioned all the paths of time."

Nyx watched, the next day, the household guard gather in the stone square and perform a complex series of movements. They were very old, the young mage with her explained. Developed by the first mage-ruler of Saphier, for far different purposes. Now, despite the blades, it was more an exercise, a dance. The movements were slow, but Nyx recognized the whirling blades, the deadly rhythms of Brand's attack on Rad Ilex. There seemed guards enough for every window and every mouse hole in the house, all wearing the path of time that lay under their feet, emblazoned in red across their breasts. They also wore the familiar silver on their wrists. The thought of such an army marching the spiralling paths of time disturbed Nyx profoundly. Yet all she saw of martial art was relegated to a dance, and all she saw of magic was the complete disappearance of the firebird.

The mage with her, Parnet, a sturdy young woman from north Saphier, with a fat braid of red hair and a milky, freckled face, said when the guard dispersed, "Perhaps you would like to see the lemon garden. The fruit is ripe now and the trees are beautiful."

"I would rather see Brand Saphier," Nyx said. She added, infected by the constant courtesy, "Please."

"The firebird is resting," Parnet said slowly. "I don't know where in the house it might be."

"I thought you were trained to read minds."

"Oh, no," Parnet said, her complacency shaken. "I mean, yes, we are, but not without careful regulations, and not ordinarily without permission. It's punishable, though experiments are always made, among the younger mages. You can see such rules prevent a good deal of confusion, as well as animosity. Some mages are inclined to temperament."

"I see," Nyx said temperately. "Perhaps, then, at moonrise?"

"I'll ask Magior for you."

Nyx was silent, swallowing frustration. They had drifted to a stop beside an immense bowl of black marble, containing water. Above the water hung a huge tapestry of a man in a plain black robe, sitting on a floor of brilliant tiles, in front of a great black bowl of water. He studied it with interest, though it held, as far as Nyx could see, only a couple of threadbare patches.

"Who is that?" she asked. Parnet answered without a hint of judgment,

"No one. It is a question."

"The man?"

"No. What you see: the real bowl, the tapestry bowl, the water, the man. It is all a question about you."

"Me."

"Few pass here without speaking. What you say about this tells something about you. Even those who say nothing tell something. It is one of the ways of grouping beginning mages, according to their perceptions of what is most important. You chose the man. Some ask what he sees in the water; others what relationship the real bowl has to the bowl of thread. I suppose that, in a land full of strangers' faces, you would see the unknown face first."

Nyx opened her mouth, hesitated. The house came alive around her suddenly, puzzle-pieces everywhere, springing out of what she had considered background. "The bowl in my room," she said suddenly. "The color. Or rather the lack of it . . . This entire house is full of questions."

"Yes."

"How fascinating." She gazed into the water, saw the color deepen in her eyes. "And there are no answers. Only responses. Some must find all that white in my chamber peaceful."

"Yes."

"And the walls of battle-scenes?"

"Some find them absorbing," Parnet answered simply. "Most of them become the warrior-mages."

"Is Brand a warrior-mage?"

"Brand is a warrior. He has no gifts for sorcery."

"Yet he can walk the path of time on his wrists."

"That is common here, for warriors," Parnet answered, with a touch of surprise in her voice. Nyx frowned down at the water. She let one hand fall to her side, touch the tiny ivory ball that held Chrysom's key. She saw Parnet's reflection, her expression open, waiting, calm. She asked abruptly,

"And is the firebird itself a question? Or do you have a few answers for that here?"

Water rippled for no reason, obscuring both their reflections. Nyx turned her head, found Parnet still looking into the water. Her brows were raised slightly, worriedly; her face hid nothing. She said very softly,

"They have been trying, as you tried. All we can do is wait for Draken Saphier."

"Who will return soon."

"Soon."

Nyx sat that evening after supper, gazing into the white bowl of water in her chamber, watching the black leaves turn and turn, fashioning, out of water and air, some mysterious path of their own. Thoughts as dark were beginning to shape their own patterns in her mind. She barely gave them form, or language, for in that house apparently not even memory was private. One black leaf had Draken Saphier's name, one Rad Ilex's, and the third the name of an unknown mage who had entered Draken Saphier's house, ensorcelled his son, cast the blame on Rad Ilex, and vanished—or who had been taught by Draken Saphier,

had learned far too well, and who, having fashioned the firebird
and driven Rad Ilex away, still lived in the house, free and
unsuspected. That mage would be among those working with
the firebird now, to guard the spell. Someone close to Brand,
who had flung him out of his world, destroyed the path back to
it, and never expected to see him again.

*Until I brought him back,* she thought. *Along my private path.*
The mage could destroy that, too, if Chrysom's key were found.

But who? And why? And what had Brand witnessed that he
had been so ruthlessly reshaped, and even human, had only the
firebird's cry to speak of it?

She reached out, turned a leaf over between thoughts, as if it
were the page of a book. Its underside was gold. She watched
it awhile, thinking of the silver paths, and Draken Saphier, who
had a power like Chrysom's, to fashion bridges across time. How
expansive was that power? she wondered. And why did one of
those patterns lead to Ro Holding? Or had the bird simply gotten
lost in the strands of time, fleeing down a path that was being
consumed by sorcery?

She turned another leaf idly; it was deep blue. Blue, gold,
black . . . What would the third color be? Did the colors have
significance, or was it another of the house's questions? If she
did not turn it, it would be any color she imagined . . . She could
find the firebird in the house, open Chrysom's book and walk the
path to the Luxour. The bird would follow. They would escape
this house of puzzles, its bewildering courtesies and maddening equivocations. At least the desert would not equivocate:
earth, stone, light, did not lie. Or did they? There were ancient
magics in the Luxour, Brand had said, complexities even there.
But Draken Saphier could be found, to free Brand from the
firebird. Only for that, it would be worth some subterfuge to
find Brand and leave. But if she fled with the firebird down
one path, just as Draken Saphier returned by another, he would
be mystified and justifiably outraged. She might put herself in
danger; no one knew her here but Brand, no one could speak
for her but a man whose memories of her might in their eyes

be hidden within the firebird's cry. She had already taken its defense, its voice; they might wonder what else she had done to it.

She shifted restlessly, touched the third leaf gently to still herself. Meguet . . . where in Saphier was she, if not in Draken Saphier's court? With a mage hiding from Draken? Where would he hide?

The Luxour. Where the magic was unpredictable, and not even a mage could find a mage. And he knew the desert. He had been born there, Brand said, among the rumors of dragons. . . .

She turned the third leaf. The door opened behind her; she turned her head, saw Magior Ilel and a strange mage in the doorway.

Magior said, "Brand will see you now."

She rose, then turned back silently, looked into the bowl. Red as blood, as dragon's fire, the third leaf . . .

"Is it a question?" she asked.

"You chose the colors," Magior said without a flicker of expression. "It is an answer."

They led Nyx through endless airy corridors, toward chambers in an unfamiliar wing. Opening her mind a little, she sensed an enormous power, like a silent cataract. She barely touched it, a hand-brush against thundering, pounding water.

"Is this where the mages are trained?" she asked, and Magior cast a startled glance at her.

"Still your mind," she instructed.

"It has been suggested before," Nyx said tranquilly after a moment. "To no one's satisfaction."

"I do not mean to offend," Magior said stiffly. "You are a stranger in Draken Saphier's house. Your own powers are unknown to us."

Nyx glanced at the shadow beside her, flung forward by the angle of light, of the nameless mage who walked noiselessly behind her. He wore the emblem of Saphier across his chest; he would know, she guessed, the deadly movements of the dance.

She swallowed a sharp comment, concentrating on her surroundings. They had moved into a corridor of rich dark wood, carved
with ancient scenes, she guessed, of Saphier's history. A great
bronze dragon clung to double doors at the end of the corridor.
Warrior-mages guarded the doors. At a sign from Magior, they
split the dragon in two, and through the open doors Nyx saw
Brand.

The room was full of dragons, carved in wood, in red stone,
in amber, painted, embroidered on tapestry, limned in ink on the
margins and frontispieces of old books on stands and shelves. The
chair Brand sat in had dragons' faces lifting out of the arms, and
dragons' claws for feet.

"You wished to see me," he said to Nyx. The politeness in his
voice chilled her until she saw that his face was as rigid as his
courtesy. The firebird's cry of fury and despair, she guessed, was
so close to the surface of his thoughts that it took all his patience
to keep it from cutting to the heart of language. He glanced at
the warrior-mage, and then at Magior, before Nyx could answer.
"Why is Han here?"

"Only a precaution—" Magior began. Brand rose abruptly, his
mouth tightening.

"No one set such guards on me in Ro Holding."

"My lord, you were a bird. Nyx Ro is an unknown quantity."

"I know her. Dismiss him."

Expression rippled across Magior's face, a mingling of worry
and doubt. The warrior-mage inclined his head, disappeared into
thin air.

Nyx said carefully, "I haven't seen you since we came here. I
wondered how you were, if returning home had altered the spell
at all."

"No," Brand said tersely. He paced among the dragons, touching an eye here, a claw there.

"It is a spell," Magior said fulsomely, "of unusual complexity
and power."

"My father will help me," Brand said. "There's no more powerful mage in Saphier."

"Where is he?" Nyx asked baldly, expecting a straight answer at least from him; his reply overrode Magior's equivocation.

"He is expected back very soon."

"Dragon-hunting," Brand said, "in the Luxour." He stopped pacing, to gaze at a jet-black dragon painted on what looked like some kind of leather shield. The dragon's eyes were tiny, malevolent, red as garnet. "So I was told. He is drawn there sometimes, to search, he says, for his heart. Or he may be looking for Rad Ilex."

"You expected Rad Ilex to be here."

"I thought he might be."

"Rad Ilex has not been seen in this court since you vanished," Magior said. "He would have been killed, that night, had he lingered a moment longer. So your father said. Only one moment."

Nyx opened her mouth, closed it, swallowing a smoldering cinder of impatience. Brand said abruptly to her, "Then why are you still here? I thought you would have gone."

"I was asked to stay," Nyx said calmly, "to speak to Draken Saphier. It seemed a reasonable request. Everyone, it seems, expects him soon."

Brand's brows pulled together hard. He was silent a moment, his eyes on her, as if he had heard, even beneath the turmoil and frustration of the firebird's cry, the equivocation in her voice. He said finally, "The Luxour is full of voices. So the mages say. The desert speaks. The stones and the silence speak. So they say. I doubt if I would hear much. But that makes it difficult for the mages to call my father home. And finding him, if he does not wish to be found, would be impossible. So I am told. It's hard for me to wait patiently. The most I can manage at moonrise is just to wait. It would be kind of you to wait with me, at least while I'm human. The mages have tried to work with me; they get no farther than you did. I don't think anyone can help me but my father, and I have very, very little patience left for mage-work. So. Keep me company. Walk with me, in the gardens."

"I think," Magior murmured, "we should keep working. Such enchantments might be unravelled quite unexpectedly."

"Perhaps the moonlight will unravel it," Brand said, "since no mage in this house can." His face was strained, taut; Nyx heard the noiseless cry emanating from him so strongly, she wondered that the dragons around them did not turn into spellbound jewels. His great-aunt heard it too, apparently; she bowed her head in acquiescence.

"Perhaps you are right," she said. "I will wait for you here."

He did not speak for a while; he took Nyx's arm, his grip tight, as if he expected the moon to toy with her shape, too. They left the house, walked on wide paths of white stone that wandered among the rose-trees. Nyx, unused to such formal progression through a garden, found it bewildering, for a mage and a man about to fly away. She laid her free hand on his hand, reminding him that she was there, and said,

"I think—"

"Not here," he breathed, and she was silent again until they passed through the courtyard of roses into a tiny walled garden full of lemon trees, soft paths of moss between fountains and moon-bright streams. He closed the gate behind them; his grip eased finally.

"It is my father's meditation garden," he said softly. "No one else comes here."

"There is little hope of privacy in a house full of mages," she pointed out.

"Perhaps. But I'm used to being private with you. No one told me you were still here. I thought you would have gone to look for Meguet."

"All they knew of me is that I brought you here. They couldn't have assumed you cared. Did you ask after me?"

"No."

"Then why are we here, whispering?"

"Because," he said restively, "your face looks changed. Wary. It wasn't only you studying me, in that tower. I had nothing else to watch but you. You do what you want, say what you think; you listen to reason, but not without arguing. Here, you pick your way from thought to thought as if you are afraid. No. Not afraid. But in danger. In my father's house. Why?"

"I'm alone in a strange land, surrounded by mages of indeterminate power, and more warriors than I've seen in all of Ro Holding. It seems expedient for me to be somewhat wary. If you have one enemy, you might have two, and one of them under this roof."

He stared at her, amazed. "Me?"

"You said yourself you can't remember why Rad Ilex turned you into a firebird. Conceivably to guard himself against something you saw, something you know."

"A conspiracy? In my father's house?"

She sighed noiselessly. "I can only guess. You tell me. You brought me here. And I can't imagine even this place being completely private. Those goldfish are probably trained to eat whatever words fall like crumbs on the water."

"No one speaks in here," he said absently. His brows were drawn again; he glanced at the moon, then down at a little fish like an orange flame rising to the surface of the water. "The guard changes at midnight. I listen for that." His fists clenched. "I can't remember," he said tightly, "how it feels to stand in sunlight. To fall asleep in a bed. To know where I was at noon yesterday. If my father does not come soon, I'll go to the Luxour myself and find him."

"Would the bird fly there?" Nyx asked curiously. He looked at her, his eyes shadowed, haunted.

"It flew to you," he said slowly. "And here it sits in this house with you, waiting, though I assume that if it could find you in Ro Holding, it could find my father in the Luxour."

"Why Ro Holding? If your father made the paths on your wrists, why would he have fashioned one to Ro Holding?"

He shook his head, disinterested. "I don't know. He didn't create the patterns out of time and space. He only forged the paths, and I don't think even he knows where they all go. I think the firebird found Ro Holding by chance, though your power drew it, once it came there. Why? Is it important?"

"Perhaps," she said evenly, thinking of the flashing blades of the ritual dance, the silver paths blazing on every wrist. Brand was silent, watching the occasional moonlit glint of color in the dark water.

He said very softly, "You could take me to the Luxour. The bird would follow you."

"If your father doesn't return soon?"

"Now."

She looked at him, startled. "Why not Magior, or one of the other mages?"

"The bird follows you." He paused; his face loosened slightly. "I follow you. I'm here with you in my father's garden, where no one else is permitted. I trust you."

"You might," she said slowly, "but there's little reason for anyone else to trust a mage who absconds with you into the desert. If you vanish twice, they will be heart-struck. They are doing their best for you."

"And their best is no better than what you did for me in that tower." His voice sounded dangerously thin. "If I have to spend one more day covered with feathers and eating mice, and wake to myself again without seeing my father, I will walk out of this house and keep walking south, and no one will know where I am. You yourself want to go to the Luxour. Rad Ilex will be hiding there. It's the only place in Saphier where he can hide from my father. And it's the place to look for Meguet."

"Let me go," she pleaded. "By myself. That way you'll be here, if your father is on his way back now. If not, I can look for him, and for Meguet."

"No." His hands closed suddenly on her arms; she felt the tension in his grip. "No. I will not wait here. I'll walk out now. I know my father's private passage from this garden out of the house. You can stay here and explain to Magior where I've gone."

"Brand—"

"Now. Before midnight. I'm not a mage. If I tell Magior, and she thinks I'm unwise, she'll keep me here. She'll find ways. I can't stop her. I am unwise, but if I don't see my father soon, if this spell stays on me much longer, I will find a new voice for the firebird, and it will cry day and night without ceasing and no one in this house, not even you, will stop it."

"All right." She touched him gently, swallowing drily. "All right. I'll take you there. Now. And I won't walk. I think I have a path to the Luxour."

"Where?" he asked, amazed.

"In my pocket." She drew out the ivory ball. "Chrysom's book."

# CHAPTER
# 12

Meguet waited a night and a day and a night for Rad Ilex. After staring down the moon and then the stars, listening for night-hunters, she finally fell asleep as the sky lightened, showing her broken airy palaces that would turn to stone at sunrise. She woke to light pounding down at her, ground shimmering with heat. She caught up the skins and pouch, and burned her feet running to shelter among the nearest stones. There she sat, shifting as the shadow shifted, her thoughts as formless and furious as the maddening heat. When night fell, she found a slab of rock to crawl onto, away, she hoped, from whatever small ferocious things might consider her supper. The first tiny lizard that slipped out of a crevice and ran over her nearly sent her tumbling to the ground. After that, she shared the stone with them, shaking them away with little more attention than she would give a fly. The inactivity was as maddening as the heat. If Rad Ilex did not bother coming for her, she assumed Draken Saphier would let the desert have her, a ghost to haunt the dream-castles. Dying alone in the middle of a desert in a strange land seemed preposterous. But if Draken Saphier told the truth, and she had helped the wrong mage, he had little reason to care what happened to her.

He might not even bother telling her if he caught Rad; he might just leave her anyway. That thought kept her awake the

**145**

second night, listening for voices, for mage-work. In the darkest hour before dawn, when even the winds drifted gently, spent, she heard a pebble on the ground below her shift.

She tensed, thinking of the small, toothed animals. A lizard skittered across her hand. She flung it away, gasping. The lizard said as it fell,

"Meguet."

She peered over the edge of stone, saw nothing. She had to wait for it to work its way up the rock again, and then, in deep shadow, it changed. Rad whispered,

"I know Draken is here. I want you to run from me. Now."

She was silent, trying to pick out his face in the dark; it might as well have been the pocked and weathered stone speaking. "Are you trying to kill me?"

"What?"

"You want me eaten by the night-hunters."

"What night-hunters?"

"The ones who can feel your running steps."

"What are you talking about?" His voice, cobweb thin, took on slightly more substance. "There's nothing but lizards in this part of the desert. And you've been sleeping with them."

She was silent, her mouth tight, controlling a flash of temper as black as the sky. She said between her teeth, "Draken Saphier says they exist. You say they don't. He told me not to move among them. You tell me to run."

"Then believe him." There was no anger in his voice, almost no sound but a taut urgency trembling between them. "Yes, there are terrible night-hunters. Yes, I want to kill you. So run from me, Meguet, quickly, because they will show you more mercy than I will. Run. Now. Run."

She hesitated a moment, still trying to see his face. Then she slid off the ledge and ran across the cool, hard ground, blind until a light exploded behind her like the fallen star suddenly showering its pale fire across the sleeping desert. She tripped on a stone, came down hard, and heard, above her panting, Rad Ilex's sudden, twisted cry. She caught her own cry behind her hand, feeling tears sting her eyes. There was another flash. She pushed her face against her arms, felt the ground shake a little, as if, deep beneath it, the dragons stirred, disturbed.

The night was still again. She heard a step. And then Draken Saphier's voice: "You're safe, now. I have him."

She rose, trembling; she sensed only one shadowy presence in the dark. "Where? Did you kill him?"

"No. I need him alive to take the spell from my son."

She brushed hair and dirt out of her face, tried to speak with dignity, though her voice shook. "Will you give me back my shoes now? I'll walk home."

He was silent. A thin, white light snapped through the air, hit the ground near her foot. She glimpsed something small, many-legged, trying to bite the blade of light impaling it. She froze, speechless, and then felt the black anger again, as if she were truly blind, and teased and teased by voices, light touches, questions without answers, without end: *Who am I, Meguet? Who am I now? And now?*

"Please." Her voice trembled badly. "Give me my shoes and let me go."

"Come." He took her arm. "You want to go north; I'll take you. You're barely fit to walk, and I owe you something for helping me, though until you ran from Rad, I was not certain you believed me." She opened her mouth, closed it, speechless again. "Come to my court." His grip was not tight, but she suspected he would not let her go. "Wherever you are going, my palace must be closer to it than the Luxour."

She answered finally, wearily, using herself again as bait to lure truth, for her own hidden face only called forth other shifting faces. "It's where I am going. The court of Draken Saphier."

His voice sharpened. "You were walking to my house across the desert?"

"I'm a stranger in your land. My name is Meguet Vervaine. Rad Ilex pulled me out of the house of the Holders of Ro Holding, into the middle of the Luxour. He took me to his village from there. He was hurt; he hadn't the strength to take me back to Ro

Holding. I recognized you because your son is in Ro Holding, in the care of my cousin, Nyx Ro, who is a very capable mage." He was absolutely motionless; she spoke to nothing, to the night. "Rad had told me certain things that made me wary of you. And you tell me things that make me wary of Rad. Whatever is between you is far too complicated for me to sort out. Perhaps Brand himself, when he is no longer imprisoned by the firebird, can make things clear."

"Ro Holding."

"Saphier is on none of our maps."

"I have heard of Ro Holding."

She was silent, aware of words scattered to a stranger's winds, like birds flying out of her mouth that could never be caught. She felt ancient, uneasy stirrings, not from the Luxour, but within her, a faint flurry of voices through the ages: *Meguet, what are you, are you doing, are you doing? I am blind,* she told them fiercely, desperately. *I am trying to see.*

The night shifted, as if it, too, had caught an echo of her past. She said quickly, "Then you will know where to go to get your son. If not how."

"Yes." She saw, finally, in the slow ebb of dark, a line or two of his face. "The mage Chrysom was born in Ro Holding. It seemed he liked to travel. He left his name in the air of Saphier's past." She felt his hand again, tighter now; his voice was imperative, impatient of distances. "Come."

Stars blossomed from the dark, shot in streaks of silver past them and back again, winding, weaving, circling, until it seemed they stood in a web of silver that was at once rushing away from them and frozen still. Draken spoke; the paths blurred together, silver into dark, except for one. He led her onto it.

They were met, in a great, orderly hall, by a turmoil. Meguet, blinking at noise made by dozens of people, brightly dressed at that hour of the morning, at the bronze lamps and mage-lights burning everywhere, realized she had walked barefoot into the house of Draken Saphier. Her hair was loose, tangled, her clothes sweat-stained and dusty, her hands scratched. Draken, seen for once in light, was frowning at the chaos. Something seemed to drag at him; there were taut, weary lines beside his mouth, between his brows. Rad, she guessed, weighed heavily, wherever he was.

Draken said nothing. He picked up a mage-light from a ledge, held it aloft. Red, smoky, sinuous lines of light whirled out of it, took shape in the air above the crowd. A dragon floated above them, wings spread, neck arched, glaring down at the gathering. It hissed suddenly; the air chilled; lamps flickered. Draken tossed the mage-light; it hung in midair, illumining silent, upturned faces. The dragon reached for the star, held it between its claws, stared into it.

"It is a question," Draken said obscurely to the soundless crowd. "Contemplate it." Then he added, "Magior."

A tall, graceful woman with a still, seamed face came to him. She bowed her head. "My lord."

"What is this unseemly behavior from my household, my mages?"

"My lord—" She touched her eyes wearily. "Your son has disappeared."

"Magior—" His voice caught. Meguet wondered blankly if the silvery path had led them backward in time instead of forward. "What—"

"I mean, my lord, again. He has been here for three days."

"Here!" He looked stunned, and then suddenly harried, his attention drawn to his restive prisoner. He asked incredulously when he was able to speak again, "Is the spell broken?"

"No, my lord. He was brought here by a mage from some peculiar country where mages, apparently, are neither trained nor disciplined. We worked with the spell, and at her insistence finally permitted Brand to speak to her. They were last seen entering your meditation garden. Before midnight, last night. Neither has been seen since. We have searched ruthlessly, my lord. They are gone."

"Where?" Draken whispered. *Nyx,* Meguet thought. The name turned her cold as stone, as if it were a spell. Nyx in Saphier.

"I believe she intended no harm," Magior was saying. "Brand insisted that no one could help him but you. She apparently has some knowledge of the time-paths within Saphier, which is perplexing because she had never even heard of Saphier before the firebird flew into Ro Holding—"

"The Luxour," Draken said, his face taut, dark with care. Then he stopped breathing, stopped thinking, it seemed. It was something Meguet had seen Nyx do: grow so still she might have been painted on the air. "And that," he said very softly, evenly, as if he were recounting the ending of a tale, "is why Rad Ilex went to Ro Holding."

"Following the firebird, my lord?" Magior asked. His eyes went back to her.

"No doubt. For whatever his purposes. But Brand—was he well? What did he say? Does he remember anything? How could he speak at all?"

"Before he encountered Nyx Ro, he said that he could not even remember his name, where he was born, or when. The spell permits him to speak only at moonrise, until midnight."

"Strange," he breathed. "And this mage helped him remember?"

"Enough so that she was able to bring him here. But he still does not remember the exact circumstances of the spell, and he still changes; he is a bird, my lord, except for those scant hours." She shook her head. "It is an impossible piece of mage-work. We did our best with it. He was becoming extremely impatient, waiting for you. I'm sure that's where they have gone: to search the Luxour for you."

"Yes." The lines were deepening on his face again: He still wore the dust of the Luxour, he had an unruly mage in his pocket, it seemed, and now a firebird to find among the dragons. He looked at Meguet. "Your cousin, Nyx Ro—is it likely she would have been so impulsive?"

"Oh, yes," Meguet sighed. "But only to help Brand. She would never harm him. I watched her working with that spell in Chrysom's tower. She may not be disciplined—she trained herself—but she is fascinated by what she can't do, what she doesn't know. If Brand told her anything at all about the Luxour, she would have felt compelled by more than the firebird to go there."

"I see," he said, unsurprised, and Meguet realized what she herself had conjured in his mind: a kindred spirit.

She added, "Nyx must have come also to look for me. I vanished with Rad Ilex; Brand would have told her to look for him in Saphier."

"My lord?" Magior said abruptly, startled, staring at Meguet. "Is this another mage from Ro Holding?"

"She says she is not a mage," Draken said, though his eyes held Meguet's a moment before he answered, and there was the faintest thread of curiosity in his voice. "What we have here is the mage's cousin, Meguet Vervaine. I found her wandering across the Luxour: She had been pulled into Saphier by Rad Ilex."

Magior's brows rose. "How terrible," she said blankly. "But, my lord, why?"

"It's complex," Meguet answered, trying to keep a straight course, in this land of tangled paths and shifting landscapes, toward essentials. "What I need to do above all is to find Nyx and go home. She is heir to Ro Holding, and the Holder will not sleep until she returns."

"And we have kept her three days," Magior said worriedly. "And now she is in the Luxour. My lord—"

"I'll find her," Draken said. "Even in the Luxour, I can find my own son." He paused, thinking with an effort; he closed his eyes briefly, concentrating on a spell, or measuring his own weariness. He had been awake at night, listening for Rad's footfall, as well as Meguet.

She said, "I will come."

"There's no need."

"I need to come."

He shook his head. "You'll slow me," he said inarguably. "You have no conception of the difficulties of the Luxour. Even mages can rarely find one another. The great stones seem to deflect power, or attract it, draw it in. The land changes spells as it changes its face."

"You found Rad Ilex," she reminded him, and felt concentration crumbling all over the silent hall. He said, lifting a hand to catch the mage-light as it fell from the dragon's claws,

"I fought the Luxour for him and won. With your help."

"My lord—" Magior whispered.

"Yes," he said tautly. "I have brought Rad Ilex with me. And now I must go back and find Brand. Magior, see that Meguet Vervaine is treated with utmost courtesy."

"But what will you do with Rad Ilex?" she breathed. "What will contain him while you are gone?"

"Where is he?" Meguet asked, expecting no answer, but the entire hall waited, without a sound, for his response.

"I trapped him," Draken said, "in a time-path I made. I tricked him into running down it, and then closed the path upon itself. It has no beginning and no end. I can hold him there, while I am away," he added to Magior. "It will be draining, but not impossible."

"My lord, take the mages to help you—at least a few!"

"No. We'll only confuse one another. I need to find Brand and Nyx Ro quickly." He handed Magior the mage-light; she stood gazing at him, an old woman with a star between her hands. "Keep the house orderly, and do not trouble Meguet Vervaine with details. Show her the gardens. Let her rest. Ask her no questions beyond what is customary to reveal the status of a stranger in the house. Do you understand me?"

"Yes, my lord."

"I will answer everything else when I return."

He vanished; so did the dragon above their heads. Meguet, sagging suddenly on her feet, was grateful for Magior's firm hold, as well as her silence, as she led Meguet through a thicket of curious gazes. Exhausted as she was, she saw the silver enclosing every wrist; everyone, it seemed, was imprisoned in the delicate weaves of time, on its never-ending paths. She made nothing more of it then, barely aware of washing, eating, in a chamber so full of light it seemed made entirely of gold. The light hardened into the golden face of the Luxour just before she fell asleep.

She woke hours later at dusk, to a vision of silver. She almost cried out, but she had no strength even for that. The tangle of silver floated, glowing, in midair, its lines blurred in the soft shadows. Rad Ilex, standing in the midst of endless layers of paths, put his finger to his lips. Half his face was masked in blood, the other half gilded with the dust of the Luxour.

He whispered, "Meguet." His voice seemed to come from unexpected, ghostly places. She swallowed, felt the blood beating through her. "Where is he? Where did he go?"

"To find Brand," she answered finally. "And Nyx. They went looking for him."

"Nyx."

"She came here."

"To Saphier?" He moved slowly, as if caught in hard, rushing currents. He changed, she saw with horrified fascination, in unpredictable ways: He grew smaller, he lost perspective, a limb would disappear around an invisible corner, reappear. "Where is he?" he repeated.

"In the desert."

He said, "Ah," very slowly; the sound died on an ebbing wave. "The desert distracted him."

"What?"

"He has lost hold of me a little. So I came looking for you. I need help."

"I won't argue that," she whispered, still amazed. "But why me? I'm no mage. And the last I saw of you, you tried to kill me."

"I was trying to save you. If you hadn't run, Draken would have attacked us both—"

"You lied to me. You said there was nothing more dangerous than lizards in the night."

"I didn't lie."

"Draken killed something. With teeth. Beside my bare foot."

She heard him sigh. "Meguet. Would you rather be in here with me? I would have said anything to make you run. Besides, I didn't lie. Draken lied. He made that thing, then killed it. I know how his mind works. Can you get your own mind off small details for the moment?"

She put her hands to her eyes, still saw him floating in the dark behind her eyelids. "I was awake for two nights, terrified of those small details. Of such details are great lies formed. What do you want from me? Draken will bring Nyx back with him, and she and I will leave. If there is a threat to Ro Holding, we will face it there."

"Of course there's a threat. You've been in this house. Armed mages wear the paths of time on their wrists, and one of those paths, as the firebird has shown, leads to Ro Holding."

Her hands slid down slowly to her mouth. The blood drained out of her face; the room darkened a little, a shadow forming against the dusk: the dragon, hunting. "But why?" she whispered.

"Saphier breeds warriors. War is our history, our heritage. You saw Brand fight me. The movements of his attack are as old as Saphier. Draken is a double-edged sword: the warrior-mage. His eye turned to Ro Holding when he found Chrysom's writings here. I showed—" He stopped abruptly; she heard his voice shake. "I showed him the path to Ro Holding."

"You what?"

"Inadvertently. He discovered from Brand that I used to visit Chrysom. That I was searching for that key. That the key held in it paths of time beyond Draken's knowledge. He wants conquest, even through time, and he wants the dragons' power to make himself invincible."

"He wouldn't need much," she said numbly, "in Ro Holding."

"He wants that key. Does Nyx have it here in Saphier?"

"I have no idea."

"If she does, and Draken realizes that, she is in terrible danger."

"That key." She felt again the sudden, blind anger at the confusion, tangled as the winds on the Luxour blowing from every direction, into which he inevitably led her. "Always that key. Draken never mentioned it. You want it. You told me that I would be in terrible danger from Draken. That he would sense my odd powers and take my bones apart to analyze them. All he did in the desert was take away my shoes. All he's done to me here is give me a bed to sleep on instead of a stone."

"He's like that. He'll bide his time. And then he'll attack. Meguet," he said urgently, at her silence. "You must help me. You can help me escape this. There's not a mage in this house who would dare raise a finger against Draken Saphier. But you would never attract his attention. You must help me, set me free to help Nyx."

"Help her!" Her voice nearly rose above a whisper. "All you and Nyx do is fight. I won't free you to go and steal that key and leave her wandering alone in a desert—"

"She knows the path to Ro Holding. She got herself here."

"I don't know how she got here. You tell me this, you tell me that—and then you tell me that I know what you have told me!"

"You know the firebird." He was breathing quickly, the time-paths blurring around him. "Its face is the true face of Saphier, and its cry the only truth. Meguet." His face darkened; he seemed to flatten, an upright shadow. "Think. Help me. I'll come back when I can. If I can." The paths vanished, swallowed in Saphier's night. Only his voice lingered, urgent, imperative, to become her own voice as his faded. "Choose."

# CHAPTER
## 13

Nyx stood with the firebird in the Luxour.

The firebird had perched above Nyx's shoulder on a ledge of rock. It watched a splash of milky silver spilling into the sky above the distant mountains. Its beak opened; a sapphire dropped. It cried jewels now and then instead of fire: a single blood-red garnet, an emerald. It left, to Nyx's bemused eye, a gleaming trail across the desert, as if it marked a path for Draken Saphier to follow.

She sensed power everywhere, as if the entire desert were under a spell, and its winds and piles of stone and vast stretches of nothing might change, at moonrise, into something completely different. It seemed always on the verge of changing. Stones shifted beyond eyesight; shadows tumbled across the ground, wind-blown, attached to nothing. Not even the ground felt solid; it seemed pocketed with echoing chambers, where things stirred, breathed, dreamed. Odd smells streaked the winds: sulphur, damp earth, even water, or some ancient memory of water. In the light of the rising moon the great piles of stone here and there took shape: They were dragon-bones and palaces; they reared, spread their wings; doors opened, windows filled with light.

The firebird cried a blue topaz. The moon slid free of the dark, jagged line of mountains. Nyx, watching, saw the bird seized,

157

pulled almost into something else at the moment of transfor-
mation. Its eye narrowed, became slitted; its feathers froze into
hard, smooth scales. And then Brand slid down off the rocks to
her side, unsurprised, by now, at where he found himself under
any risen moon.

"Did you feel that?" Nyx asked, amazed at the random, mind-
less power that had stopped for a moment to toy with a spell no
one else could even grasp.

"Feel what?" Brand asked. He scanned the dark, looking for
mage-fires, for his father to step out from behind a rock.

"Something emerged between the firebird and you. Only for a
moment."

He looked startled, torn between hope and alarm. "What?"

"Almost like a—" She paused, trying to remember what it was
almost like: the tapering head, the hard, tight skin. The word
caught. "Dragon."

He was silent, staring at her. Then he turned, impatient, frustrated. "Where is my father? I hoped the firebird would find him,
fly to him the way it flew to you."

"I doubt if even the firebird—whatever powers it has that you
don't—could isolate one mage in this windstorm of power."

He shook his bead a little, still searching. "I just see desert,"
he murmured. "Rocks. The wind feels like wind. It smells like
dragons' breath. That must be the hot springs." He looked at her.
"Now what? Do we just walk?"

"I'm thinking," she said absently, wondering if the whole of
the Luxour were on the verge of turning itself into a dragon. In
the next moment, it would become; but this moment, in terms
of its own time, had begun before Ro Holding had a name, and
might last until its name was forgotten. "No wonder Chrysom
came here. . . . He must have loved this place." She drew the
ivory ball out of her pocket, opened Chrysom's book. Many of
its paths, she found, began and ended in the Luxour; it seemed
riddled with secrets. "Yes," she said finally, choosing one. "We
just walk."

The path brought them to the springs. The water churned and steamed in the dark; mud bubbled and snorted. Wind dragged steam over them, blew it away as quickly when they began to cough. Beneath the noise of water and the exuberant wind, Nyx was aware of something deep and constant, a heartbeat within the earth, so low she felt rather than heard it. She touched Brand.

"Do you feel that?"

"What?" he asked, wary again. "Am I changing?"

"No. It's like a heartbeat."

He listened. "No." He roamed, peering into moonlit crevices, studying pale crystals that crusted the edges of the pools. He came back to her. "Nyx," he pleaded, and she heard the urgency in his voice. Time, for him, would not slow even in the Luxour.

"Yes," she said, but the wind brought her a breath of winter out of nowhere, and, wondering, she followed the chill.

Brand heard the heartbeat then; it came out of a hole in the night, a place so cold it was rimed with ice. For a moment, he forgot the firebird. "Is it a dragon?" he whispered, as if in his excitement he might wake it.

"I don't know."

"What else could turn desert into ice?"

"I thought they breathed fire. . . . I wonder if Chrysom mentions it." She opened the book again; pages riffled quickly, stopping to show her what was on her mind: *The Ice-Dragon . . . It exists,* Chrysom had written, *in a time accessible but not recommended. It is very cold, and the dragon, roused, is fearsome, a monster with night-black scales and white eyes. It will follow the time-path if you do not close it behind you.*

"What does he say?" Brand asked.

"He saw the dragon." The book misted away in her mind. "He made a time-path to it. I wonder if all his paths through the Luxour lead to dragons. . . ."

"If you free a dragon, that would get my father's attention."

"And what will I do with the dragon?"

"My father could deal with it. He always wanted to see a dragon."

"Your father might well be annoyed if I set a dragon loose into Saphier. Chrysom left them alone."

"It's not like you to be so cautious," Brand commented.

"It's not like you to be so impulsive."

She saw him smile unexpectedly in the moonlight; the Luxour was working its odd magic on him. "My grandfather was a dragon," he reminded her. "So they say. My father says the heart of power—"

"—is a dragon's heart."

"So perhaps we should look for my grandfather. See if he's in the mage's book. A dragon who could take the shape of a man. My grandmother didn't find him fearsome. If you find that dragon, my father would be in your debt. He always wanted to know his father."

She was silent, thinking of the smell of winter and the timeless dark of the ice-dragon's cave. Could it do such things beyond its own world? she wondered. Breathe a perpetual winter over a land, imprison it in ice? *A monster,* Chrysom had written. What might the other dragons do if they were loosed? She drew an uneasy breath, beginning to understand what she had dropped into her pocket, and carried so carelessly into a land ruled by a dragon's son who could forge the time-paths but not the patterns. To find dragons, he would need the patterns she had found. . . .

But it was Rad Ilex searching for the key, not Draken Saphier.

"Nyx?" Brand's voice pleaded again, this time for dragons.

"All right," she said slowly. "I'll see if Chrysom wrote of a dragon he didn't find fearsome."

She found several, after perusing the book for so long that Brand had vanished by the time she finished. She looked around, startled, for the firebird, and found Brand finally, standing inside the ice-cave, shivering, listening to the heart of power.

The path she chose ended in one of the massive tumbles of stone. The winds smelled hot and dry there, as if they were about to burst into flame. She felt no heartbeat, but an odd, shifting underfoot as if the earth were falling away like sand in an hourglass. The stones trembled a little. Nyx looked up, gripping Brand, in case she had to open a door into thin air and leave before a boulder flattened them. The bulky jumble resolved, as her eye travelled upward, into high, airy walls, half-broken turrets, moonlit windows.

"It's a palace," she breathed.

"It's just stones," Brand said. His voice was tense again; the moon was continuing its inexorable climb toward midnight. "What does Chrysom say about this dragon?"

"It is red as flame and breathes flame. However, when it understood him to be harmless, it ceased its baleful attack and permitted him to come close. Its eye, Chrysom said, seemed a portal through which he might walk."

"What does that mean?"

"It's enormous."

"What else? Did it speak?"

"It lies within a ring of fire."

"Did it speak?"

"The point is: You can't survive attack by fire."

"Chrysom did."

"Chrysom was a mage."

"Did it speak?" he asked again, patiently, and she sighed.

"It made, Chrysom said, overtures of interest in a language he found fascinating but obscure."

"Meaning what?"

"I'm not sure."

"It could be my grandfather," Brand said hopefully. "If it saw one human, it would have known what my grandmother was, when it saw her centuries later."

"How did she find it?" Nyx asked, puzzled. "Or did it find her? Did it walk its own path of time into Saphier out of some peculiar longing for a human heir to its powers?"

"No one knows," Brand said. "She was a warrior-mage, like my father, very powerful, though she did not train mages. She must have come looking for dragons; the dragon may have let her find it. But I wonder why."

"Perhaps, like Chrysom, it was very powerful and very curious. Perhaps it liked to travel. It had seen humans before, and it approached your grandmother in that shape so not to frighten her." She shook her head. "It doesn't sound like this dragon. This one likes sleeping in the hearth fire; it doesn't travel."

"More dragons than my grandmother's must have travelled," Brand pointed out. "Legends of dragons have come out of the Luxour for centuries. You saw my father's dragon-room. Some of the things are very old."

"How many dragons would it take to produce a legend?"

He hesitated. "None," he admitted. "Some say the only dragon ever seen was by a mage having a bad dream on the Luxour. But they're here," he said softly, fiercely. "Even I can feel them. Chrysom saw them."

"Yes."

"Then find another. One I can see with you. It may recognize my grandmother in me. She had long black hair and blue eyes." His hand closed lightly on her arm. "Please. I'm in no shape to worry about risks."

She opened the book again.

The next path ended under the earth. They stood in a starless black, surrounded by thunder. Nyx, casting a mage-light so Brand could see, found water everywhere, dark rivers and cataracts tearing at the reflection of her light. The mage-light hollowed a vast cavern around them; its walls and ceiling receded into shadows. Brand, his face teared with water from a misty, roaring waterfall, asked incredulously,

"Are we still in the desert?"

"Chrysom says so." She looked around, her hair shining with jewels of water. "How strange . . . It's as if the dragons create their own small worlds within the Luxour."

Drawn to the plunging water, he missed a step in the shadows; she heard him splash. "What does he say about this one?"

She consulted the book again. "This dragon is white as bone, with eyes like blue water. It recognized the human form. It is a shape-changer, an imitator, capable of taking any form—" Brand opened his mouth; she held up her hand. "It is quite old and transforms slowly, with much effort now. It breathes a kind of incandescence that shrouds it as it sleeps. The mist itself is a form of power. It seems to be a subtle labyrinth, a time-trap in which the unwary might easily become lost, if the dragon does not wish to be disturbed. Apparently Chrysom chanced on it at the right time."

"Does it speak?"

"It has, Chrysom says, the power of communication."

"Then let's communicate with it," Brand said tersely. Nyx looked past the book in her hand, at his set, tense face. "It may know my grandfather, at least."

"Well," she said after a moment, "I suppose it's pointless to be cautious now."

"It also takes up time."

"At least, if we're both trapped, I won't have to explain to your father what happened to you."

"Chrysom wasn't cautious," he reminded her. "And he lived to write the book."

"True," she said, but did nothing.

"Are you afraid of dragons?" he asked. "I didn't think you were afraid of anything."

"I seem to have grown cautious," she admitted. "There was a time when, like Chrysom, I would have taken every path to every dragon, for no reason but to see them in all their power. Then, I supposed I had no one but myself to think of, and the acquisition of knowledge of any kind seemed more important than returning home in one piece."

"I'm not in one piece," Brand said starkly. But he was listening; his eyes were on her face. He stood with his arms folded, motionless, while the dark water poured endlessly behind him.

"This is not my land," she said. "You belong to Saphier. I've brought you this far, and I am responsible for you on the Luxour. If I lose you to time, Saphier will mourn you and curse me, and if I lose us both—"

"Ro Holding will lose its heir."

"I'm not accustomed," she said apologetically, "to being this reasonable. But I have already lost Meguet somewhere in Saphier through my own willfulness, and I don't dare lose you. I can't go through my life scattering people into various bog-pools of time from which they might never return. I'm not afraid of much. But I am a little afraid of myself. And I am terrified of harming you."

He stood silently, still motionless, his brows drawn, a peculiar expression in his eyes. Then he blinked, and the expression faded. "That's odd," he said.

"What is?"

"That's all I thought I was to you: a puzzle to be solved. And so that's all I thought you were: a mage with a puzzle to solve. Now—" He hesitated.

"Now?"

"Now I wonder who you would be if I were not a man lost within a spell. Instead of dreading midnight, feeling time pass like this black water rushing away from me, I might ask you questions. For a change."

She was silent, seeing him differently now, as if for a moment, in that place beyond the world, his face was no longer haunted by the firebird within. It belonged only to him, and she knew him and didn't know him. She said tentatively, "What questions?"

"Anything. Why you're always walking out of your shoes."

"I find shoes distracting when I'm trying to think."

"Or how you knew you were a mage when you were young, and there was no one in your house to tell you what you were."

"I had Chrysom," she said. She was motionless herself, caught in his odd stillness, the little ivory ball in one hand, the mage-light at her feet. Water misted over them both, luminous in the light: the dragon's iridescent time-trap. She watched the light move in his eyes, the flick of cobalt beneath his dark, slanted brows.

"Chrysom is dead."

"Chrysom brought us here."

"Did you always follow his teachings?"

"No."

"My father's mages rarely question him. But the firebird follows you. As if you understand something more than power." He moved; his face grew clearer, chiselled out of light and shadow, the water flecked and gleaming along his cheekbones. "What do you think the firebird knows?"

"That it might be safe with me."

He blinked. "Are you saying—"

"No. Just that it couldn't fly home to safety. So it flew to me." She paused, her lips parted, remembering. "An odd choice, considering."

"Why?"

"Not so long ago, I was learning sorcery in a bog. I burned birds in my fires and read the future from their bones."

"You did."

"I thought—a mage should know everything, no matter what the knowledge entailed. So I tried to learn everything."

"Did you?"

"I learned to leave the birds in the trees."

He smiled a little, his face losing its lean, feral cast, becoming, to her entranced eye, again a stranger's face: someone who, in his forgotten past, had learned to laugh, who had been loved. "Except the firebird." He moved again, step by step closing the distance between them. Light shifted over him, caught in the folds of cloth across his chest, traced the straight line of his shoulders. "Except the firebird. Your eyes have so much color now. What causes them to change like that?"

"When I work a spell." She paused, scarcely hearing herself, wanting to reach out, touch a star of water at the hollow of his throat. "When I'm angry. When I find something—something of overwhelming interest."

"And which is it now?"

"Probably not anger."

He swallowed; the star moved. "Probably," he said huskily, "you are casting a spell."

She shook her head a little. "I'm not doing it."

"You're changing shape."

"Am I?"

"You used to look like a mage."

"What does a mage look like?"

"Like a closed book full of strange and marvellous things. Like the closed door to a room full of peculiar noises, lights that seep out under the door. Like a beautiful jar made of thick, colored glass that holds something glowing inside that you can't quite see, no matter how you turn the jar."

"And now?" she whispered. He came close; the light at their feet cast hollows of shadow across his eyes, drew the precise lines of his mouth clear.

"Now," he said softly, "you aren't closed. You're letting me see."

He slid his hand beneath her hair, around her neck. She watched light tremble in a drop of water near the corner of his mouth. He bent his head. The light leaped from star to star across his face, and then vanished. She closed her eyes and he was gone: Her own hand shaped air, her face lifted to a dream. She heard his cry deep in her mind: the firebird's voice torn free. She heard her own cry and opened her eyes. A jewel fell at her feet.

She looked at the firebird, her eyes as colorless as bone. It spread its wings, crying noiselessly as it swooped into the shadows, found stone rising everywhere, no way out. It circled furiously as she turned helplessly to watch it; its wild flight slowed, spiralled inward around her turning, and finally the light caught it, pale and fiery, masked even to itself, trying to change the dark, rushing water into gold. It settled at her feet. She knelt beside it, touched its breast lightly with her fingertips. Then she rose and opened a path back into midnight.

# CHAPTER
# 14

Meguet stood gazing at a waterfall that came out of a solid wall and vanished into stone. The water flowed noiselessly, ceaselessly, a thin, even wash that gradually fanned so wide it broke into graceful, shining threads before it disappeared. Mage-work, she decided, trying not to yawn. She had slept poorly after the sight of Rad Ilex in his prison; her dreams were fleeting, but seemed full of portents, urgent warnings that she could not quite understand. She hoped, when Magior appeared at mid-morning, to be taken to some peaceful place and allowed to contemplate grass. But Magior seemed to think she needed exercise, though she felt bruised in every bone from walking on fire, sleeping on stone.

"Is it real?" she asked, for Magior seemed to invite comment. "May I touch it?"

"You may," Magior answered. Meguet touched one thread of water gently. It separated instantly, formed a double strand. She put her finger to her mouth thoughtlessly, then flushed.

"I beg your pardon. I must have thought I was still in the desert. I am very tired."

Magior, oblivious to suggestion, moved down the hall. They were on some floor, in some wing of the vast house; Meguet had no idea how far they had gone. The long, pale corridors, the light-filled rooms, seemed never to vary. She remembered Nyx's odd house in the swamp, which seemed to ramble forever in and out of memory. She asked,

"Is the house real?"

Magior looked at her, astonished. "No one has ever asked before."

"It seems we might be walking down a single hallway, through a few rooms; only the things in them change. There's a timelessness about this place. As if it were constantly being made." She added apologetically, at Magior's silence, "My mind is still wandering in the Luxour, seeing odd things everywhere."

"Yes," Magior said vaguely. She led Meguet into a room full of gold.

It was stunning: a priceless collection of goblets and urns, vases, plates, sconces, baskets woven of flattened strands of gold, tiny, ornate tables, even a head molded out of gold, small statues of birds, lamps, a bouquet of golden flowers. As Meguet stared, the gold took on the hues of the Luxour: dust and light so rich it could not possibly fall for free. She followed Magior across the room; Magior stopped in front of a round gold table standing on three legs. On top of it stood a simple bowl carved of black wood.

Meguet looked at it, aware of Magior watching her silently. "There must be a land," she commented finally, "where wood is more important than gold. But somehow I do not think it's Saphier. What is this? Some kind of test?"

"In a way," Magior said calmly. "There are no answers. Only responses. Some see the wood more valuable than the gold. Others find its presence troubling, want it removed."

"Do you always test your guests?"

"No."

"Then why me? Because I am a stranger from another land? Is my presence troubling?"

"No," Magior said quickly. "Only the circumstances which brought you here."

"You mean Rad Ilex."

"I mean Brand Saphier. Rad Ilex is no longer a question; he

exists only in Draken Saphier's mind. I know you are tired and need to rest. May I show you one more room? And then, I promise I will take you into the gardens." She moved without waiting for an answer. Meguet, bewildered, followed her down an interminable hallway, up a staircase or two, down another corridor until she thought her feet would simply stop, plant themselves in the floor, and she would become one of the house's ambiguities, for other guests to find troubling and wish removed.

A dragon reared in front of her; she paused mid-step, blinking. It was attached to doors, which armed guards opened, breaking the dragon in two. The inner room was full of dragons. She stopped in the center, turning slowly, for she had never imagined them in such vivid colors, with varying expressions and forms. They were woven on banners, tapestries, sculpted of bronze and clay, painted on wood, on silk, carved into chairs, screens, boxes. She tried to see them all, tried to look everywhere at once, until her eye was caught by one and it drew all her attention.

It was painted on a shield: a dragon black as shadow, with wings of shadow, and blood-red eyes of such malignity that, staring at it, she felt her heartbeat. Behind her, Magior was so still she might have vanished.

"Is it real?" she asked finally; her voice sounded thin, tense.

"Why that one?" Magior asked abruptly. "Why not others of far more beauty, far more mystery?"

"This one is terrifying. What terrifies also fascinates."

"So does beauty fascinate. Why do you fear this? It is only imagined: None of them is real. Why choose this, as the one truth in the room?"

Meguet turned. She closed her eyes briefly, felt the weariness in them, hot and dry as dust. "I don't mean to offend," she said. But the old woman frowned.

"You are more than just a stranger. If I had to place you, I could not be sure . . . But you felt the power, as we walked down the hall?"

"What?" Meguet shook her head, perplexed. "I don't understand."

"The mage's power. Your cousin felt it."

"I'm not a mage."

"Perhaps not. But Draken was right to ask me to question you. Your responses, even allowing for your unfamiliar surroundings, are not innocent."

"Innocent of what?"

"Experience," Magior said. She read the expression in Meguet's eyes; the lines moved on her face.

"Draken asked you to do this?" Meguet breathed.

"He is curious about you. You are in his house. He is always curious about those within his house." She turned. "Come. I promised to end this. I am sorry it has upset you. It was not Draken's intention."

"What was his intention?"

"To see if you possess power. Sometimes those who are gifted don't know it. Come with me. I'll take you to a more tranquil place. One without dragons."

Meguet walked alone among rose-trees. The vast house met her eye whichever direction she turned: a world enclosed, constantly looking inward toward the path of time at its heart. She could not stop her restless movements, though they led nowhere. In the distance, through the roses, she could see the movements of the household guard, a bright army wielding spinning shafts of light as they performed their ancient ritual. "Ritual" was the word Magior had given her: It was, she explained, little more than a meditation exercise. The meditators outnumbered all the inhabitants of Ro House. And that number, she had been told, did not include the warrior-mages.

She watched them as she paced, guessing that she herself was watched by someone, somewhere. It did not, she admitted to herself, take extraordinary subtlety to weigh the dangers of one mage, however powerful, against an army trained to march through time. The dragon, red-eyed and malevolent, loomed in her mind: destroyer, death-giver. That dragon she had recognized, of all those Magior had shown her.

*The Dragon hunts the Cygnet.*

But which dragon? Draken Saphier? Or the dragons of the Luxour which Rad Ilex wanted so badly to see?

Draken wanted the key, too. So Rad had said. Better, she thought coldly, to let the mage loose the dragons into Saphier against that army, than to watch its bloody dance across Ro Holding. Rad had been in the Luxour looking for dragons; Draken had been searching for the mage who had ensorcelled his son. Draken had saved her life, even knowing she protected his enemy. Still, he did not trust her: He had had Magior question her. How far, Meguet wondered uneasily, would he permit his curiosity to go?

*The Dragon hunts the Cygnet.*

Draken Saphier was in the Luxour, looking for his son. Who was with Nyx.

Rad, not Draken, had come to Ro Holding to steal a key. Rad had named Draken Saphier as the threat to Ro Holding, yet he himself dreamed dragons on the Luxour, longed to set them free. Draken, he said, wanted Chrysom's key. Yet Rad had ensorcelled an entire court to obtain it. So he had ensorcelled Brand Saphier, both Brand and Draken insisted, and his own spell was not strong enough to contain Brand's rage within the firebird. But it was the firebird's magic that had wounded Rad: It had been made, he said, to kill.

She sank down wearily on a stone bench. Did Nyx have the key with her? she wondered. She might have brought it to bargain with Rad for Meguet. Or she might have simply dropped it into her pocket and forgotten it was there. Was Draken only searching for his son? It was Rad who had talked of the key, of dragons; Draken had spoken most passionately of his son.

But he knew of Chrysom, of Ro Holding. He had brought Meguet into his house, and for all Meguet could see, every door was guarded. He would find Nyx, bring her back with him. And then what would he do?

*The Dragon hunts the Cygnet.*

She pushed her fingers against her eyes, blocking light, and the dragon rode the dark behind her eyes. She smelled roses. The dark became her shadow, with a red rose lying in it. *Choose,* the mage had said. *The rose or the sword.*

*Choose,* the colorful, motionless dragons around her had said, and she had found the face she had been warned to fear.

She stood abruptly, the images growing clear in her mind. The red rose. The black dragon. She drew breath, feeling her hands grow icy with terror, for she had made her choice about Rad Ilex before she ever learned his name. In Chrysom's tower she had wielded his rose against a dragon of thread; he would have the key now, if he had not paused to protect her from his own sorcery. If she had picked up the sword, he would not have recognized her in that brief, tense moment; he would have loosed the dragon, distracting Nyx, then taken the key and fled, leaving Nyx frustrated but safe in Ro Holding, never knowing what Rad had stolen.

If she had picked up the sword.

The rose had cost them all. But the mage was still asking her to choose between the sword and the rose, for if she refused to help him, he would be at Draken Saphier's mercy. There had been no mercy in the firebird.

The red rose. The black dragon.

*The Dragon hunts the Cygnet.*

She had seen the dragon's face.

Rad Ilex had left a rose in her mind. Draken Saphier had left a dragon, and it was not one of the Luxour's half-dreams, entrancing in their mystery, floating between worlds. A dark and killing thing, she carried in her mind: It had, of all the dragons in Draken Saphier's house, come alive within her heart and spoken.

*The Dragon hunts the Cygnet.*

She was in the dragon's house.

Magior took her back to the mages' wing that evening. She recognized the long, dark hallway, the great bronze dragon at the end of it. She asked, trying to keep her voice calm, controlled, "Is Draken Saphier back?"

"No," Magior said, as the dragon doors were opened for them.

"I am taking you to supper with the warrior-mages." Meguet felt her face whiten. Around her the dragons seemed to come alive; their golden, glaring eyes, their brilliant wings, their breaths of fire burned the air with color. Magior glanced at her, as if she felt the sudden chill in Meguet's mind. "It is considered an honor."

"Then," Meguet said numbly, "I am honored."

"They will treat you with all due courtesy. There is no need to fear them."

"I'm hardly used to the company of mages. Nyx is the only mage I know." And Rad Ilex, she remembered, growing cold again at the thought that he might appear, bloody and helpless, floating above the mages as they ate. Guards opened tall red doors on the other side of the dragon-room; murmuring voices, the smell of food spilled into the air. Meguet walked blindly forward into a sudden silence, as faces turned curiously toward her, the stranger from the land at the end of one twisted strand of silver around their wrists.

"This is Meguet Vervaine, of the court of Ro Holding," Magior said, leading Meguet to a chair. Even the long tables were placed in a square; what seemed a hundred mages faced the intricate spirals and coils of Saphier's emblem patterned in the floor. They wore the emblem, Meguet saw, on their breasts, each path colored by a different thread. "She is," Magior continued as they sat, "quite weary from her ordeal with Rad Ilex in the Luxour and is not to be overly troubled with questions. Those of you who saw her at Draken Saphier's brief return know already that she is not a mage, though she is kin to the mage Nyx Ro. She is, however, by the standards of Ro Holding, a warrior, and has shown interest in the movements of the warriors' ritual."

Food, borne by a hand and a sleeve, appeared on Meguet's plate; she stared at it, wondering what she could possibly be expected to do with it. The mage sitting on her left, a woman with white-gold hair and a hawk's restless, hooded eyes, said kindly, "The movements of the warriors' dance are quite old. I take it you have no such tradition among your warriors in Ro Holding?"

*We barely have warriors,* Meguet thought starkly, then stilled her thoughts, lest the mage forget her manners and listen. She said, trying to find her usual composure, as if she had not fallen out of the sky into this elegant and dangerous land, "No. Only games and exercises involving appropriate weapons." She hesitated; the hawk's eyes watched her, waited for the trembling in the grass, the revealing word. "You call it ritual. In Ro Holding, while Brand Saphier was with Nyx, I saw him use that ritual to try to kill."

Again there was silence, even from the far table; the still eyes gazing at her reminded her of the dragons. Magior asked, her voice dry, precise, "Whom? No one of Ro Holding, I hope."

"Rad Ilex."

"Brand's father teaches him many things," the strange mage answered smoothly. "He is extraordinarily skilled and proficient. As tired as you are, I am sure it would be as tedious for you to listen to an account of a warrior's training in Saphier, as it would be for you to disclose your own warriors' training. In battle, as you know, everything becomes a weapon."

"You must eat," Magior murmured. "How will you recover your strength?"

Meguet picked up her fork, ate a tasteless mouthful. A man at a side table, with the stamp of Draken Saphier in the bones of his face and his black hair, commented, "The ritual originally involved ceremonial blades carved of bone. Since they could be played, it is assumed that the dance was performed to music."

"Perhaps a hunting ritual," someone else suggested, and the ensuing argument, tossed back and forth across the tables, brought to light an endless list of ancient and startlingly named battles.

"Much of the music in Saphier," the mage beside Meguet said, "originated in the battlefield, or the training field. In the Battle of Toad Stone, whistles made of raven bones were blown, to scare the scavenger birds from the dead."

"Toad Stone?"

"Two clan families fought over a great stone that resembled a toad. They revered the toad as kin to the dragon, a link between worlds, a messenger, perhaps. The dragon, in Saphier, is the symbol of all power: the power of magic, of battle, of art, of birth. I would imagine it means the same in Ro Holding."

"There are no dragons in Ro Holding."

"Some say there are none in Saphier. I meant in tales."

"There are no tales of dragons," Meguet said reluctantly, as if the mage might deduce from this no standing army, no fleet of warships, no revered toads and almost no mages.

The hooded eyes widened a little. "How curious. What, in Ro Holding, symbolizes power?"

*The Cygnet,* Meguet thought, and wondered if she would survive that supper to breathe under its familiar stars again. "In ancient tales," she said, "the sun symbolized the fury of war."

"And now?" the mage pressed, her gaze, intense and curious, searching for what Meguet strove to hide.

"Now it just grows crops."

"But under what symbol do you fight now?"

"Another ancient symbol," she said desperately. "A random grouping of stars. Is it the dragon you carry into battle? Or is it the symbol on the floor, there and within the square: the patterns that your warriors dance?"

The golden eyes flickered slightly. "The symbol," she said vaguely, "is not at all ancient, unlike the ritual. If you were stronger, I could show you one or two of the exercises the warrior-mages are taught. They are quite simple."

"I'm not—"

"So you say. Magior seems less certain. The exercises are designed to wake dormant power through physical movement, and then to channel that power, focus it, and release it as a weapon. The waking and release of power occasionally surprises those who think they have no such gifts. Magior rarely makes mistakes about those with potential for power."

The room was silent again, as if, Meguet thought, the mages' attention were tuned, beneath their lively conversation, to her voice. She said more calmly than she thought possible, "I have no such power. And I have no interest in it. My place in the

Holder's house is bound by ancient traditions; I have no desire to trouble those traditions by changing my ways, even if it were possible. You understand tradition in this house, I know."

Magior moved her cup an inch, found no argument beneath it. "Perhaps," she said slowly, "you should consider the matter. In a day or two, if Draken has not returned, and you are stronger, we will broach the subject again. Tradition has its uses, and its limits. It ceases to be useful when it stands in the way of knowledge."

"I would not want," Meguet sighed, "to cease to be useful to the Holder."

"No. But—Enough. You have scarcely eaten. We will trouble you no more with such matters tonight."

In bed at last, exhausted with fear, she could not sleep. She lay staring into the dark, wondering if she could get out of the house without being seen, find her way back to the Luxour before the mages began to pick her apart. But if Draken returned with Nyx, if Meguet abandoned Nyx, if Draken found Meguet vanished . . . She tossed answerless questions in her mind for so long that the blood-stained face appearing behind its glowing silver prison seemed another dire portent.

"Meguet."

She was sitting bolt-upright, she realized, with both hands over her mouth. She dropped them. He could not seem to find her; he looked here and there as through shifting layers of time.

"Meguet. Help me."

She swung out of bed, stood in front of the floating, luminous weave. "Rad," she breathed, and tried to touch it; her cold fingers closed on air. His voice sounded weak, distant; still he could not see her. "Rad." Her voice shook. "I'm here."

He saw her finally. "You're so far away," he said. "Down a stairwell, at the end of a long hall. I'm getting lost, here. You must help me. Please."

"Yes."

"Please. Quickly. You must listen to me, you must believe me."

"I do."

"If you don't, I'm dead, and you will have Draken Saphier with his army in Ro Holding searching for that key. You're in his house, you must have seen something to make you doubt that his intentions are as peaceful as Ro Holding's heartland. He will burn across those fields of sheep and wheat until peace is a charred memory, and there is a warrior-mage in every Hold, and a dragon coiled around Chrysom's tower."

"Rad." She tried to grip the weave again, pull him closer. "Can you hear me?"

"Of course."

"Then why aren't you listening to me?"

"I'm trying to tell you—"

"Rad. I have seen that dragon. It is black as night, and its eyes are fire. Please. Help me."

He was silent, gazing at her, one eye out of dust, the other out of blood. He was trembling, she saw; the desert and the time-prison, as well as the firebird, had drained him. He said very softly, "Did they question you?"

"They have begun to. I don't want Nyx in this house. Help me find her in the Luxour. I'll set you free—tell me what to do before you disappear again." She slid her hands over the air, groping for a single thread of silver, as if she could pull the weave apart.

"Meguet. You need a time-path."

"Yes," she said quickly. "How do I get one?"

"There is a guard outside your door." She nodded; there was a guard at every door. "Open the door. Let the guard see me. I'm enough to amaze anyone for a split second. I don't have much strength in here, but I can disarm a guard who is not a mage. If he feels it, Draken will only think I am testing his power. Let's hope the guard is not a mage. Open the door."

She opened the door with shaking hands, gasped something unintelligible at the young man who stood there. He whirled into the room, a movement out of ritual, and stopped himself dead mid-step at the sight of Rad's face. Meguet swung the door shut with one foot, grabbed a bowl of water with three leaves floating in it, since the guard had nothing obvious in the dim, silvery light, by way of arms, and broke it over his head. He fell to the floor in a pool of water, a leaf clinging to his hair.

Meguet tossed the pieces of the bowl on the bed, checked the motionless body. "Not even a knife," she said, frustrated. "What in Moro's name do they use for arms in Saphier?"

"That is a mage," Rad said tersely. She stared at him, then began to move again, dressing quickly in the light, silken garments they had given her. She bent over the guard, touched the paths on one wrist. "You can't remove the time-paths," Rad said. "Just hold one. I'll open a path for you. Any warrior is taught this—it takes no power. You must walk down the path to me. Draken won't sense anything until you reach me. The path will end inside his trap. Don't enter; I'll be able to walk your path out. When I'm free, he'll know it. But I'll open another path to the Luxour, then; we won't return here."

"What about the mage?" she asked.

"What about the mage?"

"He'll wake," she said, holding the silver tightly, as if mage and time might disappear together. "He'll tell Magior—"

"Meguet. He'll tell the entire house. It will take them just long enough to find breath to say 'Luxour' before they know where we have gone. They'll come looking for us, they'll come fast, and they will be the warrior-mages. But they'll have to search the Luxour for us, and a hundred mages on the Luxour will confuse even Draken. For a while."

He was shaping time as he spoke, weaving a pattern around them, silver smoke in the dark; she could not tell if the path lay before her, or behind her eyes, within her mind.

"Trust me," she heard Rad say. The guard stirred a little under her hand. She heard Rad say something else—in her mind or beyond it—and she rose. *Come,* the path said, the frozen shining stream at her feet, and she followed it into Draken Saphier's tangled weave.

# CHAPTER
# 15

Nyx sat outside a ruined palace, listening to the dry shift and stir of dragon wings. Earlier, the palace had been a pile of stones; twilight had reshaped it, given it depth, subtle colors, ghosts. She had been reading Chrysom's book, searching for Brand's grandfather, since his father had either left the Luxour or been swallowed by it. The firebird had flown somewhere within the rocks, dropping darkly gleaming garnets like a trail of blood through the shadows. Nyx drew her mind out of dragon-paths long enough to make a mage-light so that Brand could find her when he changed. Then she wandered back with Chrysom underground, within still water, up cold barren peaks, into magical rings of mist and gold and fire. Some part of her, listening for Brand, was aware of the gently changing hues of blue above the mountains where the moon would rise. She refused to look, for that might slow the moon. She refused to let her thoughts stray, for then she would find Brand's cobalt eyes looking back at her through every page she turned. The moon took its time, leaving her adrift among the dragons until a footfall brought her out of dragons' time into her own, and she closed the book in her mind.

The moon had not yet risen, but the man who stepped into her mage-light was so like Brand that she almost said his name. And then she saw the white in his long dark hair, the lines beside his mouth. He looked at her silently, out of Brand's eyes. She rose slowly, making no ambiguous movements, for she sensed an enormous power in him, as if in his dragon's blood he had inherited something of the Luxour. He stood motionlessly, taking in what she revealed to the inward and the outward eye, before he spoke.

"You are Nyx Ro."

"Yes."

"I know all the mages of great power in Saphier, and therefore you are not of Saphier. You know my face, therefore you know my son." He paused; she saw his eyes follow the glittering path of garnet into the stones. His lips moved soundlessly. He turned abruptly, disappeared for a few moments among the caves and crevices; Nyx waited. He returned without the firebird. "It's sleeping," he said. "On a high ledge, with its face toward the moon." She saw him swallow. "I think he can get down."

"He says he's grown used to finding himself in odd places when the bird changes."

"Where did you find him in Ro Holding?"

"He flew over the walls of Ro House, and started turning cart horses into trees with diamond leaves. Cobblestones into glass. He changed my cousin into a rose-tree. He was very nearly shot. His cries were terrible."

"Yes," he said huskily. "I heard him—it—cry before he vanished from Saphier. And then what? You calmed him. You call the bird him."

She nodded a little wearily. "Brand and I have argued over this. He insists the bird is sorcery, that it has nothing to do with him. But I think he is the man and he is the firebird, and the bird cries of all the things the man can't remember, in the only language he will permit himself to use."

She heard his breath. He moved closer to her, leaning against the stones between her and the firebird's trail of jewels. He studied her silently again. Mage-light catching in his eyes revealed fine rays, like dragon's gold, across the cobalt. "You are perceptive," he commented, "for so young a mage."

"I've seen his face," she answered grimly, "when as a man he hides from memory. It's like a man flinching from fire." His own face changed, as if he had felt the sear of memory; for an instant he wore Brand's expression. "What is it?" she whispered, shaken. "What is it he will not remember? Do you know?"

He looked away from her, down at a single jewel. "I heard Brand cry out," he said tautly. "And then I saw the firebird, and the mage who had ensorcelled him. I heard the firebird's cry before it disappeared. No one else had been with them, to witness what had happened between them. No one in my court could give me the shadow of an explanation why the most gifted mage I have ever trained had cast a spell over my son. No one. I questioned everyone, often, and in every way I could, with and without language." He paused; the lines along his mouth deepened. He met her eyes again. "They had been close. That's all anyone could tell me."

"Yes." Her voice caught. "So he said."

His expression did not change, but she felt the sudden shock within his thoughts, as if it had disturbed the air between them. "He remembered?"

"A few things. The mage's name. That once he loved him and now he wants to kill him. Even the firebird recognizes the mage."

"And what more does he remember?"

"Saphier. You. That's why we came here: to search for you. He is convinced you can remove the spell because you are the most powerful mage in Saphier."

"The mage who made the spell will unmake it," he said harshly. "I have him."

She made an abrupt, uncalculated movement; her body peeled itself away from the stones, stiffening. "You have Rad Ilex?"

"I trapped him on the Luxour two nights ago."

She reached out to touch him, did not. "Please." She felt herself tremble, windblown. "Was there a woman with him? He pulled my cousin out of Ro Holding; I came to Saphier to search for her—"

"You followed Rad Ilex out of Ro Holding?"

"No, I came later. She is tall, with long pale hair—"

He was nodding. "Meguet Vervaine," he said, and for an instant she saw gold rays of dragon-light burn in his eyes. "I found her half-dead, alone in the Luxour." Nyx tried to speak, put her hand over her mouth. "I was suspicious of her at first. She tried to protect Rad Ilex, she lied about herself and him. But I persuaded her to help me trap him. She did, and so I took her with me to my court, where she is safe, cared for by my mages. She knows that you are here in Saphier, and that I am searching for you."

"Thank you." She closed her eyes, felt a burning like hot, dry winds, the merciless sun, behind them. She said again, numbly, "Thank you. I would have blamed myself forever if she had died here, alone and lost in a strange land."

"Blaming Rad Ilex seems more to the point. He brought her here. Under duress, you say. Then why would she have tried to protect him from me?"

"I don't know." She eased back against the stones, considered the question blankly. "Falling headlong into another world, perhaps she trusted no one. One mage had already terrified her; perhaps you frightened her even more. She isn't used to mages."

"I fed her, spoke gently to her. She recognized me as Brand's father and as Saphier's ruler. Still she tried—" He lifted a hand, let it fall. "It isn't important. I have you all now: Brand and Rad Ilex, your cousin and you. As you said, I must have frightened her, and it is sometimes difficult to think clearly in the Luxour."

"But where was Rad Ilex?" she wondered, puzzled. "Why was she alone? If she ran into the desert to escape him, why would she try to protect him?"

"People do strange things when they are confused by circumstance. She said, when she finally told me her name, that she was walking to my court."

"Across the desert? On foot?"

"So she said."

"But if she was running away from Rad Ilex to your court, then why was she afraid of you, and trying to protect Rad at the same time?"

"I thought," he said patiently, "you might explain that."

She brooded, her brows knit. "It makes no sense. Meguet usually makes more sense than that."

"Is she a mage?" he asked abruptly. She transferred her brooding from the ground to him.

"No," she said, surprised. "Why ask me? You recognized what I am the moment you saw me. You were with Meguet; if you were curious, you would have answered that question, one way or another."

"At first I thought not. And then I saw . . ." He hesitated. "A shadow. Perhaps it was only the Luxour."

She was silent, gazing at him, trying to put pieces together: Meguet protecting Rad Ilex from Brand's father, Meguet trying to walk alone and powerless across a desert to get to Draken Saphier's court, Meguet casting a shadow of power when she no longer had the strength to move. "It makes no sense," she said again, baffled. "If Rad Ilex left her in the desert to die, then why would she—and if he didn't, then what was she doing there? She has more intelligence than to try to cross a wasteland like this on foot."

"One or two other things I found puzzling also. Why did Rad Ilex go to Ro Holding? And how did you get from Ro Holding to my court, and then from my court to the Luxour? Rad Ilex wears the time-paths I forged for him, and so does my son. But Brand's were destroyed. So. You must have walked paths of your own making."

She opened her mouth to answer, and hesitated, unwilling, without knowing why, to open the marvels of Chrysom's book to Draken Saphier. As the answer hung in the air between them, she saw his eyes change, and she realized that he had known the answers to those questions even before he had found her on the Luxour. His eyes caught mage-light, turned gold. Dragon's eyes, she thought, frozen under the strange, inhuman gaze, and then: Meguet was born knowing what to fear.

She remembered the figures standing in the doorway of Chrysom's library, as the time-paths slowly misted the world with silver: the young man with Meguet's hair, and her heritage, with the warning to the Cygnet in his eyes. . . .

The stones and shadows were misting around her now, washed with gold; the pale mage-light burned gold. The key floated in a dark, secret place in her mind. But the dragon-eyes permitted no secrets; the key might as well have been in her open hand. It turned slowly in her mind, as if touched by invisible hands, that could not, for the moment, break through its mystery to open it.

Then the dragon closed his eyes; the gold melted into shadow and stone and light. Nyx blinked, saw Draken frowning deeply, concentrating, but not on her. She took a step away from him, another. He did not notice, lost in some private, harrowing moment. At her third step, his eyes opened. The taut lines of his face loosened; he sagged against the stones, spent and amazed.

"I've lost him," he breathed. "How could he escape a time-path looped back into itself?" He was silent, working out an answer; so did Nyx, in case the knowledge came in handy. But it only mystified her. "He had help," Draken said flatly, and Nyx felt herself grow cold with fear.

"No," she said quickly. "Not—"

"No one in my house would have helped him. No one else."

"She wouldn't have. She couldn't have. She has no power."

He shook his head impatiently. "She wouldn't need power for that. She'll be with him now."

"No."

He pondered, his eyes human again. "The Luxour," he said at last. "They'll come here. It's the only place in all Saphier where he can breathe a moment or two longer, though he is dead now, as he runs." Then a ghost of memory haunted his face; he whispered, "Brand." He turned away from Nyx, slumped against the wall, his face hidden in one upraised arm.

She heard a sound: stones shifting, dragon-claws scraping over them. It was Brand, she realized, climbing down from the fire-bird's roost. The garnets had vanished. Standing within the dragon's golden eyes, she had not seen the milky rising of the moon. Draken lifted his head, listening as Brand followed the path of the mage-light through the stones to Nyx.

He stopped when he reached the light; she saw him rock on his feet, as if a wind had pushed him. Then he made a sound, a broken word, and slid to his knees at his father's feet. Draken bent to pull him up, then knelt himself, as if even he could not bear the weight of all the bird's enchantments, and drew Brand into his arms.

Brand, lifting his face from Draken's shoulder, found Nyx, and stretched one hand out to her. Draken's shadow lay between them; she could not bring herself to move. Draken said, bringing Brand to his feet,

"Nyx Ro said she found you in Ro Holding."

"The firebird found her." His eyes clung to her a moment longer, and then returned to his father. His hold on Draken's arms tightened a little. "She gave me the only hope in the world of finding you again."

"Yes. I did not know how or when or where I would see you again, since your time-paths were destroyed."

"Nyx has a book. The ancient mage Chrysom of Ro Holding fashioned time-paths all through the Luxour. I made her bring me here to search for you. When we could not find you, I made her search for dragons. For my grandfather."

Draken looked at her, his expression unfathomable. "And did you," he asked, "find dragons?"

"No."

"Nyx decided that, even for a desperate man in the shape of a firebird, the dragons were too dangerous."

"That was wise of her." He touched his son's hair lightly, let his hand drop to Brand's shoulder. "What a strange thing to find in Ro Holding: the paths to the dragons of the Luxour."

"And equally strange," Nyx said tightly, "to find on a warrior's wrist the path from Saphier to Ro Holding."

They both looked at her as she stood alone, the mage-light casting her shadow wide and dark across the stones behind her. Draken seemed only thoughtful, but Brand, troubled, left his father abruptly.

"Nyx." He put his hands on her shoulders, frowning, then kissed her, as if to change the expression on her face. He succeeded only in changing his father's expression. "How can you believe that my father will be anything but grateful to you, to your house, to Ro Holding, for caring for me?"

"How could I?" she wondered.

He held her a moment longer, searching her eyes, tuned to the undercurrents in her voice, but not understanding them. He turned to his father again, said tautly, "Help me. Please. Nyx tried to remove the spell, Magior has tried—I can barely remember day, and I am beginning to hate the night. It's like drowning, every midnight, night after night after night. Only Nyx has made it bearable."

"I see."

"You can remove the spell. You taught Rad Ilex everything."

"Rad." Draken's mouth tightened. "For a day or two I had him trapped."

"You found him?" Brand said sharply. "Where?"

"Here in the desert. But he managed to escape." He touched his eyes. "I am sorry."

"Free me." For a moment Nyx, used to all Brand's expressions, barely recognized him: He wore the cold, intent, merciless face of a warrior of Saphier. "We'll both find him."

Meguet, she thought, chilled, and a stranger's eyes flicked at her, as if responding to her fear, yet hardly seeing her.

"He must be here still," Brand added. "Where else could he go without leaving Saphier? Unless he went back to Ro Holding. But he wants Chrysom's key, and Nyx has it here. He must have known she would come here to find Meguet."

Nyx closed her eyes, heard Draken say, "Chrysom's key."

"His book. The key is the book. Father—I am only human by moonlight, only until—"

"Listen to me." Nyx, wondering if she could fray into wind before either of them noticed, opened her eyes at the urgency in Draken's voice. He took Brand's face between his hands. "Listen to me," he said again. "I will try to help you. But I may fail."

"No."

"Listen. I know Rad's power. The Luxour shaped it. Before he could speak, he understood the language of these winds, the stones; he heard the dragons breathe before he knew the word for dragon. I don't know what of all this vast and unpredictable power around us went into the making of that spell—"

"Why?" Brand whispered. He was trembling; Nyx saw a streak of silver run down his face. "Why did he do this to me? I can't remember."

Draken shook his head. "I never knew," he said bitterly. "I only saw you after you had changed. When your human cry became the firebird's cry. You will remember. Look at me."

They were both silent. Nyx, sensing all Draken's attention on his son, was caught in the spell of the Luxour as its magic responded to Draken's making and unmaking. Their shadows, etched lean and black across the ground, changed shape: A great dragon spanned the circle of light, its black wings closed, its long neck bent toward the thing it held mesmerized beneath its gaze. The shadow of the firebird lay beyond Brand; winds shifted it, colored it yellow, red, peacock-blue. Then the dragon's wings lifted, opened, folded around the gaudy shadow, swallowed it into blackness. Nyx, staring, raised her head abruptly, startled by a movement above her head. Something shifted in the night: A head as bright as blood rose clear against the moon. Fire streamed out of it, washed red across the stars. The great head disappeared. Nyx found Brand again; spells flowed over and away from him like tattered rags: an owl wing, a lizard claw, a lion's face, his father's face, a dragon's misty, glittering breath.

Then the magic flowed elsewhere, left their shadows intact, shifting, as Draken's hands fell from Brand's face, and Brand, white, tearless, took a step back from him.

"I'm sorry," Nyx heard Draken whisper. And then she opened Chrysom's book, chose a dragon at random, and ran.

Whether Draken tried to follow her or not, she was unsure: What leaped at her like a great wind, nearly tangling the strands of the path in her mind might easily have been the raw power sweeping across the Luxour, forming its own spells around anything magical. She found herself in the deep caves, among the roaring waterfalls where Brand had forgotten, so briefly, the memories that constantly reshaped him. Her own memories threatened to distract her; she felt the sudden loss of him like a hollow in the air beside her, a silence where his voice belonged, stone where her eyes expected his face. But she had no time for such unusual feelings; she had no idea whether Draken would pursue her or Rad Ilex first, and she had to reach Meguet before he did.

She turned another page, opened another path. This one ended among the stones and dream-palaces, too close to where Draken had found her. She opened another path instantly, and fell into a place so black she thought she had reached the ice-dragon's hole torn out of the night between the stars. But the air was warm, tranquil; she caught her breath a moment, reading a phrase or two about the dragon hidden within this shadow.

*. . . a small and exquisite creature, with scales like gold leaf and shining copper . . . its eyes are azure. By temperament elusive but not unfriendly . . .*

She opened its path back into the Luxour, and came face to face with a warrior-mage.

He carried ritual blades; they and the time-paths on his wrists glittered like frost in the moonlight. His black garments flowed on the wind; odd colors seemed to flame and break free from them, then fade into night. With mages' sight, they recognized one another.

"Nyx Ro."

She stopped herself from vanishing before he attacked; he sounded only surprised.

"Yes," she said tersely.

"Draken Saphier is looking for you and his son. Where is Brand?"

"He flew ahead," she said, hoping it was somewhere near midnight. The mage looked disturbed.

"Rad Ilex is loose in the Luxour. It's not safe for the firebird to wander."

"How—"

"Meguet Vervaine is with him," the mage said without expression. "Your kinswoman. The warrior-mages are searching the Luxour."

"She was obviously under duress," Nyx said quickly. "He ensorcelled her."

"Most likely," the mage agreed politely.

"How many of the warrior-mages are out here?"

"All of them." He shook his head a little, fretfully. "Magic blows like sand in your eyes, here. It's hard to distinguish minds, even faces, from the lies the desert tells. Even those of us searching together got separated. You must not lose the firebird."

"No," she said, and he vanished, leaving a shining, faceless ghost of himself imprinted on the wild winds. She opened a path hurriedly to anywhere, and nearly scalded herself in steam from a boiling pool.

She backed away from the heat and cloying smell, and found a slightly cooler place where she could think. Surrounded by the bubbling pools, the mists, she felt hidden for the moment. She wiped steam-slick hair out of her face, and wondered starkly how, in a desert full of wild magic and mages who could barely find each other, she could possibly locate the two who had fled there to hide.

The Luxour itself had shaped Rad's power. So Draken had said, and if Rad could wear the faces of the desert, stones and dragon-dreams and shadows, and empty his mind of all but the constantly shifting winds of power, then even Draken with his dragon's eyes and relentless mind would have trouble picking him out of the air. But how Rad could hide Meguet, Nyx was unsure. Rad might transform her into a moon-shadow, but not even he could hide her thoughts. Nyx would be on her mind, Ro Holding, the Cygnet; words foreign to Saphier would drift into Draken's mind. If the warrior-mages did not find Meguet first. Like Draken, they would search for her to find Rad. Would Rad,

knowing that, abandon Meguet to plead coercion and duress to
Draken Saphier? Meguet would more likely fight what would be
the shortest battle in her life. And if Draken didn't kill her, he
would use her to force Nyx out of hiding.

And to yield the key. She stirred, remembering her own danger,
and made herself as transparent as the steam billowing around
her. But what, she wondered, would he do about Brand? Rad
Ilex, she was certain, had not cast that spell. If not even he
could remove it, Brand would wrench the firebird's voice out
of the Cygnet's labyrinth, and its fire from Nyx's hold, and sear
the burning desert itself with his despair.

But the firebird had attacked Rad. Brand had named him the
maker of the spell.

Meguet had tried to protect Rad from Draken.

Rad knew who had cast the spell. He had been there.

She felt her body shocked into visibility; even in the steam,
her skin was cold.

No witnesses, Draken had said. No one else saw, but he and
his son and Rad.

Three leaves. One blue as Brand's eyes. One gold as the
Luxour. One as red as the black war-dragon's eyes.

She whispered, "Draken."

As if she had summoned him, he began to shape himself out
of the mists in front of her.

She ran before he had a face. But his mind's eye saw her
and the random path she had pulled from Chrysom's book. He
pursued her, a single burning dragon's eye in the dark, a force
like night-wind at her heels. He could, she remembered with
horror, forge his own paths, not from place to place perhaps,
but from here to nowhere. As quickly as she shaped Chrysom's
path, he reshaped it, cutting through her weave of silver, leaving
her on an edge of nothing, or turning her own path back on itself,
until she lost all sense of Chrysom's design, and guessed that
the path she fled down would loop through itself to lead her
inevitably, strand by shifted, twisted strand, to the Dragon of
Saphier.

In desperation she opened another path, and then another, flowing away from that. She shaped a third, a fourth, flinging them into the dark, and running without knowing what dragons waited at their endings. She opened others, sending filaments of silver like crazed nets to catch a drifting moment and open it. She gave Draken no time to alter them before she spun another, sent it branching away into the unknown. Finally, she opened two that, by some luck, were so close they seemed almost indistinguishable. She fled down one, leaving Draken to snarl the other until he wove it through itself and then found he had trapped nothing.

So she hoped. The path she followed remained true to Chrysom's pattern. She had no idea where it led; there could be no worse, she reasoned, than the dragon hunting her. When the path ended, she closed it behind her, let it fade back into possibility, and then into a dream that only Chrysom's key would bring to life. Stranded on some island of time within the Luxour, she turned to face the dragon.

At first she thought she was alone. She stood at the mouth of a cave so massive even her mage's eye could not find walls or ceiling. But she smelled earth, wet stone, heard the slow drip and trickle of water. She took a step forward, sensed something where her eye saw only air. Tentatively, she let her thoughts flow around it: It might have been the ghost of stone that had once filled the cave. As she had with Chrysom's tiny jars, she let her mind drop into it.

She seemed, for an instant, made of light, as if the sun burned behind her eyes, and all her bones were lucent and bright as fire. She could not speak or think; she was as formless and bright as air at noon in the Luxour. Then the sun blinked, and she felt cold stone beneath her face, her body, and realized she had fallen. She pulled herself up, shaking, stunned, blind, waiting for the pain to begin, the punishment for touching fire. But she felt only the cool breath of the cave. She opened her eyes finally, and saw the dragon.

Its shadow had been burned into her mind, it seemed; her eye shaped a darkness against the dark. The heavy bulk of its head loomed above her; it could have swallowed her and scarcely noticed. Its huge eyes glittered faintly, flecks of light as colorless as stars. Its voice filled the cave or her head, slow, ancient, dry, dust blowing across dust.

"Who are you?"

Her own voice sounded small, trembling in the vastness. "I'm sorry—"

"Answer."

"Nyx Ro. A mage. I came—I was running—I didn't see you. I didn't mean to disturb you."

She heard its breath, long and endless. "Nyx Ro. Running. From where? To where? Answer."

"I was running away. From another mage."

"What mage?"

"Draken Saphier."

She had no idea what those words might mean to it: The act of running would not occur to it, and she could not imagine anything it would be compelled to run from. A great nostril, vague and colorless, expanded slightly; she heard a hiss from it. "When humans run, they run from the greater to the lesser fear. They do not run down the spider webs of time where unknown dragons wait. How did you find me? Answer."

"I have a book of paths—"

"You did not make them."

"No."

"I eat paths of the makers I dislike." It seemed to shift. A hollow echo rolled through the cave; light sparked as its scales dragged across stone. Still she could not see its color. She swallowed.

"You eat power."

"I dislike minor annoyances."

She made a movement, half a step. "I won't disturb—" Black moons sculpted out of the dark descended behind her, slid together and locked. She stood ringed by dragon-claws, and wondered if some of the minor annoyances it ate were human. She said carefully, "I would not make much of a meal. You have already terrified me. Your power is like the Luxour's, ancient and unimaginable. You don't need to threaten me, any more than the sun needs to threaten. I must get back to the Luxour. Those I love are in terrible danger. If there is a price I must pay for disturbing you, just tell me."

It made another sound, a faint, distant rumble. "Who disturbs the Luxour? Answer."

"Draken Saphier. And his mages."

An eyelid descended; stars vanished, reappeared. "A dust storm. A random shift of rock. The Luxour will survive that."

"Yes." Her voice shook again. "But Brand Saphier may not. And Ro Holding may not—"

"Human names. Human dreams."

"That's all I know. That's what I am. I have no dragons' time for loving. While I stand here in your hold I am disturbing you, and those I love might cease to exist. Please let me go. Tell me what I must do. I will leave you in peace; you'll never see me again. Please."

"You woke me. Nyx Ro. Weaving my secret path out of mages' fire."

"Destroy the path behind me," she said desperately. "I don't have the power to make such things, only to follow them.

"Who does make them? Answer."

"He is dead."

"Who else?"

"No one."

"Why have you come here? What petty breath of storm across the Luxour sends humans running in fear beyond time? Answer."

She drew breath, held it, feeling as if its thoughts had looped back through themselves, trapping her within some answerless question. There was no place where she could hide herself from its bright, relentless eye. It would burn the leaves of Chrysom's book inside her mind; it could turn her bones to gold and hoard them until trees grew on the Luxour. She searched for an answer it had not already heard, and remembered at last the word for what she fought.

"The dragon's son," she said.

The dragon was silent. She waited a moment or two, listening, before she realized that the black around her held no more subtle shades of dark, nor did the stillness hold more questions. She turned, trembling again, and opened Chrysom's book to fashion a simpler path back to the Luxour.

# CHAPTER
# 16

Rad Ilex took one step onto the Luxour from his time-path and vanished. Meguet, looking for him wildly in the moonlight, saw winds, shimmering veils of dark and silver, swirl around her. She closed her eyes and heard Rad's voice.

"Meguet."

"What?" she said tersely. She opened her eyes, saw nothing now but the vast, wind-swept desert.

"I've made you invisible." For a moment, she was afraid to move; she stared rigidly ahead, lest she look down and find she stood on nothing. "Don't be afraid," he added. "You can see yourself. I can see you."

"I can't see you."

"Wait."

Slowly he shaped himself out of air and night; she saw the strange winds glide over him. He said softly when his face became more than a blank shadow, "I'm using the power of the Luxour to do this. It's a turbulent force all across the desert. Draken will have trouble isolating me from it."

"What causes it?"

"The dragons, I think. They breathe power; they dream it; it escapes from all their private worlds into the desert. I can disguise myself in it. But hiding you will be more difficult. Look."

She looked down and saw a moon-shadow the strange power had shaped, that clung to her invisible heel: a black swan, its wings outstretched. She swallowed drily. The shadow peeled away, flew into the wind.

"Will he see—"

"I don't know. The magic creates itself constantly, especially when it responds to other sources of power." She stopped searching the night for the shadow of the Cygnet, and met his eyes. "I can hide from Draken Saphier. Perhaps I can hide you. But you cannot hide from the Luxour."

He was worried, she realized, and with reason; she felt the ground drop away again, as if she stood on nothing. "It's a power," she heard herself say, "that rouses only in defense of the Cygnet. When Ro Holding itself is in grave danger."

She saw his grim face tighten. "Now?" he demanded incredulously. "In the middle of the Luxour with a hundred mages and Draken Saphier alert for any hint of power?"

"If Draken threatens Ro Holding, or Nyx in such a way that Ro Holding itself is threatened, then by my heritage I must fight for the Cygnet. Even on the Luxour. Even against a hundred mages."

Another shadow formed, broke away from her: a black rose. She heard his breath. "How were you trained? And by whom?"

"No one," she said simply. "I was born. I am the Cygnet's eye, its hand. At such times. Now, I'm only a woman in a desert in the dead of night, facing danger without even a sword."

"A sword. You saw how much use that was to you in Chrysom's tower."

"I know. But it would make me feel better."

"If I could risk it, I would make you a hundred swords. But if you raise a weapon against the warrior-mages bearing the ritual blades, they will fight back. They are fast, ruthless, efficient. You saw what Brand could do. And he's not even a mage."

She nodded, her eyes wide. "They lied to me."

"Who?"

"The warrior-mages. They said the dance was only ritual. I didn't believe them and they knew it."

"They are preparing for war. They don't care where. They want to experiment with an attack through time: an army of mages and warriors and dragons that can appear and disappear seemingly out of nowhere. Ro Holding is as good a place as any to begin."

She stared blindly at the ground, trying to think. "We must find Nyx."

"And that key, before Draken does. I can hide it forever from him among the dragons."

"They will still have time-paths," she said starkly. "Who will hide Ro Holding?"

He shook his head, scanning the desert. She saw nothing move in the moonlight but dust; they might have been the only people on the Luxour. "I'll do what I can."

"Can you find some water? With your face like that, you look already dead."

"Oh." He touched it; the dark mask of blood and dust vanished. His own face, taut with weariness and pain, was no more comforting. He stood silently, letting his mind wander, she guessed, for a long time. He seemed to draw strength from the desert's power, calm from the ancient, unchanging mountains; his face eased a little as he contemplated the thing he loved. He stirred finally; she said,

"Now what?"

"There are a dozen mages prowling nearby, but neither Draken nor Nyx."

"I don't see anything," she said, shaken. "Can they see us?"

"I can't see them either. But I can tell the difference between a warrior-mage's power, and the Luxour's. That's what keeps me safe. To them, I am another random thought of the Luxour."

"And what am I?"

"In danger," he said. "Let's search among the stones and pools; it would be easier for her to hide there than out here."

They emerged from another silver path onto the banks of a steaming waterfall that poured down steps it had carved in stone

washed with all the colors of opal. Rad was silent, searching
again, Meguet guessed, while the damp, cloying mist billowed
around them and away, finding nothing of them to cling to. She
heard Rad breathe finally,

"I think she's here. . . ." Then he vanished again within his
thoughts. Meguet watched the colors in the water swirl, form
a reflection of her face. The reflection slid leaflike down the
steps before it broke apart. A warrior-mage appeared out of
nowhere, stared into the water. He turned abruptly, searched
the mist. Meguet, not daring to breathe, turned her thoughts
to steam, stone, crystal. Then the mist itself leaped at him,
poured, burning, into his mouth as he drew breath to scream.
He fell backward into the scalding water and followed Meguet's
reflection into deeper water. Meguet saw a silver path begin to
form in the air above him, break apart as he sank. One of his
ritual blades spun out of the water, snagged on the crystals along
the bank. She eyed it, but seemed oddly incapable of moving.

She heard Rad's whisper close to her ear, and started. "I found
Brand. The firebird. But I can't find Draken."

She allowed herself to move finally, tried to touch him. "Let's
find Nyx. She must go home. She won't leave until she knows
where I am."

"She won't leave without you," he said, startled.

"I must stay. I can't hide behind the walls of Ro House and
wait for Draken Saphier to bring his war there. If I must fight,
I must fight here."

"You'll die," he said incredulously.

"Either here, or in Ro Holding. As I would have died defending
Chrysom's tower, if Draken Saphier had come to steal that key
instead of you. It's my heritage."

"It's ridiculous," he snapped, but no more, for the mists,
snatching at Meguet's thoughts, whirled into a high white
tower covered with what, at first glance, seemed to be red
roses, but which changed, to Meguet's horror, into the black
dragon's malevolent, flame-red eyes. They looked everywhere,
the eyes of Draken Saphier; they saw through mist, through

Rad's spell, through her mind into the Cygnet's eye. . . .
"Come," Rad said, gripping her. She could not move. He
pulled her roughly away from the image, and down another
silver path.

Here they were surrounded by bubbling pools; even the mud
spoke. Meguet could scarcely see the wall of yellow rock rising
above the mud-pools, which she might have touched with the
point of a broadsword. She waited while Rad searched the place;
his thoughts came back to her.

"You must leave," he breathed. "You'll kill us both."

"Then leave me."

"No."

"Were they real?" she asked. "The dragon-eyes?"

"One might have been. Draken knows how to play with the
Luxour's power. But only as a man with one finger knows
how to play a flute. I still can't find him. Finding him will
be dangerous enough, but it's far more dangerous not knowing
where he is."

"Hide," she suggested after a moment. "I'll bring him to you."

He looked at her darkly, but said only, "You'll do that soon
enough as it is. I want the key first. And then you and Nyx Ro
out of Saphier. Then I want Draken Saphier. In that order."

She did not bother to answer. She saw something move in the
solid wall of yellow stone. Mist, she thought, a trickle of water.
But something made her reach out to grip Rad, warn him silent.
Her fingers closed on nothing; he had vanished even to her eye.
The dark shifting became a crack in the stone. The crack widened
as she stared. Then the face of the rock tore like paper and a dozen
warrior-mages emerged.

She was surrounded in an instant; their whirling blades spun,
plunged into the ground around her, elongating into a high,
deadly cage so tight she cut her forearm, turning. The teasing
desert gave one blade swans on its hilt, down its blade; she
reached for it desperately. It snapped silver light, numbing her
hand. She stumbled back, cut her shoulder on another blade.
She caught her balance desperately, stood trembling while the

mages appeared and disappeared into the mists, searching for
Rad Ilex.

The ground around her turned to boiling mud. It swallowed the
mages' blades, along with one mage who, leaping for Meguet,
turned visible in midair as a wave of mud flung itself up and
shaped him before it slapped him down. Steam blew everywhere,
glittered with fine grains of silver and gold. Meguet, feeling a
hand close on her wrist, pulled against it. It pulled harder; the
silver grains snaked into a pattern around them. The pattern
shattered like glass. She heard Rad cry out; the grip on her wrist
slackened, tightened again. Light flashed, bright and painful as a
flashing mirror; the island she stood on melted beneath her. She
had no time to scream before she was dragged into mud. Like
the mist, it found nothing of her to grasp. Silver wove in the
murk; she could see again suddenly, as the mud pool faded. Still
Rad remained invisible. Or was it Rad? she wondered suddenly, panicked. Was it Draken Saphier instead, leading her down
the time-path? She pulled free abruptly; a flock of tiny swans
formed themselves out of the silver path, soared upward, flew
in a ring around her. She stopped, tense, her eyes wide, searching
nothing.

"Meguet."

It was Nyx. The swans scattered at the word, turned back into
silver. Nyx appeared a moment later, pale, and dishevelled, her
eyes full of color, but, to Meguet's eye, unharmed. Nyx took a
deep breath, closed her eyes. "Meguet," she said again. "What a
place to find you in. A lake of boiling mud."

"Nyx." She felt, saying the name, as helpless as she had ever
been in her life, finding the heir to Ro Holding underground in
a strange country, while a deadly storm of magic raged above
their heads. "Do you have any idea what kind of danger you're
in?"

Nyx nodded. "I know exactly what kind of danger I'm in. And
so are you and so is Ro Holding." Her voice sounded composed,
but as she touched Meguet's bleeding forearm, Meguet saw her
hand shake. "You're hurt."

Meguet ripped a length of silk loose from her torn sleeve impatiently. "Nyx, listen to me—" She stopped abruptly, searching the soundless dark beyond the time-path. "Where's Rad Ilex?"

"Still battling mages." She took the silk, wound it methodically around Meguet's arm. "I thought he would be safer without you."

"He said so, too. But he wouldn't leave me."

"You might as well be carrying a blazing torch, the way power is escaping you."

"I can't help it. Rad complained, too." Nyx checked her shoulder; Meguet shrugged away. "Nyx, listen."

Nyx folded her arms, stood quietly, her eyes colorless again. "I'm listening."

"I want you to give me that key and go back to Ro Holding before we take another step in the Luxour."

Nyx raised an eyebrow. "You do. While you do what? Battle the warrior-mages of Saphier with your good intentions? Don't be preposterous."

"Then give the key to Rad and go home. He can find the dragons, bring them to the Luxour to fight Draken."

Nyx was silent a moment, her fingers tight on her arms. Her eyes slid away from Meguet's, the expression in them unfathomable. "Does he imagine them to be so obliging? To rouse themselves to fight for or against Draken, at the whim of whichever human reaches them first? They are very dangerous."

"I don't know." Meguet rubbed her eyes wearily. "I don't know what he thinks, except that this is what he wants. He takes power from the Luxour, he says. Maybe that would persuade them. At least he could hide the key from Draken. Or you could. Hide it on some path and go." Nyx remained unmoved; Meguet's voice rose. "Nyx, you are heir to Ro Holding!"

"I might as well be heir to the moon if we can't stop Draken here and now. I know what he wants. I'd go home only to sit in Ro House and wait for him and his army of mages and dragons to knock at the gate. I saw your kinsman with his corn-silk hair appear in Chrysom's tower just as I left with Brand. He came to warn me."

"Then why did you leave? Nyx, what possessed you to come here?"

"What possessed you to think you could cross the Luxour on foot to Draken Saphier's court?"

"I had to find the danger—I couldn't see it sitting safely in Rad's village."

Nyx shrugged slightly. "And I couldn't see what the firebird saw, by sitting safely in Chrysom's tower. Nor could I find you. A minor point to you, perhaps, but it seemed important to my mother. What was the warning you were given?"

"I saw a dragon of night and stars across Rad's doorway, in the morning light. At first I thought Rad was the danger—he knew too much—and Draken, when he found me in the desert, was persuasive. I didn't know—I was confused—"

"With reason."

Meguet paused, remembering the dragon, her hand straying to her shoulder. "I doubt that Corleu even knew the word for what he was compelled to warn you of. The Dragon hunts the Cygnet. That is the warning."

"I thought as much." Nyx gazed at nothing, wandering a tangled path of magic or memory, while Meguet contemplated their dubious fates grimly. "Brand," Nyx said softly. The color washed into her eyes at the name. "He might stop Draken."

"Why should he?"

"It's complicated," Nyx said, and nothing more, seeming, for once, at loss for words. Meguet, looking at her, found the unspoken words in her eyes.

"Nyx Ro," she said incredulously, the blood startling through her. "He's a warrior!"

"So? You love a Gatekeeper."

"At least he is part of Ro Holding." Meguet laid a hand on her forehead, where the headache was beginning, and added crossly, "Moro's name. Brand himself barely knows who he is. Other than the son of a ruler who wants to scorch the four Holds of Ro Holding with dragon-fire. Is he Saphier's heir?"

"I forgot to ask."

"Oh, Nyx, really."

"Such things are unimportant in Ro Holding. You know that. I never knew my own father's name."

"That's because your mother fell in love discreetly and in private, and not, I would imagine, in the middle of a strange land with a man who spends most of his day in a tree." She was holding her shoulder as she spoke, frowning at the nagging pain. "You love him for the color of his eyes."

"Most likely," Nyx said temperately. She drew the ivory ball out of her pocket, opened it, and extracted something that looked like a brown, withered hand.

"What is that?"

"Olem root. From Berg Hold." She applied it gently to Meguet's shoulder. A numbness washed across the pain; the scent of cloves and earth and mint seemed to quiet even the flickering ache behind her eyes. "Country magic. It will cling there until the bleeding stops, and then it will drop away and wither again. A trifle gruesome, but it works."

"Yes," Meguet sighed. "Thank you. So. Brand will stop his father from destroying Ro Holding for your sake?"

"Not exactly for my sake," Nyx said, but did not elaborate, nor did she allow expression into her eyes. She took the amber earring from the ivory, hung it from her ear. Gold fire shimmered across it, faded. "As you say, we hardly know each other. But," she added on a breath, "he knows his father even less."

"What—"

"We must find the firebird now. Quickly."

"Draken will be with him."

"Draken was alone, when I saw him last. I'm hoping the Luxour separated them."

"What about Rad?" Meguet asked anxiously, as Nyx shaped the silver pattern into their future. "Should we leave him on his own?"

"He would only distract the firebird. I want all of Brand's attention." She listened a moment, for what Meguet could only imagine: dragon's breath, the silent voices of the mages, the footsteps of the dragon-lord. "Come."

Winds, desert, stars, spilled around them at the path's end. Meguet saw the broken palaces rising up against the night. The transparent, elusive colors in a dragonfly's wing illumined windows, flickered away. In the next moment, the palaces were only stones.

"Should we hide?" she whispered to Nyx. "Are we invisible?"

Nyx shook her head. The wind tossed her hair into dark, tangled paths; for an instant her eyes reflected moonlight. "I want the firebird to find me."

"What if the mages find you first?"

"That's a risk I'll have to take. Meguet—" she breathed, as stars sparked in the ground around Meguet, shifted to form a familiar constellation. "Will you stop that?"

The Cygnet rose above their heads, star-fire marking its wings, its cold bright eye, until the winds picked the stars apart and they fell like fading embers into the dark. "It's the Luxour," Meguet said a little wildly. "I can't control it."

"I can't either."

"What do you want me to do? Should I hide?"

"Go wait among those stones. Maybe their power will disguise yours."

Meguet left her alone, barely more than a shadow in the desert, using a power at once simpler and far more complex than any mage's power to call the firebird. Turning as she entered the nearest mass of stones, she saw tiny black swans form and fly out of her footprints in the dust. Appalled, she moved deeper into the stones.

Moonlight pulled her own shadow from the dark; she looked up and saw again the haunting shift from jumbled stones to the sagging walls and broken towers of a great ruined palace. Her mind wandered down an imaginary time-path and found the palace again, in a moment so close to the Luxour's time that the two worlds of desert and palaces, made unstable by enormous, random powers, were constantly overlapping. The moonlight in the high windows grew filmy with butterfly colors. The colors washed away; the cold light poured down stone. She heard Nyx's voice.

She walked soundlessly to the opening in the stones, looked out. The firebird had come to Nyx; as it spiralled around her, she coaxed it down. It came to rest finally in front of her. It gazed at her a moment, motionless, crying neither sorrow nor fire. And then it changed.

*He is free,* Meguet thought, with wonder and then, as the stones around her shifted, he changed under her eye: She saw the broader, more powerful line of his shoulders, the white in his hair. She felt something flash out of her entire body; the winds took her fear and shaped it into the dragon's shadow.

Nyx vanished. Draken simply turned his head, looked at the stones where Meguet was hiding, and Nyx appeared again.

"No," she said sharply.

"Then give me what I want."

"Where is Brand?"

"Where I left him. Give me the key. Then I will set you and Meguet on the path to Ro Holding. You can go home."

"And wait for you." Her voice shook with anger. Draken said very softly,

"Yes."

Meguet felt her body flash again. This time her own rage shaped the shadow that flew, soundless and dark as night, with its coldly burning eye on Draken Saphier. She flew and did not fly; she felt the power gather in her again, as the black swan neared him. Blue light flickered along its wings. He must have heard the winds part for it; he spun suddenly, flung up his hand. The black dragon formed against the moon and stars, its red eyes flaming. It opened its mouth, swung its long neck down and caught the black swan as it flew into Draken Saphier.

He cried out, as the blue flame rippled over him. Then the dragon broke the swan's neck and tossed it away. Meguet, still caught in it, felt herself grow limp and thoughtless with its death, falling farther and farther away from a point of light that grew small, so small she could scarcely see it, though it seemed, as she fell, the only important thing left to do.

Then the hard ground shaped under her again; someone gripped her, shook her. "Meguet!" She opened her eyes. The world was still black, but she recognized Rad's voice. She lifted her head, saw Draken rising. She heard a strange noise beside her; Draken, hearing it also, vanished just before the mage-light struck.

So had Nyx; the light snaked across the air where she had been, and picked one of the warrior-mages out of nothing. Her ritual blades and time-paths caught the light, flared brighter than the moon. Then she seemed to lose all light, become a piece of nothing darker than the night. She fell without a sound. Another mage appeared beside her; power snapped back at Rad. The stones shook around them; a shard flicked across Meguet's cheek. She flinched, heard Rad breathe something.

"Stay here," he said, and vanished. She stumbled to her feet, gripping stones to keep her balance, and looked out.

She saw a calm and empty desert. Then both Rad and Nyx seemed to waver in and out of the air, as if they were being pulled into eyesight and constantly pulling themselves back. As the silent struggle gradually and relentlessly worked them visible, the warrior-mages appeared around them, still as monoliths in the moonlight.

Draken saw her. He was an eye in her mind instantly, blood-red and unblinking, staring everywhere she fled, forcing her finally into a maze where she took every wrong turn she could make, and every wall that stopped her turned into the dragon's eye and forced her on. Once she turned and stood in its glare, refusing to move. The eye turned to fire in her head; from some far place she heard her own voice. She ran.

Abruptly, she could see again. She was on her knees, clinging to stone, trembling as if she had been running for her life through the maze of palaces on the Luxour. Draken had turned away from her to watch the firebird come.

It flew fast, and it flew straight to Rad Ilex.

He could not seem to move; he could only watch it, his head

uplifted. He tried to speak; he could not. The bird's silver claws shone like ritual blades; they were open, curved, and dropping toward his heart. Nyx's face was turned toward the bird; she too struggled to speak. Meguet, freed from Draken's attention, walked the maze in her mind to what the dragon had sought: the eye of the Cygnet.

*Nyx,* she said, from that secret place, and Nyx met her eyes.

Power swept through her, from the Cygnet to the Cygnet's heir. Nyx shook free of the web of minds that held her, and cried to the firebird,

"Brand! Not Rad! It's your father's spell! Remember!"

The firebird faltered above Rad. It tore its voice out of Ro Holding and screamed, falling as if it had been shot. Brand, his face rigid with the firebird's fury, rolled to his feet and leaped in a single unbroken movement, at his father. Draken, startled, nearly unleashed mage-fire; he pulled it back quickly as Brand's body struck him. He staggered, regained his balance and gripped Brand. The back of his hand, coupled with the weight of time-paths, whipped across Brand's face. He fell like the firebird had out of the air, and lay still.

A few of the warrior-mages stirred; Meguet heard an indrawn breath. Draken met their eyes, said calmly, "It was necessary. He will understand." He looked at Nyx. "The key."

Her eyes flicked at Meguet, leaning drained and helpless against the stones. She bowed her head. Something small, burnished with amber fire dropped into her hand. Draken, his eyes on it, stepped toward her. She flung the amber at his feet.

It exploded with all the firebird's beautiful enchantments. For a moment Draken vanished among them: a scattering of garnet roses, a diamond snowfall. But as he picked himself out of the spell he had made, the mages held Nyx, shaped her back into the waning moonlight as she tried to vanish. Draken, shaking gold leaves out of his hair, stepped across Brand's body to her.

"Perhaps," he said, "you will give me something to fight after all in your peaceful kingdom. You and your cousin who is not a mage."

He held her eyes and held out his hand. After a long time, during which she stood like the warrior-mages, a standing stone beneath the setting moon, she reached into her pocket for the key to all the dreaming worlds.

# CHAPTER
# 17

The first of the dragons appeared at dawn. Nyx watched the line of light above the mountains turn fiery with sunrise, and listened to Brand breathe. He might have been the firebird still, his bruised face empty, his thoughts hidden from her. Twice she had heard him try to speak in the night, then stop. He sat beside her on bare ground. The mages had tied his hands behind his back, while his father roamed the time-paths. They did not, Nyx guessed, want to use power against Draken Saphier's powerless son. Rad slumped against a rock near him. A web of power, spun from mage to mage across the circle, trapped him in its intricate strands; Nyx caught a glimpse of it in the dawn, fine-spun and dangerous, each tendril clinging to Rad, trembling a warning at his every breath. It vanished from eyesight, then; the mages hid it from the light of day. She felt no such elaborate constraints on her; they knew she would not leave Meguet or Brand. The mages had left Meguet free; they watched with cold curiosity the odd enchantments the Luxour pulled out of her. She was mage and not mage. Nyx they understood; they might not, Nyx feared, let Meguet return home. Meguet sat near Rad, leaning against the same rock. She watched the sunrise absently, frowning a little; Nyx wondered if Meguet saw, instead of the rising sun, the great shining prism hidden within time, which was the Cygnet's power and its eye.

She heard Brand's breath catch. An eye had opened in the distant mountains: a second sun, red-gold, flaming through the harsh, barren crags. A crag unfolded, extended itself upward in a broad sweep of gold. Another eye opened. The true sun rose above them. Shadows scattered away from the mountainside as the dragon's face emerged. A second crag broke away, moved upward into the sky, to catch the wind. The dragon shrugged itself out of the mountain, soared upward, light sliding like molten gold across its bright scales. In that moment Nyx felt the slackening of the mages' guard. It did not matter; as they watched the dragon burn across the morning, no one could have moved.

It came straight to them; its vast shadow, flung forward, reached them first. It seemed, as the earth darkened beneath its broad underbelly, to have swallowed the sun. Then it veered, loosed the sun from beneath its wing. It settled on top of the steep ruin of stones near them. It stretched its wings in the light; gold shook into their eyes. Then it faded into itself among the rocks, its brilliant, craggy profile to the light. One eye stared down at them, wide and ruthless as the sun.

Nyx felt a touch, and started. Brand had shifted closer; his shoulder brushed hers. She looked at him; the dragon had wakened something in him besides the firebird's silent, endless cry.

"My father—" His voice caught. He began again, softly, but Nyx sensed the mages' attention riveted on them. "He won't stop this, until he finds his own father. The dragon-mage."

"I know."

"Such monsters will make a wasteland out of Ro Holding." He closed his eyes, his face twisting. "Why must he take Ro Holding? There is a land for him at the end of every path."

"He glimpsed the power in Meguet," Rad Ilex said wearily. "It's mysterious, beyond his control, beyond his experience. He will take apart Ro Holding to find the source." Meguet's eyes flicked to him. She turned her face away abruptly, her mouth tight. He reached out with some effort, as if he lifted stone instead of bone, and touched her. "I'm sorry. If I hadn't dragged you here with me—"

"If I had just let you take the key," Nyx said bitterly.

Meguet's head bowed. "If I had not picked up the rose."

"It's my father's fault," Brand said with savage lucidity. "None of yours. Any of you." He struggled impatiently with his bonds, and added dispassionately, "I would like to kill him."

Nyx asked tentatively, "Do you remember—"

"Everything." He stopped. He raised a shoulder, brushed it against his swollen cheek, where a few fragmented time-paths had imprinted themselves in blood. He looked at Rad finally and said again, "Everything. You told me this would happen. That you needed to leave Saphier to look for Chrysom's key, and you told me why. You had told my father, in all innocence, that it existed, and then you realized that all the innocence was yours. You knew he would kill you for the key. I didn't believe you. Then he came in and I saw his eyes. Dragon's eyes. You had already opened a path to Ro Holding. He—I—" He shook his head. "It becomes confused here. He tried to stop you—I tried to stop him—I don't know how I thought I could." He swallowed, added huskily, "He was no one I knew then. Not my father—No one. He had transformed himself. He was the dragon. And I became the firebird."

"He made the firebird to kill me," Rad said, and then was silent, as if words, like his hands, were fixed to the mages' web of power and had become too heavy. He lifted his head suddenly; Nyx, following his gaze, saw a piece of morning sky detach itself and fall. Against the gold-brown desert its shape became visible: a sky-blue dragon, smaller than the first, with eyes like cloud. It dropped onto another pile of stones, and vanished again; with difficulty she saw it settle itself, now stone-brown and grey, flecked with black, a rock-dragon hidden among the rocks. "I envy him," Rad whispered. "Seeing all their private worlds." Only Brand stared at the ground, seeing nothing. "Brand," Rad said, again with effort, and Brand turned his dark, empty stare at him. "He didn't know you either, then. You were someone for him to use. He would have used anyone."

"Don't defend him," Brand said fiercely. "Not to me."

"I'm not. He barely glimpsed then what he is bringing to the Luxour now, and if you hadn't been there, he would have turned himself into the firebird to stop me."

"I was there. And so were you. He had no mercy for either of us. It was cruel. And unforgivable."

"Yes. I'm only explaining why—"

"Power. I know my father that well at least." He made a sudden, furious attempt at the leather thongs binding his wrists. The mages watched impassively. Nyx, her throat aching suddenly, reached out to loosen them. Light charred the ground under her hand; the snap of air numbed her fingers. She started to rise, swallowing anger, to plead with the mages. Meguet's eyes caught her, wide, warning, and held her still.

"But why," Nyx asked Rad, when Brand had calmed himself, "did Brand become human again, those few hours every night? Why would Draken have done that?"

"I don't think Draken did," Rad said softly. They watched a crimson dragon, long and sinuous, flicker in and out of time, its scenting tongue bright and quick as lightning, burning and vanishing. The winds of the Luxour finally dragged it into shape; it took its place on another ruin. "Brand and I met in secret at moonrise. Draken transformed him into the firebird at midnight. I remember hearing the changing of the guard, how the familiar ritual noises frayed apart at the cry of the firebird. I think Brand broke his father's spell every night trying to remember the significance of moonrise, of midnight. Not even Draken could cast a spell more powerful than love, or rage, or grief."

Brand shook suddenly with a terrible, noiseless grief. He bowed his head, hid his face behind his hair; Nyx saw the tears fall on the barren ground like rain. She eased closer to him, slipped her arms around him. He dropped his face against her. Her hold tightened; she felt her own tears slide into his hair. The mages cast no spell to stop her. She held him until his trembling eased, and her own eyes were hot, heavy. She sat back; he raised his head, shook the hair out of his face. He leaned forward, kissed her; she tasted his tears. He said softly,

"And so the firebird found you."

"If the firebird had come to Ro Holding a month or two earlier, it would never have come to me." Her voice shook. "In some ways, I was as ruthless as your father. The small birds in the back swamps of the Delta know. Meguet knows."

He rested his face a moment longer against her dusty hair. "My father does not intend to war against swamp birds," he said wearily. "And whatever you did to Meguet, she still loves you and she is still alive."

Another dragon broke into the morning, this one building itself out of a line of stones half-buried in the ground. It was huge, as grey as smoke, with a flattened, predatory skull. Its eyes sparked light like diamonds; they looked as hard and cold. One of the mages whispered uneasily to another as it took to the air. Its shadow slid slowly over them; it circled and settled on a massive rise of stones as grey as itself. Something in the distance disturbed it, perhaps an image drifting out of the winds. Its jaws opened; a colorless light flashed out of it. One of the piles of stone exploded, left a ghostly image of ruins where it had stood. The shock of boulders hitting the ground rocked the mages on their feet.

"Moro's name," Meguet whispered. Nyx watched her tensely, wondering if she were about to vanish to fight a dragon that made even the mages wary. Another appeared. This one Nyx recognized: A drifting wall of steam among the pools tore itself open to reveal an empty blackness, a hole in the shape of a dragon, with eyes like stars, and breath that froze the rocks it settled on. A few cracked; fragments rattled down. It curled and breathed; the hot morning light slid like white fire over the ice on the dark stones.

"How many more?" Meguet asked rigidly.

"I'm not sure."

"A dozen? Two?"

"Maybe. Not that a dozen more or less matters much."

"Draken can't control them all," Rad said. His head jerked, as if a strand of the mages' web had tightened around his throat. He swallowed, leaned back silently.

"He is looking for his father," Brand said. "His father will control them."

"I hope," Nyx murmured. Meguet turned her head, looked at Nyx without fear, without hope, simply recognizing the frail bonds of time and memory between them. With a shock deep in her, as if something named Ro Holding had suddenly ceased to exist, Nyx realized that the Luxour might hold the only moments they had left. All for a firebird, she thought numbly. All for a key. For a challenge to a mage on a warm summer day. She stared blindly at her eyeless shadow, felt sorrow, heavy, motionless, endless, begin to replace her bones.

More dragons became visible: one of air, translucent, its bones pale light, its wings faint shimmerings of heat; another, formed of twilight cloud, with scales of deep purple, blue-grey, violet. A white dragon, carved of ivory, it seemed, and as delicate, shaped itself out of steam and rode the wind to its distant perch. The stones were filling with dragons, watching the desert like birds of prey. A cobalt dragon flew out of the broken roof of one of the palaces, and then a black one with rust-red wings broke out of the palace's shadow, its great, ax-shaped head lowering on its long neck to study them as it passed.

And then Draken Saphier came out of a flash of silver.

He studied the dragons surrounding them, their heads and great winged bodies etched in vivid, powerful lines against the sky. He said to the mages, "There are others. I haven't found my father. He may be one hidden in a misty time-path with dangerous properties for the unwary. Have they been quiet?"

"The dragons, my lord?" With a start, Nyx recognized Magior.

"Our guests. What have I missed from Meguet?"

"A comment or two, my lord."

"I can imagine." He took a ritual blade from her, walked over to Brand. His shadow fell over his son; Brand lifted his face. Whatever his eyes held made Draken toss the blade on the ground. He squatted in front of Brand, held his shoulders. "Listen to me—" He dodged spit, said again, patiently, "Listen." Brand gazed past him, motionless now. "I was aiming that spell at Rad Ilex. You flung yourself in the way, in some misguided attempt to protect him. You fled before I—"

"You," Brand said furiously, "destroyed my time-paths so that I could never return to Saphier! So that I could never speak the truth, never say that you had made the firebird out of me to kill Rad Ilex."

"That's not true," Draken said gravely.

"What's not true?"

"That I never wanted you to return. I would have searched for you in every world we conquered."

Brand's face flamed. He rolled so fast, his father barely had time to move; his sharp kick caught Draken Saphier in the chest, but only hard enough to stagger him. Brand, his hands tied, was off-balance as he rose. Draken spun around him, slid one arm between his wrists and jerked upward on the leather thongs. Brand gasped. Draken forced his rigid arms higher; the blood ran out of his face; his eyes closed.

"Listen to me," Draken said again, very patiently, and Nyx thought coldly: *Either here or in Ro Holding.* She flung power across the web and ducked into her own shadow. Meguet, moving faster than the eye could follow, was a blur, picking up the blade Draken had dropped. Nyx's power tangled in the web; it became visible for a second, a flaring crosshatch of light that dissipated just before it touched Draken. Meguet, nearly invisible, brought the ritual blade slashing down between Brand's wrists. It cut through the leather, but Draken misted away at its touch. Meguet vanished as he reappeared; the Cygnet, blown across the winds like black flame, marked the place where she had been.

Then a strange light sprang down out of nowhere, peeled layers of wind and power and time itself apart like paper to find her, force her, pale and shaking, back into eyesight, despite all the Cygnet's power. Nyx, stunned, dragged her eyes away from Meguet finally, traced the light through the air above their heads, through the bright morning sunlight, up stone and the shadow flung by stone, to its source: the dragon's mouth.

Around her no one moved. No one spoke. Even the mages were staring upward. Rad Ilex might have unbound himself from their loose and fraying concentration and slipped away, but his eyes too were on the dragon slowly rising on the stone pile above them, unfurling its wings to fly.

It had risen with the sun, Nyx remembered: the golden dragon with the red-gold eyes. It had perched up there all morning without a claw or a wing-bone moving, its great eyes smoldering down at them, unblinking, until it had opened its jaws and caught Meguet with a flick of light as easily as a swamp toad catching a butterfly.

It dropped off the stones; the sky darkened as it flung its shadow over them all. It came down fast, for all its bulk; still no one moved, not even Draken, for it held them all with its fiery eyes. It could have landed on them, or scorched them all to ash, stray shreds of power for the winds to play with; no one could guess what it might do, and no one lifted a finger to stop it.

It vanished. So did the light holding Meguet. Nyx still searched the sky for it, her eyes bewildered by its absence, until movement among the motionless mages drew her attention back to earth.

A strange mage walked among them toward Draken. His hair was gold, his eyes were amber flecked with red. He wore a robe of dragon scales that drifted and glowed like the strange desert winds. His face was clean-lined, hard and powerful, like the desert itself, a thing so ancient it had been scoured by wind and sun and time of everything except its essence.

He stopped in front of Draken, studied him expressionlessly. Draken's face lost color in the light; Nyx saw him try to speak, falter. The dragon spoke first, his voice low, sinewy, harsh with unexpected inflections. "You are mine."

Draken's eyes burned, the dragon's gold in them reflecting light. "I am Ragah's son."

"She gave me no name," the dragon said indifferently. "She asked me to name her and I did. A word that means 'night-fall.' For her hair, and her powers that waxed by moonlight. She sent a message to the dreaming winds that she wanted a dragon-born child. I heard her dream in my dreams. She haunted the desert, she sent her wish on every wind, and I dreamed and dreamed until she roused me, drew me out of my world into this place. And I remembered the human-born, the human shape. And now you are here, Ragah's son, rousing dragons with your dreams."

"I was looking for you." Nyx heard the wonder in Draken's voice. "I didn't know I had already found you."

The dragon sighed, a long, slow, lizard's hiss. "You have found me." His burning, light-filled eyes moved to Brand, standing in Draken's shadow, and to Meguet, who still held Magior's ritual blade. He turned then; his slow, unblinking gaze swept around all the mages' faces. His hand opened. Nyx saw the mage-web become visible, shining, all its strands linked to Rad. The dragon's hand closed. The strands snapped in his grip, vanished. Rad gripped the rock, pulled himself to his feet, trembling with exhaustion, or with wonder. "You have dreamed," the dragon said to Draken, "of dragon-wars and found me."

"Teach me," Draken breathed. "Teach me. The heart of power is the dragon's heart. You have all the power of the Luxour in you, all the power of the dragon-worlds, all the power of time. You haunt my dreams, your shadow spans my life. I have looked for you since I was born."

"You woke me."

"Yes."

"And you brought me here."

"Yes."

"For this." His face tightened; deep, bitter lines formed. "For this." He looked at Nyx. His eyes were endless; they had seen forever, and they left her breathless, as if, meeting them, she had begun a slow fall off the world. They went to Brand again, who gave him only an expressionless, unyielding warrior's stare. The dragon sighed again. "What will you give me to teach you?"

"Anything."

"Your son?"

"Anything." The word flicked across Brand's face; he closed his eyes. "Everything."

"Seven years."

"Seven. Twelve. A lifetime."

"Seven I will take from you. In return, I will teach you what you need to know before I will permit you to call yourself my son."

"Yes," Draken breathed.

"If, in seven years, you have not learned what you must learn, I will kill you." Draken opened his mouth to answer, did not. "Answer," the dragon said. Nyx, staring at him, felt the cold silken touch of dread and wonder glide over her.

"Yes."

"So dragons treat their children. So I have learned from you, as I waited on that bright, high place, listening to your son. As I woke in my quiet dark to listen to the mage who, running for her life away from you, found herself faced with me. All these small, disturbing human voices. Because of you, I was wakened; because of you I listened, having nothing else to do. You taught me."

Draken was silent. He turned his head, looked at Nyx, as did Brand, Rad Ilex, and the entire circle of mages, everyone but Meguet, who had closed her eyes at the thought of the Cygnet's heir running headlong into a dragon's lair. "You? You found my father?"

"I didn't know," she whispered.

His attention moved to Brand. He seemed uncertain, suddenly, as if, not seeing the firebird, he did not recognize his son. "Brand?" he said. The hard, set face with Draken's hair, his eyes, gave him nothing.

"You wanted paths to find us," the dragon said. "You woke us, brought us out to use us. To burn, to annihilate. There are those among us who crave such work. Like you, they do not discriminate. They may begin here."

Draken moved a little, as if a wind had pushed him lightly. "In Saphier."

"You have brought us into your land." His slow, burning gaze swept the mages again. "They could not begin to fight us."

Draken whispered, "You would not destroy Saphier." Something besides the memories of his dead and blackened past touched Brand's face, altered the white, stiff lines of it. His eyes glittered faintly, with a shock of hope or horror, Nyx could not tell.

"It is a place," the dragon said indifferently, "to begin."

"No." The wind pushed harder, moved Draken back a pace. The mages' voices murmured around him, shaken, protesting.

"You'll find another country. Take Ro Holding instead. What does it matter where you rule, if you have conquered time?"

"It matters."

"Why?"

"Saphier is the dragon's face. The Luxour is its heart. Saphier's history is my past, my future. The Luxour is my heart."

"You have no heart," the dragon said contemptuously. "This stone has more heart. I should kill you now, let them burn Saphier to ash and rubble. Shall I?" he asked Brand, who started under his sudden gaze. "Shall I? Answer."

Brand's hands clenched. His mouth tightened; his silence wore at Nyx as she sat tensely, neither moving nor breathing, listening. It wore at Draken, who seemed to hear in it, or in himself, something of the firebird's endless, anguished cry. "He is your son," Brand said finally. His voice shook. "How do dragons treat their children?"

Lines that were not bitter shifted unexpectedly across the ancient face. "Who taught you to riddle with dragons? Your father? Does he know the answer to that riddle? Tell us the answer, Ragah's son. Guess if you do not know. How do dragons treat their children? Answer."

Draken, his eyes on Brand's rigid face, started to answer, stopped. He lifted one hand, hid his eyes from what he saw. "With lies," he said. "With ruthless cruelty. They make their children love them, and then twist their love into hate, their trust into fury, their innocence into despair and grief. So dragons treat their children."

"No," the dragon said softly. "You are wrong. So humans treat their children."

The mages' voices fluttered like leaves in a treeless place. In the distance, the great, grey dragon rose on its rock pile, sent a flash of deadly light at whatever had annoyed it. The ground shook as the dragon-fire scarred the Luxour; stones whirled into the air. Draken watched them fall; they struck the earth like random heartbeats. He said, his voice sounding weary, almost as ancient as his father's, "I have nothing to give you for Saphier but my life."

"A poor price."

"All I have. Spare Saphier. I beg you."

"It made you. You are its past, its future."

"It made Rad Ilex. Something good must dream its way out of the minds of dragons into the Luxour, into the air of Saphier to shape the likes of Rad Ilex, who of all my mages defied me. And Saphier made my son. In spite of me."

"There is a price," the dragon said, "for Saphier."

"And all in it?"

"All."

"Take it," Draken said harshly, and bowed his head.

The air ignited with silver. Paths tangled with paths, melted, converged, tore, until it seemed to Nyx that they were all trapped in Chrysom's impossible black box, where all the threads of time led into one another, and no path opened beyond the chaos. The image of melted, burning threads of silver imprinted itself on the air for moments after the time-paths had vanished from every wrist.

"There are no more such paths anywhere in Saphier," the dragon said. "Except one." He held out his hand; the gold and ivory key lay in it. Again the hard lines of his face eased; he looked at Nyx. "The mage—what was his name? Chrysom. He was a gentle man. I dislike burning books."

Nyx's face shook. She put her hands over her mouth; the burning tears slid down between her fingers. Meguet, tearless, stunned, turned to her as at a touch, seeing what she saw: Time, nearly ended on the Luxour, was shaping its path again toward home.

"I will take the key," the dragon said. He added an after-thought, "And you, my twisted son. For seven years. And I will take the dragons back. But who," he wondered of the mages, "will watch these human dragons for me?" The mages, under his eye again, turned to stone. He lifted a finger, spun a thread of fire. It streaked through the air and caught Rad Ilex.

Rad, white, silent, ringed by fire, stared into the dragon's eyes. The winds died; time stilled on the Luxour. In an hour, or in the next breath, Rad moved again, turned to the mages of Saphier. The dragon-fire parted, looped around his wrist, burning gold and red and all hues between. He said nothing. He didn't have to, Nyx thought. Only he and the dragon knew what power had passed between them, and no one seemed likely to test him.

"In seven years," the dragon said, "Rad Ilex will come to me for Draken Saphier. Do not force him, by any intention or act, to find me sooner than that."

In the motionless ring of mages, someone moved: Magior stepped forward. "And who, my lord," she asked humbly, "will rule Saphier? It is best for Saphier if you choose."

"Who will rule in your place for seven years?" the dragon asked Draken Saphier. "Answer."

Draken was silent. An errant wind scattered a handful of dust at his feet; briefly, his noon shadow shaped the firebird. He swallowed something bitter, painful, the lines on his face running deep, before he lifted his head, held Brand's eyes.

"Brand Saphier will rule," he said. "Now and for the rest of his life. I know Saphier. I will not have it tear itself apart choosing between the dragon and the firebird." He added, so softly that even the Luxour stilled itself to hear, "If in seven years you have any desire at all to find me, look for me here. The Luxour seems the only thing that I have ever loved."

Brand's expression blurred, as if the magical winds had reshaped it briefly, and then shaped again the warrior's mask. The dragon said to him,

"Is human justice served between father and son? Are you content? Answer."

"No," Brand said huskily. His own hands clenched; expression shook again into his face, and, unexpectedly, into Draken's. "There is no justice for this. Nothing will ever quiet the firebird's cry."

Draken nodded wearily. "I hear it now," he said. He turned away from Brand, to his father.

"Come," the dragon said, and Draken vanished. A black dragon with eyes of cobalt and gold lifted itself into the winds above Brand. From the jumbled stones and palaces the dragons rose, soared into the air, shapes of fire and shadow, a progression across the bright sky as strange and gorgeous as the firebird's enchantments. As the dragon-mage led them back into their secret worlds, the Luxour sent a shadow after them, a memory in the wind: the Cygnet, with its wings of night, its starry eye, following dragons across an unfamiliar sky.

# CHAPTER
# 18

Nyx saw the face of the firebird one last time as the dragons disappeared: The cry filled Brand's eyes, then left them empty, searching the barren desert for something he had forgotten. She took a step toward him. His eyes found her then. He waited, drained, motionless, for her to come to him, the terrible emptiness in his eyes slowly filling again with memories, dragons, the magic of the Luxour. She put her arms around him, heard nothing for a long time but his breathing, his heartbeat. Finally she heard his voice.

"Can you stay?"

She shook her head against him, her own face colorless, expressionless. "I must go home."

"Then how will I see you again?"

"There is a way," she said, but for once she doubted herself. "There is always a way." She shifted to see his face; it was set, but more in determination than despair. He even smiled a little, crookedly.

"I have never made things easy for you."

"I never liked things easy." She held him again, tightly, aware this time, of all the silent, watching mages. "Will you be safe?" she asked him.

"The dragon rules Saphier," he said softly. "For seven years.

223

Even the most powerful of the warrior-mages will be wary of that. I trust Magior. And Rad. They will help me. Saphier's future has always been its past. I don't know how to change that. Perhaps only the threat of dragons can change Saphier's ways. The threat of something more dangerous than itself." He dropped his face against her lank, dusty hair, kissed it. "Some day," he whispered, "we will find that cave full of waterfalls and dragon-mist again."

"I'll find a way," she promised. Her throat ached. "Chrysom did it. I can do it."

"I can't. This time you will have to come to me."

She looked at him, saw his face, his father's face, even something of the dragon's hard, powerful face. "If Saphier's heart is the Luxour, and the Luxour is the dragon's heart, perhaps it is more your grandfather's heart. He found something of Ro Holding to value. Something of Ro Holding's peace."

"So have I," Brand whispered. He bent his head, found her lips, coaxed peace from them until the winds of the Luxour, hot and fuming and enchanted, swirling around them, seemed to her the winds of home. He raised his head finally; she felt him draw in air as if he would swallow all the magic in the winds.

She loosed him reluctantly. "Come to me," he said, and she nodded. He cast an eye over his mages then. Some were watching him, astonished; others dreamed across the distances, searching for a glint of dragon-wing. Most had clustered in small groups, to unravel the events that had so abruptly changed the path of Saphier's future. Nyx looked for Meguet. She stood beside Rad Ilex as he spoke with Magior; Nyx saw him lift one hand, draw it lightly down Meguet's hair. She stiffened slightly, then met Nyx's eyes. She looked too tired to stand; her face pleaded silently: *Home.*

"We must go," Nyx said to Rad Ilex as she joined them. Magior, her face seamed with fine, troubled lines, said to Nyx,

"Draken Saphier cast a spell, it seems, over his entire house, as well as his son. We were all ensorcelled by his vision. The dragon was wise to destroy the time-paths. It is still a very powerful vision."

"There are other visions," Nyx said wearily. "Perhaps the dragons of the Luxour will dream up something for the mages of Saphier to do besides war."

"Yes," Magior agreed, but doubtfully. "It will take some time to change. Saphier has always been"—she gestured toward a sudden feathery sweep of distant steam—"volatile."

"Saphier," Rad said grimly, "has a choice between inventing peace or ceasing to exist. A more merciful choice than you would have allowed Ro Holding."

"Yes." Magior cleared her throat. "I know. Force is its own justification. It exists primarily because it is capable of existing. Now that we are made powerless, I can find no justification for what we had contemplated. I thought I was too old to change. Too old to see Saphier in the light of anything but its own history. We will need help. Your ideas, Rad, and Brand's. Even Draken's. Perhaps, in seven years, he will be alive to advise us."

"You would trust him?" Rad asked sharply.

"I would trust his father," Magior said simply. "If he permits Draken to live, he will have changed the heart of Saphier itself." She paused, her eyes on Nyx. "Perhaps, with Brand, it is already changing."

"So will Ro Holding," Meguet murmured, "if you manage to find each other again."

"Across mountains and seas and endless wastes," Nyx said, seeing them spread across the distance between Ro Holding and Saphier, each mountain, each ocean, pushing them farther apart. "And worlds," she added speculatively. "And time." She put a hand to her eyes against the vision, felt Meguet's hand on her shoulder.

"There is always—"

"A way," Nyx finished. She looked at Rad, wondering how anyone so haggard and spent that he could scarcely cast his own shadow, could possibly be standing upright. "Is there a way home?" she asked him. "Will the dragon permit you to use Chrysom's time-path back to Ro Holding?"

He nodded, and held out his hand: What he had sought in Ro Holding lay in his palm. "One last time," he said with an effort. "Then I must return the key to him. Or he will come back to Saphier looking for it, and he will not be pleased. You'll have to help me open the paths. I can hardly open the book itself."

Nyx was silent, thinking of the key holding all the mysteries of the Luxour, all Chrysom's innocent, secret journeys. So was Rad; their minds touched inadvertently, holding the same key. They pulled back; their eyes met. Nyx said ruefully,

"Now I would be content for either one of us to keep it."

"Yes." He reached out to Meguet, held her wrist as he had when she had been pulled so precipitously into Saphier's history. "So," he said without looking at her, "I must return you to your Gatekeeper." She said nothing, did not move, until he finally raised his eyes. She said softly,

"I will never forget the dragons. Or the Luxour."

"Or the rose?"

She started to speak, then stopped. She smiled suddenly, and a little color came back into his drawn face. "Or the rose that got us into all this trouble."

"Now you know why I dropped it there."

"Now," she said, "I know why I picked it up."

He held her eyes, using her, Nyx realized, as his calm focal point of concentration. She turned abruptly, for one last glimpse of Brand standing in the Luxour, stones towering behind him in a tumbled jagged disorder that seemed to be always on the verge of order. In the next moment, in the next . . . Surrounded by mages, all their thoughts and ideas pulling at his attention, he detached himself for a moment, stood alone, saw only her. The Luxour slowly misted from gold to cobalt-blue to black, until the only clear thing in the world was the silver path to Ro Holding forming beneath their feet.

Chrysom's tower, building around them out of the mist, seemed, for a moment, another rising of stone at the moment of change. It did change into a palace and remained changed, though Nyx noted, with an instant of surprise, without the firebird. Her throat tightened. Rad's white dragon waited for him still; she freed it. It leaped gracefully to its place across Rad's heart. Together she and Rad fashioned a path back to the Luxour while he still had strength to think. Meguet had not even that left; Nyx found her a moment or two later, sunk deep into a leather chair and fast asleep.

She paced a step aimlessly, bewildered by the silence, some part of her still expecting to see the firebird. Her bones ached with exhaustion, but she could not bring herself to leave the tower. It seemed the only bridge between two worlds, and a broken one at that, but all she had. Memories crowded into her mind, far too many for the tower to hold; she had no other place to keep them. She touched her face, and still moving, found a tear on her fingers. Her hand shook, her whole body trembled. She looked at Meguet, who had escaped the world somehow; not even Nyx's tears brought her back. She was trapped, it seemed, like the firebird, by memory: impossible to go back, yet equally impossible to open the tower door, leave the past behind her. She forced herself still finally, stood in a drift of sunlight, her arms tightly folded to stop her trembling. Still she could shape no path, not even into the next moment.

The door opened abruptly. She caught a glimpse of her mother's face, chalk-white and delicately lined, before the Holder gripped her, shook her a little, and finally pulled her into an embrace that took her breath away. She blinked, vaguely aware that her mother was holding her upright; her bones preferred to spill onto the floor.

"What happened?" the Holder was demanding, her attention divided between Nyx's frozen face, her torn, dusty clothes, and Meguet, dressed in the same peculiar fashion, with blood on her sleeve and her face as pale and still as ivory. "What happened?"

"I fell in love," Nyx said.

Meguet woke out of a dream of dragons. A black dragon had been trying to tell her something: not the red-eyed dragon of war, nor the dragon with the human eyes that had been Draken

Saphier, but one with a gentle voice, and eyes as cold and pure as stars. Or had it been a dragon? she wondered, in the moment between sleeping and waking. Something dark as night that flew . . . She opened her eyes then and found the night.

Memory returned slowly: She had fallen asleep in a chair in Chrysom's tower, not, as her bones felt, on the stone floor of a cave in the Luxour. Nyx was safe, Ro Holding was safe, time had been breached and sealed again. She gathered herself wearily, piecemeal, and stood. Nyx had left a candle lit for her. In the dark yard beyond the south window, she saw another flame. She moved toward it thoughtlessly, as if to walk to it on air, before her mind woke and told her what it was.

She turned and took the stairs instead.

She wondered, as she crossed the quiet yard, what time it was, what day it was. Midnight might have come and gone; there was no firebird to cry against it. There was still a Gatekeeper; she saw a taper flame, trembling in the sea air, rise to light his pipe. The flame vanished suddenly, as if he had dropped pipe and taper to stand, a dark figure against the torchlight at the top of the turret steps.

She did not see him come down. He was just there, with her in the yard, holding her face between his hands.

"Meguet," he said, and she felt his swift, fierce embrace, as if he could not bear even a shadow of night between them. She held him as tightly, feeling for the bone beneath his face, the bone beneath her hands, feeling for his heartbeat against hers. "I thought I lost you," he whispered.

She shook her head. "I came back." He said no more, turning his face, bone by bone, against hers to find her mouth. For a moment she wandered with him beyond time, beyond memory, beyond weariness and terror. A stray touch made her wince; she dropped back into time.

"You're hurt," he said, his hands sliding lightly down her arms, loosing her.

"Only a little." Draken's relentless eye tracked her suddenly as she ran down the secret paths in her mind; she hid her face against Hew's shoulder, added numbly, "I should be dead. And you should be trying to bar the gate against a hundred mages, and dragons of air and night and stone that could tear this house apart with a breath and toss it into the swamp. And the dragon-lord of Saphier, Brand's father, who caused all this trouble."

She felt him shudder. "There's been nothing at the gate lately but what's expected, familiar. All the odd enchantments went with you and Nyx. We had a warning. And then nothing, not even a lost swamp-bird. Blue sky and tranquil seas. And a Gatekeeper going blind trying to shape you out of thin air. You vanished out of the world with a mage who gave you a rose—"

She lifted her head, blinking. "I was dragged." She could see vague lines and shadows on his face in the torchlight; she could not see an expression. "Into a desert. Like no place I have ever been, not even in dreams. Dressed for supper in a hot, barren, nameless wasteland where there were dragons or maybe not, with a dying mage on my hands."

He made a sound, touched her again, gently. "Let's go up," he said, "where I can see your face."

They sat in the turret, a dragon's eye of a moon watching them from over the swamps while she told him where the rose had led her. She could see him clearly then, in the taper-light, the shadows beneath his eyes, the ghosts of worry and care still haunting his face as he listened, one hand linked in hers, so still she scarcely heard him breathe. When she had wakened herself again in the chair in Chrysom's tower, he moved finally. His lips parted; he didn't speak. One hand reached toward a taper, dropped. She said very softly,

"You opened the gate between Ro Holding and Saphier."

He met her eyes; still he didn't speak. Then she heard his breath, long and slow like tide.

"I am Gatekeeper," he said finally. "In the light of day or in the dark, in the end it's me, standing here, making a choice to open or not."

"Nyx said she was warned, just as she left with the firebird, that there would be danger to the Cygnet. You let her go."

He picked the taper out of its sconce then, lit his pipe. "I promised her I would."

"Even when—"

"She gave me a name. The place where you were lost, where she would go to find you if she found a way. I never saw the dragon's shadow behind the firebird, only the strange mage, and the firebird, who cried questions without answers here in Ro Holding. And only you, vanishing like that, dragged to anywhere by a mage who got past my eye."

"Did he? Or did you let him in, too?"

He shifted, putting the pipe down, and turned to her, grasping both her hands in his. "He found his own way in. As he had, you said yourself, many times before. Chrysom made this house, and its gate, and maybe left a door open somewhere, for the mage he liked. If I had stopped Nyx from going, then what? We would have had at least one dragon at our gate, and maybe we can move the house across Ro Holding, but not Ro Holding itself to a safe place. The Cygnet flies alone among the dangers of the night. It doesn't live quietly in some safe place. And neither, as you of all of us know best, does Nyx."

She opened her mouth, found herself wordless. The house, she decided, in that tangled moment, had its mysteries, and she was one of them and so was he. Mysteries, by their nature, behaved in mysterious ways. She settled back, calmer now. "Sometimes," she said, "I know you as well as yesterday. And sometimes not at all."

He watched her, his own face calmer, still holding her hands. He leaned toward her; she met him halfway. The moon disappeared between their faces, reappeared now and then, in various phases, until a step disturbed them, and as they drew apart, the full moon grew again between them.

Nyx stood at the top of the steps, looking tired but composed. "My mother sent me to find you," she said to Meguet. She held out a hand as Meguet straightened. "She doesn't need you yet. She only wanted to make sure you hadn't vanished again." Meguet eyed her narrowly. Nyx had dressed for supper in familiar fashion, but supper was long past, and small jewels flashed askew in her hair, and a button dangled by a thread.

"What have you been doing?"

"Trying to find Saphier." She tucked a strand of hair behind her ear. "What else?"

"How?"

"In books. And other places."

"What other places?"

"Odd places." Her eyes went to the Gatekeeper. "Hew—"

"What other places? That box of Chrysom's?"

Nyx drew breath, loosed it. She folded her arms, leaned against the stones. "Don't worry. I'm being careful. I've figured out how to come and go; I don't get lost inside the box and I don't go far down any of the paths. None of them," she added wearily, "are at all familiar. Hew—"

He was shaking his head, his brows crooked. "I'm sorry." he said gently. "You found your own path there before; I can't do that for you. All I do is open and close."

"Well." She pondered, her eyes on the stars, while the Gatekeeper shifted past Meguet in the tiny turret, came out to stand beside Nyx. He lit his pipe again. "Assuming it's on the same world, in Ro Holding's present, and not its past or future—which I can't entirely rule out—it must be somewhere. Not even Calyx can find it, and she's been searching records as old as the house."

"It's just as well," the Gatekeeper said, "from the sound of things, that the Dragon hasn't flown itself into the household records before now."

"I suppose." Nyx yawned; her eyes looked colorless and luminous as the moon. Meguet, watching her through the open turret arches, asked with some sympathy,

"What does your mother think of all this?"

"She seems unusually resigned. I suspect she hopes that I'll never find Saphier and that I'll forget about Brand. Perhaps. Anything is possible. But expecting me to forget Brand, and the Luxour, and the dragons of the Luxour, and the dragon-mage, and all that wild, unfocused power that shaped even the Cygnet out of our thoughts, is expecting too much. There is, I reminded her, a precedent. Chrysom also loved the Luxour."

"So did I," Meguet said softly. "For a few moments. When I saw it through Rad's eyes."

"You didn't tell me that," the Gatekeeper said. She met his eyes across the torch fire.

"No," she said, smiling a little. "I felt it was wrong of me, wanting to see dragons. Things that lay beyond the Cygnet's eye."

"How do you know they do?" he asked curiously. "Or do you know at all?"

She was silent, gazing back at him. "I don't," she said, and got to her feet abruptly. "None of us would have recognized a dragon before now. And perhaps I never saw the Cygnet among the stars only because I didn't expect it to fly anywhere in Saphier's sky."

She stepped outside the turret; Nyx was already searching the night sky. "The Dragon hunts the Cygnet," Nyx murmured. "Behind the constellation? Or above it? The black war-dragon with blood-red eyes."

"I saw it," Meguet said wonderingly. "The constellation in Rad's doorway. The dragon of night and stars. It never occurred to me it might be—"

"There," the gatekeeper said, pointing over the sea, "just on the horizon. That red star. Two red stars. And look. One star its breast, one star the tip of its outflung wing, those stars its claws, and those, that faint cloud of stars, its breath of fire. And that star over there, perhaps its tail? Would that be it?"

"I see it," Nyx breathed. Her fingers, chilled, closed on Meguet's wrist. "There. South and west above the sea."

"I see." Meguet was staring at the Gatekeeper.

"Is that what you saw, Meguet?"

"Yes."

"So Saphier lies somewhere beneath the dragon's eye. I can sail there—"

"Please," Meguet breathed.

"I'll send explorers," Nyx conceded. "Messengers. Even my

mother would approve of that. As much as she approves of any of
this. I'll take Chrysom's box to Rad Ilex; perhaps he can help me
find a path between Ro Holding and Saphier. A private path . . ."
Her voice trailed into silence; she contemplated the dragon's eyes
a moment before she asked slowly, "How would a man born in a
swamp in the Delta in Ro Holding recognize a dragon?"

"I was wondering that myself," Meguet said. And then she felt
all thought fade away until she was barely air, barely night within
the night. She was touched, it seemed, by the light, flickering,
changing winds of the Luxour. "Were you there?" she asked the
Gatekeeper. His face was in shadow again; she could not see his
eyes. "On the Luxour? All those dark swans flying out of my
night-shadow, all those winds stealing magic out of me. One of
those swans wasn't wind. One was real." He didn't answer. "Tell
me," she pleaded, her voice still spellbound, her bones shaped of
stars now, at her elbow and ankle, throat and amazed eye. "Tell
me that you saw the dragons. That when I say dragon, that's what
you will see: the flight of dragons across the Luxour under the
noon sun."

He started to speak, stopped. Then he shifted into light, and
she saw them in all their terrible grace and power flying through
his eyes. He drew her against him tightly, perhaps to hide what
he had seen by day, perhaps in memory of what he had fought
by night. "Gatekeepers don't leave the gate," he said at last into
her hair. "But what my heart does, flying out of me in terror
or wonder or love, only you can tell me, because it will follow
only you."

She felt his heart fly into her; her mind filled with dreams and
memories of the soft touches of wings, the rustlings and night-
murmurings of flight. Her hand brushed his wrist; his fingers
opened, linked with hers. She whispered, "Then follow."

She led him down the turret steps. Behind them, Nyx stood in
the moonlight, waiting as patiently as stone or time, for the slow
dance of constellations to reveal a path by star and water into the
Dragon's dawn.